DEAD COLD
An Invitation to Murder

A DETECTIVE MAGGIE FLYNN MYSTERY

By

Lisa Fantino

Wanderlust Women Travel Ltd.™
Harrison, New York

This book is a work of fiction. Names, characters, businesses, organizations, places, events, historical or otherwise, and all incidents are the product of the author's imagination or are used fictitiously. No procedure is exact since all is a work of fiction. Any resemblance to actual persons, living or dead, events, or locales is entirely coincidental.

Copyright © 2025 Lisa Fantino
All rights reserved. No part of this book may be reproduced in whole or in part in any form. Please do not participate in or encourage piracy of copyrighted materials in violation of the author's rights. Purchase only authorized editions.

The scanning, uploading and distribution of this book without express written permission is a theft of the author's intellectual property.
Thank you for your support of the author's rights.

Hard Cover First Edition: March 2025
Published by
Wanderlust Women Travel Ltd.
600 Mamaroneck Avenue/Suite 400
Harrison, NY 10528

WanderlustWomenTravel.com

Cover design by Lisa Fantino with Canva AI apps
Author photo by Chris LoBue

AuthorLisaFantino.com

Hard Cover ISBN-13: 979-8-9855486-3-1

"The life of the dead is placed on the memories of the living."

~ Marcus Tullius Cicero

Prologue

"When the needle hit my carotid artery, I thought the worst he could do was rape me. I would recover, eventually, with help. But how do I move on from murder? There's no one who can hear my silent cries, no one who can help end this nightmare, no one who can help me now.

"Early tomorrow morning, police will come to my house, the house my grandfather built and the home my parents cherished, the home where I was raised and the last home I'll ever know.

"Nice officers, men and women, who always say that doing the family house call to deliver the death notice is the worst part of their job, in a job chock-full of ugly, will tell my widowed mother that me, her only child, her daughter has been found...dead!

"As her world collapses into a black hole within the secure walls of our home built on love, Mom's heart will implode. She'll internalize her pain, as mothers often do, until her emotions boil over, bursting through the surface, cracking her generally stoic façade into a grid map of every sleepless night, every worry, every heartbreak, everything unsaid, and every regret never expressed. Her cries will be so deep, primal, sounding like the dark echoes off the blackest depth of a bottomless ocean. A tsunami of sorrow will flood her world, yet no one will hear her screams. Her cries for help will remain only hers, now locked away, forever, inside her maternal vault.

"You see, last night, I died alone, just steps from our secure home, only the angels were left to guide me home, after the devil himself squeezed the very life out of me. Then he just disappeared into the damp darkness of a night so inky black that not even a raven could see its wings."

Chapter One

Snow usually blankets the city in an easy calm, muffling the constant drone of New York City, silencing the buzz that is inherently the Big Apple. Whether it's one in the morning or one in the afternoon, you can close your eyes and actually feel the muffled pulse of the city once it dons its white teddy bear coat for winter. But not this year. This year it is notably different. There is a pall hanging low on the horizon, ominous, threatening anyone who crosses its path. It's unseen, creeping stealth-like among the natives, creating an indiscernible discomfort, an uneasy chill blowing a cold wind down the mighty Hudson River and across to the East River.

"Well, would ya look at this," said the veteran nurse to the young nursing student as they stepped into the snow-bright night at the end of their double shift. It's as if the falling snow bends the light in such a way that looking up makes a new day possible, brighter unlike when a thunderstorm clouds the sky, darkening all hope of anything good on the horizon.

"It's snow pretty, get it?" Brittany asked, laughing at her own question.

The night skies glistened a bit brighter because of the snow.

"Yeah, give it a New York minute and watch it turn to filthy grey slush," said the older nurse, hardened by life at just forty years old.

"Awe, spring's right around the corner, hang in there," Brittany said, trying to offer emotional support to her colleague. The woman was a skilled trooper in the infectious battle wreaking havoc on the country's left and right coasts while avoiding the hearty plains in the middle, at least for now. She knew the ugly descending on New York but all Brittany could see was a chance to help people.

"I think I'll walk home," Brittany said without seeking support of her own. She hoped to shake off the day's germs in the cool night air before heading to her boyfriend's place. She wanted to spare him any possible exposure to the pernicious bug sweeping across New York like a derailed freight train, mowing down anyone in its deadly path without mercy.

Brittany was to graduate nursing school in just a few short months. She lived to help people, but no amount of training or nubile enthusiasm could prepare anyone, even the most seasoned physician or trauma nurse, for the world of hurt this flu season.

She pulled up the hood from her puffer coat, up and over the knit skull cap she was already wearing and started walking toward East 233rd Street. She would've called Mike but why make him come out in this mess when she could be at his place in less than twenty minutes. Besides, the walk would give her time to decompress rather than carry her day across her new boyfriend's threshold. She valued what she had with her new man in this new relationship, and she didn't want to test the theory of all-in or nothing so early in their dance.

She soon realized that trying to stay dry was a futile effort as the snow turned to sleet very quickly. A car's horn startled her awake as she was about to step off the curb without looking. The streets were unusually empty at one in the morning and her head was elsewhere. It happens, we all do it, especially preoccupied New Yorkers.

Brittany was ready to be apologetic to the driver as the car stopped short and the driver opened the passenger side window.

"Oh, hi," she said. She was taken aback but relaxed slightly when she recognized the driver.

"Get in," he said. "I'll give you a ride. You can't walk home in this mess."

"Gee, thanks," she accepted with gratitude. "I wanted to shake off the long day and I don't need to add pneumonia to my list of bugs to avoid this year.

"This is really nice of you," she continued, settling into the passenger seat. They had only just met a few weeks ago and she didn't want to give him any ideas nor did she want to tell him where she lived.

"Where can I take you or would you like to go for breakfast?"

And there it is. She sensed during their friendly but brief chats that he was looking for a date and a relationship, but she had Mike, and this guy was just so nerdy and weird and now he was just plain creepy.

"I'm sorry, I can't," Brittany said. Her hood had fallen back from her neck and onto her shoulders. She was so tense that she could feel her carotid artery throbbing and hoped he wouldn't notice.

Do I tell him I live with my boyfriend? That I have a boyfriend? That I need to go to the gas mart to buy milk for my mother? Oh Lord, how did this night go from snow beautiful to so sketchy in such a short time?

"My boyfriend's waiting for me at home," she said with as much conviction as she could muster. "We live at the top of the hill, so you can just drop me at the gas station. I need to grab some milk anyway."

"You have a boyfriend?" he asked bitterly, his words charred by the bile creeping up the back of his throat. Another rejection? He would end this tonight.

"Does he know you've been flirting with me?"

She couldn't engage him in conversation. There would be no meaningful dialogue in this car tonight. This was his soliloquy. She just needed a quick escape. Yet, rolling along at forty miles per hour seems slow until you try to jump from a moving car at that speed.

"I asked you a question," he said, grabbing the back of her head with his right hand, knocking off her skull cap in the process. He stopped short at the curb and immediately shifted the car into park to face her squarely with no risk of harm to himself.

What was that? She felt a prick at the side of her neck, just where she was sure that artery was pulsing through her skin, revealing her anxiety in one heart-pounding beat at a time.

Thump, thump, thump.

She could feel the throbbing, but she couldn't hear anything. Everything was muffled.

"What did you do?" she said to him.

She knew that feeling. It was an injection, the prick that could send you to oblivion and whether you woke or not was at the whim of the injector.

Thump, thump, thump.

She had a pulse. Her heart was still beating but for how long? She began to lose feeling throughout her body. It started as her toes went numb and worked its way up toward her neck.

Thump, thump, thump.

She couldn't move. She couldn't wiggle her toes. She could barely lift her arms. What had he done?

Mike, Mom, I am so sorry. She sought forgiveness in the spiritual sense because hope and prayer were her last thoughts and feelings, and the only things you hold onto until no hope remains.

"It's lights out for you, you stupid bitch. No one plays me or teases me."

She was stuck to the seat as he came around and opened the passenger side door. Her eyes could see the bright lights of the gas station on the corner. She guessed he had pulled up to the curb near the ballfield across the street.

Why didn't I say goodnight to my mom? Why didn't I call Mike? Why didn't I walk home?

Why? Why? Why me?

She couldn't move but her mind was racing toward a million regrets.

He pulled her to her feet and dragged her out of the car and along the wet sidewalk. Her legs had tightened. Her body wanted to run but she could not. She knew that without his elbow supporting her that her legs would buckle. She would collapse right there, face down in the slush, no chance of running away as much as she wanted to.

Come on Brittany, think of something. Think. She imagined he was going to rape her. She could see the lust in his eyes, blackened and brimming with fire. Piggish and drooling at the mouth, ready to feed like a bloodthirsty vampire.

"I have Covid," she whispered, just barely.

"What did you say?" He wanted her to repeat it, but she could not. She barely uttered it the first time.

"Covid? Yeah, who doesn't have it? I do too," he lied.

He wasn't just bitter, he was vengeful, resolute in his plan to make her pay for rejecting him when she had no intention of ever pleasing him. She had never led him on. She was just being friendly.

She fell to the ground as they neared a large tree set back from the busy road and close to home plate on the park's baseball field.

She looked up to see she was surrounded by weathered trees rising to the white sky as the slush fell into her eyes, momentarily blinding her view. She could see the abandoned birds' nests, which once held new life, now resting precariously on bare branches without expectation of anyone returning home tonight. She blinked her eyes rapidly to clear the slush as it landed on her eyelids and closed them again when she saw him hovering overhead, as if closing her eyes could make any of this go away.

"You think you're an angel!" The sarcasm and bitterness oozed from his lips and slobbered onto her face as he straddled and hung over her. The irony of her image as a snow angel in the slushy grass was not lost on him.

The last thing she felt was his spittle land on her cheek as he grabbed both ends of her scarf and pulled tighter and tighter, snuffing the very air from her lungs until all that was left was the spirit of an innocent taken way too soon and the deadly muffled silence of the wet snow falling on the grass around her lifeless body.

Overnight, gentle flakes had turned to an unforgiving sleet, cutting sideways, not like the sharp blade of a knife through butter, but like the burning of a branding iron, raw and merciless. And this was just the beginning.

"Damn, it's nasty out there," said the rookie officer, stuck on foot patrol, as he returned to the station house, not the house where he lived but his home nonetheless where his family in blue resided, his band of brothers and sisters. No one was out except the police and the media telling everyone else to stay home. He was eager to leave the city behind and head north to the suburban sanctuary of his parents' home.

"Hey, kid."

"Good evening, sergeant," he said panting out of breath as if the cold caught up with his young lungs. He shook off the last vestiges of his wintry shift in the lobby of the building that stood on the corner of Simpson Street, just off East 167th Street, and only six blocks from Yankee Stadium, as the crow flies. The building, once known as Fort Apache for the violence which gripped the surrounding neighborhood from the 1960s through the 1980s, now housed the Bronx Homicide Squad. For two decades, the violence in the neighborhood was so terrifying that even gypsy cabs gunned it through redlights, not waiting to be the next target, while it burned to the ground around them. It was like driving through a war zone for those who survived to tell the tale. Not a pretty look for The Bronx, not pretty at all.

Now, in the twenty-first century, gypsy cabs had become organized ride shares and the old limestone Fort Apache had become the dilapidated home for detectives chasing killers with a handful of patrol officers to help out or stand guard, whatever the job called for to protect and serve.

"Here, you need this more than I do," said the desk sergeant, handing the kid the hot chocolate she had just made for herself. She remembered being in his shoes and empathized with him having to walk a beat in the bone-chilling slush of a wet March night. These days nothing was easy about joining the New York Police Department.

"It's really strange this week," he said, taking a welcome first sip of his hot chocolate.

"What's that, officer?" she asked, already focusing on making herself another cup.

"There's no one on the streets and half the people walking around look like they're dead or dying! It's ominous out there."

"Well, look at you, my little rookie, using big words like ominous," she mocked him with the loving praise of a den mother. "Make sure you get a flu shot kid. This is a bad flu season, and one flu can wipe out even the toughest crime fighter.

"Now, go get changed and clock out before someone else calls in sick and I have to hold you here for ominous overtime," she teased him with all due respect for any kid brave enough to join the NYPD in this anti-cop climate.

The city's emergency call center had seen a recent uptick in the number of 911 calls for people in distress. Patrol officers and emergency medical technicians had seen more than one mother, son, spouse, girlfriend, explain that their daughter, father, wife, boyfriend went to bed with just a cold and apparently died in their sleep. That's just not normal, not even in the worst flu season.

January and February were the height of it, every year. Epidemiologists could almost predict the severity of the flu's attack on New York City by looking at Latin America where its flu season started about six months earlier. Yet, most people, most medical professionals, did not track it. This year, however, the alien invasion was not blowing from the south, it was coming in from a different direction, the far east.

Chapter Two

Maggie could already smell the coffee as she stepped out of the shower. She smiled as she drew a heart with one finger on the steamy mirror before wiping it down, all girly and romantic, the opposite of the hard-edged costume she wears daily to protect and serve. She had started nesting with Jackson Barrow Spencer just after Christmas. Their occasional sleepovers, usually at Maggie's condo in suburban Mamaroneck, had become more like weekend getaways in the 'burbs.

They had eased into a comfortable place in their relationship after only four months. While neither of them yielded in most fights on the job, the opposite was true with each other at home. He nuked the skim milk for her morning latte, and she picked the silk ties he wore with a casual elegance to match his bespoke suits. When it came to coffee, he was a dark roast, black, no sugar all-American and Maggie was a skim milk latte with half a sugar Irish Italian-American, or Sicilian-American if you ever asked her directly.

Jax was a great cook. He loved and worried about his detective girlfriend and she ate up the attention like a kid licks a salted cone full of dark chocolate gelato. They challenged each other mentally and made each other laugh but they were different enough, just enough, to keep it from getting boring.

He was listening to 1010 WINS on the radio while he made *panettone* French toast for her very early 6:30 a.m. wake-up call. Oh, the things men will do on a Sunday morning for the women they love!

The news from Seattle was grim. A guy traveling through Wuhan, China, carried home a souvenir that was literally let out of its cage, accidentally on purpose. Believe what you want but Covid was a biological assault on the west, starting in Europe and now stampeding its way across two oceans and nearly fifteen thousand nautical miles to New York. Release the flying monkeys, bats, raccoon dogs or whatever other vermin were on the pathogenic menu. This was going to get really ugly, really fast!

Maggie stopped at the kitchen island to take in the view. Jax continued at the stove with his back to her, wearing just sweatpants and not much else which made breakfast even hotter. She smiled quietly, admiring every ripped edge of his back which she had ridden like a pony less than eight hours ago.

"I can feel you staring at me," he said without facing her. Their routine was easy, dancing to a tune only they could hear. He found himself working remotely from Maggie's place more often, making it easier for his strong, independent crime fighter who now had to brave much more than bad guys stabbing passengers in the subways. As general counsel for Sotheby's, Jax was able to work from anywhere with his laptop and a good internet connection. He liked the life they were building together, and the ease of their relationship just worked from the start.

Maggie had never yielded to anyone until she met him, but her world quickly changed when she met Jax as a source on the Gianni Costa case which rocked the world of fine art. The death and fraud of the Costa affair, a case of true crime, had become their real-life romance. When security with another person is easy and comfort and respect are automatic, there's no need for either person to submit because love yields in the natural ebb and flow as the relationship grows. It's not corny. It's simply the truth, their truth.

"What's this?" Maggie asked about the gift on the kitchen counter. The rectangular present was neatly wrapped in elegant gold foil paper with a matching bow. Her instinct said it was a painting, but it wasn't a holiday, her birthday or their anniversary, at least not one that she could remember.

"Open it," Jax said placing her latte on the other end of the counter.

"Oh, now, I know what it is," she sang her words lyrically. Her joy was beaming across her face like a little kid on Christmas morning.

"Really, my lovely little wiseass, what would that be?"

"A painting, definitely a painting…because you moved the coffee out of the way, all the way out of the way, so it must be a really expensive painting." She laughed passionately and loudly, which lit up his day.

He just smiled, looking very much like a male Mona Lisa in that moment, all-knowing and enjoying the secret, soon to be revealed.

"You think you're such a hot-shot detective, don't you?"

"No, I know I'm a hot-shot detective, so I'm probably right."

Maggie opened it carefully to find the work of another artist she admired, not as old as a great master but a wonderfully talented contemporary artist from California, Aaron Westerberg. They had first seen his work in the lobby of a Beverly Hills hotel, of all places. It was a quickie weekend business trip for Jax, and Maggie tagged along. The portrait of a woman in a rose-colored frock caught their eye amid the stark lines and neutral color palette of the lobby's furniture. Both of them appreciated Westerberg's skill and classical influences, playing with the dark and the light within a character as reflected in her surroundings.

Maggie was speechless when she opened the monochromatic painting, carefully framed and wrapped like a treasured jewel. It was the portrait of a young woman in a pensive repose. Westerberg often did these smaller color studies as he planned and created the larger paintings which appeared in galleries across the country. Maggie found the studies more intimate, as though the subject was still isolated from the world, in a colorless gloom. The woman was not yet ready to meet society, until the artist polished and dressed her, seductively or modestly, hiding more of her secrets, submitting to his complete control until he was ready to share her with the world in all her rose-colored glory.

"She's you," Jax confessed. "Spirited, yet sophisticated. Pensive and thoughtful yet completely *pazza*, crazy and funny."

Maggie was speechless. He was the only man who could still find ways to make her heart skip a beat and speak Italian at the same time.

"So, detective, did my sixteen-inch package make you smile this morning?"

"You are so twisted and so optimistic, just two of the reasons I love you."

She kissed him on the cheek, not wanting to take her eyes off the work which was now propped up on the metal canister of coffee from Naples. He had embraced her in a bear hug from behind, kissing the top of her head, knowing he had done good, knowing that if he hung onto her long enough the scent from her cologne would linger with him until she returned from work, safe at home.

"By the end of today, if I survive dinner at Uncle Bobby's, we would have spent just under 175,000 minutes together, including the bumpy start last November." Jax said.

"I think that's a big deal since neither of us has ever had a relationship last more than a day in the last two years," he added with a smirk, a raise of his eyebrows and a tilt of his chin to the right. The reality was definitely not lost on him.

Maggie could not disagree and blew him a kiss, still mesmerized by the new art in her collection. She never had a collection of anything, except meaningless relationships, until Jax. They were both career-driven, holding the world at bay, not looking for anyone or anything more than their next transaction or next case until their worlds collided during the Costa affair. That's when Costa, an Italian art philanthropist, wound up dead and Jax suddenly became Maggie's inside man in more ways than one.

The only thing that worried him now was the other man in her life, Detective Lieutenant Bobby Stonestreet. The venerated retired flatfoot was Maggie's godfather who had been watching over her since her father had died of a sudden stroke six years ago.

Detective Lieutenant Sean Flynn was his former partner and best friend. He was family. And tonight, Jax and Uncle Bobby would meet for the first time, over the usual Sunday dinner which Maggie rarely missed unless duty called.

Maggie and Jax had met about six months earlier, and their first date was a black-tie fundraiser for The Met at The Cloisters following the closing of the Costa case. Jax had helped Maggie, and her partner, Detective Sergeant Tommy Martin, navigate the close-knit web of the art world, where nothing is as it seems, and the high stakes can be deadly.

Maggie had promised Jax and Uncle Bobby that they would all meet just after the new year and in Maggie's hectic world, the first of March was close enough to meeting her commitment. Jax was a quick study. He knew that he would have to fit into her world if their relationship was to flourish. He would answer to Uncle Bobby and her work family, not too intimidating since they all carried handcuffs and guns.

Chapter Three

Maggie hoped the day would start slowly, at least until she could wash down a second cup of coffee following the hurried latte at home with Jax. It was early, just about 7:30 in the morning, so she managed to find an actual parking space outside headquarters. Simpson was a congested, narrow street typically crowded with police cars, private cars and unmarked cars parked helter-skelter in organized chaos. She parked her Signal Red Kia Rio outside the building and made her way through the lobby with a lift of the chin and a mumbled greeting to the desk sergeant before climbing up to the penthouse, otherwise known as the detectives' squad room.

The sun rose on the dreary day as she drove down from Westchester County. It didn't do much to brighten the darkness, or lift her mood, and it was just as gloomy inside the squad room. The space was empty, lights out, no one home here where rickety forty-year-old metal desks stood sentinel against the grit and grime of the outside world. The silence was eerie except for the hiss of steam emanating from the ancient cast-iron radiators. She glared over as one spit out, seemingly at her, fully aware that those heating gatekeepers would outlast the city's eventual doomsday. Even New York City's rat-sized roaches ran from the spitting steam of antique radiators.

The Bronx homicide squad was the busiest in the five boroughs, but it was woefully ill-equipped and under-staffed with only one detective for every four murders compared to Manhattan, with one detective for every two murders. It's hard to imagine reducing a life down to statistics but when you're fighting crime, one less detective could literally mean the difference between life or death.

Her partner, Detective Sergeant Tommy Martin was stuck upstate at his family's cabin. He had texted her last night that they had about eight inches of snow and couldn't make it down his mountain. He was snowed in with the wife, their brood of five kids and their golden labradoodle named Sherlock. Maggie knew he would much rather be at work than trapped in the woods.

Detective Sergeant Lou Lopez also called in overnight for a personal day. The two senior detectives had more than sixty years of service between them in the NYPD, so they were entitled to more than the occasional day off.

Maggie had made detective just shy of four years ago and Hank Summers about six months earlier, and both were promoted to detective second grade after closing the Binky Killer case. Hank's usual partner was Lopez, but he lucked out today and became the highest-ranking detective on shift by default.

"Good morning, sunshine," Hank said as he carried a tray of coffee straight to Maggie's desk with a pair of buttered rolls. They had turned a bit soggy since the corner food truck could do little to shelter itself, or the buttered rolls, against the wet sleet blowing sideways.

"I hear it's you and me against the world today," he noted, carefully placing the coffee in front of her with the roll, and a handful of scrunched-up, dampened paper napkins from his pocket.

"Skim with half a sugar, right?"

"Shame on me for doubting your listening skills?" Maggie said, mocking him. The pair teased each other endlessly, like brother and sister, but had nothing but respect for each other and the rest of the squad. These guys were her work family, and they never made her feel inferior as the only woman on the job. It actually bothered Maggie that other women thought they were owed something more simply because they had boobs and a vagina. She learned early on that you're not owed a damn thing in this life. Her dad always taught her to work hard and never give up until you reach your goal. She truly believed that women, like other minorities, who thought they were owed this or that, or reparations or compensation, actually hurt themselves more by crying about injustice and demanding equality. They'd be better served spending more time performing better and outsmarting their male counterparts. You get what you work for and not what you beg for!

"Maybe we can catch up on some paperwork and keep the captain happy, while the criminals seem to be sleeping late this morning," Hank suggested.

"Base camp to mission control. Anyone awake up there?" The voice of the desk sergeant broke through their morning solace, invading their inner sanctum via the overhead speaker.

"Pay no attention to the woman behind the intercom," said Maggie.

"Dead body at home plate up on Indian Field and you're up at bat. Do I have your attention now?" the sergeant asked.

Maggie and Hank grabbed their coats and ran down to get the details, knowing full well their coffees would be cold, their rolls a mushy blob, and the partially drafted reports scattered like ticker tape across their desks if they ever returned to the house later today.

"Quick, hop like bunnies before the rain washes all of the evidence away," the sergeant suggested to them.

Hank asked the sergeant to radio patrol to make sure the scene was cordoned off so that no one swashed through the mud disturbing already compromised evidence.

This was going to be a long day, and it was only eight o'clock in the morning.

Chapter Four

The two detectives had never worked as a team before today, but with Tommy and Lou out, Maggie and Hank were entering new territory. All four detectives had previously worked together on the Binky Killer case, so this was not their first date, so to speak, but they needed to read each other's thoughts and that takes time like the slow dance of any important relationship. However, they did not have the luxury of time this morning. It was baptism by fire as they drove to Woodlawn, with lights and sirens blaring, reaching Van Cortlandt Park in ten minutes.

The two patrol officers, who were first on the scene, had been flagged down by a passing jogger. Having cordoned off the area with nothing more than a nearby garbage can and a few large rocks, they now stood under a nearby oak tree, looking like a pair of drowned water rats trying to shield themselves from the wintry mix. The alternating sleet and rain made any hope of protecting the crime scene nearly impossible, leaving the poor victim, shielded only by a torn garbage bag they had taken from the trunk of their police car, looking like a muddy mess rather than a snow angel.

The two officers had taken some photos with their phones, but the pictures were barely usable since raindrops collected on the lens. Maggie thanked them for their efforts, understanding that foot soldiers in The Bronx get more knocks than kudos. The jogger who found the body was still on the scene and explained, again, as he had done to patrol, that there were no footprints around the body when he arrived. Any earlier prints which could have been helpful if made in the slush were erased by the rain that followed. The jogger also grabbed a photo since the rain had let up just enough for him to take a shot before a second downpour pummeled the scene. He texted the photo to Maggie who watched him delete it from his own device at her request to not share it with anyone.

The Crime Scene Unit, CSU, arrived in short order and immediately set up a tent over the body. Crime was always messy when Mother Nature came to play. They began bagging and tagging what little evidence they could gather. Soon footprints zigzagged across the scene, behind the scene, in front of and around the scene, making the area look like the intricate pattern of an Amish quilt, while not disturbing the body until the medical examiner showed up.

They all imagined the victim worked at nearby Misericordia Hospital, since she was wearing medical scrubs under a red puffer coat and the hospital was just down the hill.

"Looks like she was strangled with her own scarf," Maggie said as she squatted next to the young woman. She carefully balanced herself so as not to slip in the mud pit which had spread proportionately to the deluge and the numerous people stirring the pot. Hank held a giant golf umbrella overhead shielding Maggie as much as protecting the scene. The lanyard around the young woman's neck held a laminated ID card which identified her as Brittany Jenkins, Nursing Student, Misericordia Hospital.

Detective Maggie Flynn looked down at the corpse lying there in the rain. The victim was a young soul, fighting the good fight in a city set to lose control. An eerie sensation came over Maggie and she could not shake it off. She had seen her share of dead bodies on the job, but this one unsettled her, and she could not pinpoint why.

"What did she do to lead her here last night, Hank?" Maggie asked her temporary partner.

"It was sleeting sideways, freezing slop, the kind that slices your skin," Maggie continued looking down, staring at the young body. "She should've been home not here. Definitely not here. Was it pure hate or angry love gone terribly wrong?"

"Look at her scrubs," Hank directed her to examine the dark spots which stained her white scrub pants.

"It could be from work. But it's not a lot of blood." Maggie replied. "Or it could be the killer's if we're lucky."

Speak to me, Brittany. Who did this to you?
What led you here?
And who's waiting for you at home?

Maggie had never met the victim before tonight but suddenly she was the homicide detective's top priority. She didn't need to look away, not even for a brief glance to the side, or up or down, which generally gave a cop just enough time to regroup emotionally to allow him or her to do their job. There would be enough time for that, later, away from the scene. This morning, death was the star attraction because this young woman was most assuredly the victim of a fallen angel, since only the devil's spawn could be this vile.

Maggie put on gloves and retrieved Brittany's cross-body bag which was lying next to her in the mud. She then yielded the scene to CSU, just as the medical examiner arrived.

She steadied herself as she rose, and Hank caught her by the elbow to keep her from falling into the mud.

"You, okay?" he asked.

"Yeah, I'm good," Maggie said shaking off her uneasiness.

"You wanna talk about it?" Hank pushed her for more, purely out of concern, since she seemed unusually ruffled by this dead body in particular.

"I just did," Maggie was tougher than a life sentence when someone pushed too hard. Hank needed to get used to that.

"Damn your independence, woman," Hank said in a stern voice, atypical for him when speaking to his colleagues and more in line with an older brother admonishing a kid sister.

"You call or scream, or holler, if you need me, you got it?" he said, ushering her into the passenger seat of the squad car.

"Ahh, don't worry about me."

"Are you kidding? That's part of the job," Hank emphasized clearly while closing her securely into their mobile office inside the squad car.

Maggie had suggested that Hank deal with the ME while she examined the contents of the handbag inside the dry car, so as not to compromise any further evidence.

Looking through a woman's handbag is as sacred as it gets, sort of like peeking behind the altar or inside the sacristy of a Catholic church, Maggie thought. Not even her close friends would think to rifle through Maggie's bag. The same could not be said of Maggie with her professionally inquisitive mind often grating her friends and family the wrong way.

Brittany's young life was about to be examined with the unease of a proctology exam in front of strangers. Nothing would be off-limits, no stone unturned. Her secrets would be exposed in an effort to find out who killed her and why.

Inside the bag, her driver's license revealed Brittany had just turned twenty-five last week and that she lived a few short blocks from the scene. She never expected the year ahead to be cut short.

Why was such a pretty, young woman walking alone late at night? was the thought on Maggie's mind. This neighborhood was not as safe as it used to be, but she could certainly walk home from the nearby hospital pretty quickly and was pretty certain to be left unscathed.

Maggie rolled down the window as Hank approached under the soggy umbrella, rain dripping from every spoke, splashing Maggie as it bounced off the car roof with a splat and into the now open window.

"The ME says she was strangled, and the body was staged. Choke marks under the scarf may yield fingerprints in the autopsy."

The scene was now cordoned off, at least fifty feet back from the body, with yellow crime scene tape, as lookie-loos stopped and stared. Not even the rain would keep nosy neighbors and passersby from staring at a corpse, especially in The Bronx where most natives over the age of eighteen had sadly seen at least one dead body in their time. The forensic technician had traded the contaminated trash bag for a tarp and covered the body, offering Brittany a modicum of dignity as she remained lying in a muddy mess on this playground where kids usually play ball and vent off steam. Now all the field gave off was the putrid smell of decomposing leaves hanging in the morning air.

"The jogger says he knelt down to see if she was really dead and not just injured when he came upon her, but he didn't touch her," Hank continued.

If you have never seen a dead body before, humans have an innate curiosity to get a closer look and to feel the body. But death ain't pretty. Poor Brittany did not go without a whimper. She died with her eyes wide open, staring at her killer dead ahead. The shock of her last moment was literally written on her face, imprinted on her eyes as her last view from this life into the next.

When Brittany left her house yesterday, she never imagined it was her time to die. Now, Detectives Flynn and Summers would have to make the house call that all officers hate to make. There is never an easy way to tell anyone that the center of their world was just ripped from their lives and the love torn from their hearts.

Chapter Five

Cops lose all track of time when working a case. Hours fade away. The day escapes them as they focus on the instant, the moment that someone's life was snuffed out. And until tomorrow's autopsy, the exact time of death would be a guess, at best.

The rain had finally stopped, and by two o'clock the overcast day cloaked Woodlawn with a grey shroud. They pulled in front of a neat cape cod style house on East 236th Street at the corner of Kepler Avenue. The red, heart-shaped solar lights which lit the front walkway mistakenly sensed it was dark outside and lit automatically because the sun had failed to rise brightly this morning. They likely remained there from Valentine's Day, still inviting love into the tidy home with a welcoming front porch. Instead, death came knocking this afternoon and they were about to forever change the lives of whoever lived here with Brittany.

The death notice to a family or a loved one is never easy, never pleasant, and it always, always leaves an imprint on the soul of the officers just as much as on the victim's survivors.

Brittany's mother answered the door unaware of how her world was about to fall apart. She melted into Maggie's arms when the detective delivered the news. Mrs. Jenkins was now all alone, her only child killed just three years after cancer took her husband.

Maggie helped the middle-aged woman to the sofa as Hank went into the kitchen to get her a glass of water.

Who? What? Where? Why? How? The survivor's questions were always the same. They never understood how something so evil could happen to someone they loved. And for a mother, in that moment, it was like ripping her heart from her chest while it was still pumping, and she could no longer breathe. No parent wants to outlive their child, and no child should die so violently.

Mrs. Jenkins explained it was not unusual for Brittany not to call when she worked late, and she would often walk home alone. The hospital was less than a mile away and nearly a straight shot along a well-lit, heavily trafficked East 233rd Street. She did not expect Brittany home last night because she had plans to visit her boyfriend, Mike Scavi, who lived close by. It was a new relationship and Brittany seemed very happy.

"He's a nice boy," said Mrs. Jenkins. He's quiet and works for his uncle's construction company. They've only been dating about two months."

She didn't know much else. She believed they met at one of the Irish pubs on Katonah Avenue. It was where all of the neighborhood kids hung out and where all of the old-timers seemed to fade away on a corner bar stool.

Brittany was in her last year of nursing school at Mount Saint Vincent College in Riverdale. As a result, she spent more time working at the hospital than on campus, where she had a close-knit group of friends. She was supposed to walk with her class at graduation in May.

Maggie and Hank asked her if they could call anyone before they left, and she just shook her head no. No, there was no one left. No, she could not believe this had happened. No, not her precious daughter, her only child. But yes, this was her new reality.

Mrs. Jenkins barely heard them as they left the house, telling her this was just the beginning of their investigation when she knew that her world had just ended.

Chapter Six

"Are you thinking what I'm thinking?" Hank asked Maggie as they walked toward the car. The Scavi Construction company was notorious for its old-school ties to the mob and Brittany's boyfriend just happened to be a Scavi. And while it was true that the New York Mafia was not what it was fifty or sixty years ago, if it smells like Locatelli and tastes like Locatelli, it's Locatelli.

"Let's see what the kid says and does," Maggie suggested.

They decided to walk the two blocks to Scavi's apartment and volleyed their approach along the way. If Scavi was innocent, then he didn't know that his new girlfriend was now dead cold, icier than this New York City winter had been. Maggie would employ the gentle touch, at first, and then become the hard-assed detective if the situation warranted. Either way, Hank would mollify his usual sarcasm when dealing with any person of interest and provide a softer, saner complement.

Maggie had secured Brittany's phone at the scene and had it with her. She knew there was a frantic string of texts from Scavi to Brittany overnight, his searching curiosity spiraled into troubling anxiety as the late night turned into early morning based on the time stamps of each text.

The foyer intercom and buzzer system indicated there were six units in the mid-sized red brick building. They pushed Scavi's button, and he buzzed them in without asking who it was. Neither detective thought this was odd if he was innocent since he expected it would be Brittany.

His apartment door was already open as they stepped off the elevator onto the second floor. Mike stuck his head into the hall with eyes of hopeful expectation staring toward the elevator, but those eyes quickly turned to despair. All he could do was shake his head from side to side and whisper, "no, no, no," as the two detectives walked the short distance toward him. He could see their shields displayed on the waistband of their pants, each pushing their jacket aside to give him a clear view, always displayed as an introduction, but now harbingers of something much less cordial.

Mike Scavi learned, from a young age, not to answer questions from any cop without a lawyer present. It was his family's mantra. Yet, this was different. His heart was ripped to pieces as he learned that he would never see Brittany again, never kiss her, never laugh with her. Their future together reduced to yesterday.

Who? What? Where? Why? How? These were the same questions they had faced from Mrs. Jenkins a short while ago. Real life writing a script for the next true crime drama.

"We were supposed to meet her friends from school today," Mike explained their plans. "They'd all been together nearly four years and were tight, very tight, and it was time for me to meet the girlfriends."

"Did you know any of them before?" Maggie asked, as Hank casually canvassed the well-appointed, tidy bachelor pad.

"No, we were only dating about two months, and we kept it just between us until recently," he replied. "Britt said she wanted to show me off to her friends to silence their questions. You know how girls can be!"

"You have a nice place here, Mike," Hank said. "My bachelor pad looked more like animal house when I lived alone."

Mike thought it was odd that he was commenting about décor at a time like this. Hank knew his questioning was targeted to disarm and unsettle Mike, divert his focus, throw him off his game. That is if he was playing the lying game. Unless someone is a skilled criminal or a professional liar, like a poker player, it doesn't take much to cause a crack in their story with the slightest push.

"I usually work from home as a freelance software designer. I need to be organized, or I don't do my best work."

It had to be the truth, Hank thought. This kid was grieving and could not spin that tale in a heartbeat, even if his last name did end in a vowel.

"I don't even know her friends' last names or digits," Mike said. "I mean, do they even know? Does her mother know?"

He was starting to ramble as his disbelief became disconsolate grief. He had not shaved in two days and his mop of curly espresso brown hair was in disarray. "What do I do now? I don't know what to do. What am I supposed to do?" He started rambling.

"Who's with Mrs. Jenkins?" he asked. "She doesn't have anyone around here. I should go to her, but I've met her only once."

Maggie had now gone into the kitchen to get the kid some water and Hank sat on the sofa next to Mike. It was a well-choreographed dance between the two seasoned detectives who understood how the investigation worked and who were at the top of their game. While they were not partners officially, they were already moving as one.

"Hey, man, you don't need to do anything," Hank offered him some support by moving closer without touching him. Hands off was the new paradigm for police departments across the country, especially in New York. "Just breathe," Hank told him. He spoke slowly hoping that by slowing his pace, the kid would also calm down.

"We'll have more questions as the investigation progresses," Maggie said, handing him the glass of water. "Can you come down to the precinct tomorrow to meet with us? I can't give you a time just yet, but we'll take your number and call you as soon as we know."

"Hey Mike, Mrs. Jenkins said you worked for your family company, Scavi Construction, is that correct since you just said you're a software designer?" Hank wanted to button it up before they left.

"Oh, yeah, but only once a week. I go in to help my Uncle Al do payroll on Thursdays."

"And Mike, we told Mrs. Jenkins, and now you, that this story will likely break on the evening news tonight and be on tomorrow's front page if nothing else newsworthy breaks," Hank explained the news cycle of crime as he handed Mike his card. "Detective Flynn and I will be working most of this evening, please call us if you think of anything, like if Brittany had any trouble at work, or on campus, or anywhere else."

This time yesterday, Brittany was still alive. Yet, murder never takes a holiday and now even homicide was overshadowed by the greater evil of Covid killing thousands, stealing one slow breath at a time, a serial killer on a global scale.

Chapter Seven

It was five o'clock by the time Hank and Maggie walked back to the car and drove the short distance to Misericordia. Hank called the Mount Saint Vincent Campus, identifying himself to campus security, to obtain the Dean's direct phone number on a Sunday evening. He had to notify the college, allowing them to beef up campus security, as they saw fit, and arrange to meet with the Dean or administrator of the nursing school tomorrow.

Maggie stopped to quickly text Jax and Uncle Bobby that she would be late for dinner and that they should start without her.

At least start on the apps and save some for me! She didn't need to text more, and they didn't need to read more, since they all had the same love language – food!

The two most important men in her life, the most important people in her life, now meeting for the first time without her. It just didn't seem right but that was Maggie's world. Her godfather knew it firsthand and Jax was getting used to it begrudgingly.

"Hi, hun, caught a case and won't be getting home till late, so eat without me." Hank had called his wife and piped her through the car's speaker. Maggie just stared at him once he hung up. He could feel her eyes and knew what was coming next.

"New roommate?" she asked.

"New wife," he replied.

"And when did that happen, Detective Summers?"

"She got me drunk on Valentines Day and we flew to Vegas overnight." He could barely contain his laughter. His eyes remained dead ahead with the hospital roof on the horizon as he drove down East 233rd Street, along the northern edge of the vast Woodlawn Cemetery.

"Does anyone know? Even Lou?"

"No, you're the first."

"Oh, how special. We're bonding by sharing our secrets," Maggie quipped.

"Well, tell me more. Who is she?"

"Some chick I'd been hanging out with in Yonkers," he said nonchalantly. "I left Queens and moved in with her."

"Some chick? That's how you describe your beloved bride, the love of your life? Men!" Maggie expressed the exasperation of all women over noncommittal men.

"Next stop, Misericordia Hospital." Hank desperately wanted to change the subject.

The casual conversation turned on a dime and ended as they pulled into the circular driveway at the hospital's front entrance. Police cars and Con Ed utility trucks – they can park anywhere!

Chapter Eight

Maggie had called the hospital en route, so the nursing administrator was expecting them and had pulled Brittany's personnel file in preparation.

"I was born here," Maggie said to Hank as they walked past the rent-a-cop standing outside the main entrance after displaying their detective shields.

"When, yesterday?" Hank's sarcastic humor was always at the ready.

As soon as they stepped through the revolving glass doors into the lobby, they were greeted by yet another security guard who took his job way too seriously. Yet, the two detectives had not been to a hospital in months and were completely unaware of the new protocols put in place as the medical centers were fraught with overcrowding and managing a bad flu outbreak with too little staff and not enough patient rooms.

The guard ushered them into a private elevator to minimize their risk of exposure. The smell of death, the cries of outrage hung in the halls, busy, hectic as people were moved on stretchers in a well-orchestrated procession to isolate them from healthy visitors.

The ride to the administrative floor was silent, deadly quiet in fact. The elevator doors opened onto a pale, ivory-colored hallway that stretched on with a countless number of office doors, all closed, none apparently brimming with activity.

The nursing administrator was casually dressed, neat but not polished, in jeans and a button-down shirt. Normally that would have been unusual but not this Sunday night in the middle of a flu outbreak that was likely Covid. The front lines knew before the powers that be were willing to make the official pronouncement that a virulent killer was on the loose.

"Good evening," Debra Feingold said, the administrator peeking her head out of the door which displayed her name in gold letters, now ajar with the expected arrival of the two detectives. She handed each of them a surgical mask to wear and said she needed to keep everyone safe on her watch, as hard as that was becoming.

"We're in for a world of hurt in this city," she said in frustration. Her voice grasping the sharp edge of sarcasm which she held like the sword of Damocles over the heads of hospital executives and politicians searching for funds and equipment, dragging their feet and playing the blame game.

"More than one hundred thousand people across the globe are already infected, thousands more are dead or dying, and politicians are rationing masks and test kits with the hope of what? That this will just go away?"

"Now, poor Brittany. What happened?" Feingold asked, trying to refocus her thoughts and help the investigation in any way possible as the detectives provided the cheat sheet version of the facts of the case.

"Brittany was going to be a great nurse," she said. "She was enthusiastic, willing to learn and take direction, and most of all empathetic and caring.

"I can't tell you how many patients she sat with, holding a phone or an iPad so their families could say their last goodbyes, albeit virtually. It never discouraged her."

Brittany had worked the day shift but volunteered to do a double, working late last night, when staff started calling in sick. They were severely short-staffed.

She frequently walked home from work but when it was late, her boyfriend picked her up or she caught a ride with a co-worker. The administrator had asked around but there was no one on site from last night as the shifts had rotated twice since Brittany left.

"I was able to reach one nurse at home and she's available to come speak with you tomorrow or you can call her this evening," she suggested. The administrator hesitated calling off-duty staff members for two reasons, the first was that everyone was exhausted, pulling double duty, and the second was that gossip would spread around the hospital faster than the flu.

She explained that one nurse saw Brittany get into a car at the back entrance of the hospital, on Carpenter Avenue, at the end of her shift. She did not recognize the car, but Brittany seemed to. It was a beat-up, grey Honda Accord.

Hank's alarm bells went off. That car was the most stolen car in The Bronx this year.

Chapter Nine

The detectives compared notes about Mike Scavi as they headed back to headquarters to drop off the squad car. Neither of them could see him as the killer even though he lived just one block from where the body was dumped.

"His family may be mobbed-up, but my gut says this kid is squeaky clean," Hank said.

"Yeah, and he's up here in the north country, living with the Irish, and not his family in Country Club. That says a whole lot," Maggie suggested, offering a little insight from her dual Italian-Irish heritage and the clichéd neighborhood cliques of The Bronx.

Back on Simpson Street, they stopped at the desk long enough to get the sergeant up to speed. They had already called Captain Ernest Bradshaw from the car to fill him in and sent a data sheet down to headquarters and the public information officer at One Police Plaza at his direction. The PIO controlled the narrative, no matter the day, the time or the case and this story would certainly break on tonight's eleven o'clock news.

It would have been a slow news day under usual circumstances but not during the viral Armageddon taking place. The weather was awful, and people were hiding at home scared to catch whatever bug was floating around. The media, on the other hand, was scared to catch a producer's wrath for failing to find a new angle in the already magnified coverage of the bad flu season. The outbreak gave new meaning to the hackneyed phrase going viral. Yet none of that mattered because the murder of a young nursing student on a soggy Bronx baseball field would be front and center no matter what the news load of the day, on any day.

Maggie checked Brittany's phone into evidence before leaving. The other items, including the handbag, gathered at the scene, had been turned over to CSU, preserving any chain of evidence before they left.

"I think we should ask the boyfriend to come in around 9:30 tomorrow and see if the ME can push back the autopsy for a few hours," Maggie suggested. They had both been on the clock for twelve hours and they were unlikely to reach anyone else worth speaking with on a Sunday night.

She called Mike Scavi and Hank called the ME's office. As luck would have it, bodies were piling up faster than the dying leaves of an autumn in New York. You see, when an otherwise healthy person dies at home, an autopsy is mandatory in the boroughs, and it seems a lot more people have been dying at home lately. So, it did not matter to the ME who got cut up first. They agreed to meet at the ME's office around one o'clock tomorrow afternoon.

As they left, exhausted but energized by the rush of a new case, Hank yelled after Maggie, "Mags, good job today. I enjoyed working with you."

"And congrats again, to you and the little woman," Maggie jabbed back.

They knew tomorrow started a new week with new assignments. Captain Bradshaw might keep them together to work the case or not. The only constants in this global epidemic were change and death.

Chapter Ten

The surge of adrenaline which fuels the drive to chase any breaking case does not burn off quickly and Maggie found herself at Uncle Bobby's Yonkers apartment faster than expected. It was late, nearly eight o'clock, by the time she arrived. She did not bother ringing the lobby buzzer or the bell on his apartment door. She just used her key.

She could hear the booming voices of her two favorite men as she stepped off the elevator, getting louder as she neared the apartment door. It was the sound of joy which she needed at the end of a day like today.

Uncle Bobby and Jax were well-deep into Sunday night college hoops and brewskies. March Madness would soon take over the sports world and team positions for the tournament would soon be locked, throwing many New Yorkers into a betting game of selecting the winning team in bracket basketball. The gambling tradition was a crapshoot, but everyone enjoyed the chase around the office, around a social group, or around many college campuses, each group pooling their bets for the sole winner. It also promoted an early bonding moment between Bobby and Jax who were now arguing like two old friends recapping the day's earlier games. They were so passionate about their favorite teams and plays that they barely noticed Maggie, who tiptoed in, as quiet as a church mouse, against the backdrop of the loud mansplaining of college basketball.

"I see you two are getting along," she said. Both men jumped off the couch to give her a big hug and a kiss, Jax held her a little tighter as Uncle Bobby moved toward the kitchen.

"Come on, let's eat," he said as he ushered them to the small dining room table. His apartment was only about 900 square feet but a wall of windows with commanding views of the Hudson River sparkled at night despite the glare from his wall-mounted sixty-inch television in the adjacent living room. The expansive wall of windows made the world outside look magical, like fairy lights glimmering off the water, no matter the reality.

Uncle Bobby was already plating their *osso buco*, the braised veal shank was still so tender and falling easily off the chunky bone. She had told them to start without her when she called earlier but that fell on deaf ears because Sunday dinner was sacrosanct in her family and Uncle Bobby was definitely family and Jax would be soon, or at least she hoped so!

Jax was already pouring Maggie a glass of merlot before she could sit down, which didn't go unnoticed by Uncle Bobby. Jax was certainly good for her, and she was surrendering. Jax anticipated her needs and cared for her, which was appreciated by her overprotective godfather. He liked this guy, he really liked him. He knew her dad would too!

Both men knew better than to ask about her long day and Jax knew her well enough to go home after dinner, to his apartment tonight on the Upper East Side, and not expect another sleepover.

Chapter Eleven

Maggie was parking her car in her Mamaroneck garage with about forty minutes to spare before the start of the eleven o'clock news. She ran upstairs, placed her gun in the small safe inside her nightstand and undid her bra, as she did every night, before doing anything else. A girl has got her priorities and unbinding the tension just tops the list on so many levels.

She washed away the ugly of her day with a good soak in a lavender Epsom salt bubble bath before the news would surely create a new knot at the nape of her neck. The tension rose each time a reporter grasped for straws on a breaking news story and hyper guestimated the facts. It was the ongoing push and pull between the police and the media, both serving the public in their own way.

She snuggled into her Derek Jeter t-shirt and then into bed without Jax to help soothe her soul. She pushed the power button on the TV just as the clock hit 11:00 p.m.

Good evening! Breaking news tonight in The Bronx. Police are investigating the murder of a young nursing student whose body was found on a baseball field in Woodlawn. Details coming up.

Maggie always needed to power down after catching a case like today, the incomprehensible death of a young victim with so much promise and life ahead of her. She didn't know how long the surge of new information, or questions about the case, would ripple through her system, but tonight she was finding it very hard to sleep.

No one but Jax knew that she nuked a cup of skim milk for forty-four seconds, no more, no less, with a teaspoon full of honey.

It took the edge off while she watched a love story like "A Walk in the Clouds" or "P.S. I Love You." She hadn't done that in a long time. She didn't need to do that with Jax as her teddy bear. His bear hugs silenced the noise outside and inside her head where the endless drone of a ticking clock amplified minute by minute as the killer got further and further away from the moment that he silenced a vibrant voice. Maggie was always chasing that clock and tonight it was pulsing, more like pounding away, louder than usual.

She and Jax had been spending more and more nights together, but he was smart enough to give her space, one of his many attributes which she adored. He wasn't a needy man. He loved her independence, but he knew when to force her into the submission of a warm embrace and just hold her without expecting anything in return.

This case was troubling on so many levels, and one was just gnawing at her gut tonight. She set the timer on a calming app, hoping the gentle rhythm of ocean waves would lull her to sleep. She would deal with the haunting shadows tomorrow which would come soon enough.

Chapter Twelve

The sun rose too early as it did every morning when you work long nights. The twilight sounds just before sunrise were the automatic alarm clock which greeted Maggie before she was ready to greet the day.

What makes birds sing at four o'clock in the morning? She wondered. *And they always seem to stop their night song as soon as I have to get up as if they did their job for the day!*

She hit the snooze button one too many times as the grinding garbage truck began lifting the dumpster to haul away the remnants of daily life. How did the day start so early, and she wasn't even out of bed yet? She never had enough time for herself or a morning walk to the beach and back. It's not like the Long Island Sound was blessed with the tranquility of lapping ocean waves, but water is water, and it always calmed and energized her at the same time. The self-proclaimed spiritual gurus of social media called it meditative drifting.

She used cologne instead of a shower and hoped no one would notice if the night sweats, which had her tossing and turning instead of dreaming, would perfume the squad room.

The Boiano Bakery was teeming with the usual morning crew, speaking in several different Italian dialects, yet understanding each other perfectly. Once one of them, whose chair faced the door and saw her and said, "*buongiorno,*" the others turned around and joined in the morning greeting with a usual lift of the chin.

The pastry cases were always full, whether it was seven in the morning or seven at night. Biscotti, with and without sugar, gluten-free scones, and of course, Maggie's favorite mini *sfogliatelle* were always fresh and available. The owner often teased her that everything was fat-free, and she always smiled well aware that a pinch on the lips would forever land on her hips. This was home and the smell from the backroom ovens made it smell like her nonna's kitchen on any given morning before she left for school. Everyone knew each other at Boiano's but no one gossiped, or they did it quietly and covertly. It was usual in New York where most Italian bakeries were full of people who saw nothing but knew everything. The neighborhood trivia was their soap opera. They knew the neighborhood and everyone who had a *goumada*, a sidepiece for a married guy, or a *bastardo*, an illegitimate kid they got christened at a church far away from home. It happened when the baby-daddy made a large donation to the church from an unknown and unregistered non-parishioner. It was just part of what made New York, New York.

There's comfort in the familiar. Here, at the bakery, Maggie could grab her usual skim milk latte with half a sugar, even though the counter girl always asked her, every morning, what she would like. Change was the mindset for a Bronx homicide detective. Yet if there was one constant in Maggie's life, one thing she was committed to, it was her skim milk latte with half a sugar and two mini *sfogliatelle*. She truly believed that the fat-free milk gave her permission to indulge in breakfast pastries.

The guys at the back table stopped talking in Italian just long enough to hold up a copy of the New York Post, hitting the front page with a pointed finger to call Maggie's attention to the headline, *Killed at Home Plate*.

Half the guys were old school from Naples which had its own official language, not a dialect like the rest of the boot. The other half were generally Sicilian, as tough as they come. And while they knew that she was also tough, no one can face death on a daily basis without it twisting your innards, including your sense of humor.

"And she's out!" One of them uttered while the rest just smiled or silenced a chuckle.

Maggie rolled her eyes and smirked as the guys tried to make her laugh. She carried a deadly weapon and she knew how to use it, but she was sweeter than the Irish sparkle in her jade green Sicilian eyes, quite deceiving since she was always armed and ready to take down any man, or woman.

"Did you guys drive through New Rochelle yet?" One of the village sanitation workers asked anyone who was listening, anyone who stopped in for their morning coffee and a daily catch-up. "I just drove through. It looks like a freakin' war zone. I mean the National Guard is there and everything."

"It was only a matter of time," said Maggie. "The Westchester courthouse has been full of sick attorneys for the past month."

"That's nothing new," three of them joked in unison.

"No, seriously, an attorney in New Rochelle has been sick for weeks, walking around the courthouse, doctors' offices and the neighborhood until he was unfortunately hospitalized." Maggie offered up inside information. "It seemed the poor guy went to a large funeral in New Rochelle and possibly infected hundreds of people as he walked around spreading monkey bugs everywhere."

"I thought it was a bat not a monkey?" One of them questioned their favorite detective.

"Nah, it was a pangolin, whatever the hell that is," said another voice in the crowd.

"Whatever it was, my guess is they'll need to lock down the whole state soon," Maggie speculated.

"Hey Mags, be safe out there," they yelled after her as she ran out the door. They worried that such a pretty young woman was on her own on the streets, amid a new kind of hell, the likes of which New York had never seen.

Chapter Thirteen

The ranks of the Bronx homicide squad had thinned considerably in recent weeks due to illness and detectives being called away from their normal assignments to fill in the gaps elsewhere. The morning squad-call was reduced to Captain Bradshaw, Hank and Maggie and one other team working on a bodega snatch and grab. This was the Bronx homicide squad now, chasing two-bit thieves, with everyone doing double duty and different duty now. Sean McGuiness and Trey Fuller had pulled the short end of the stick for the bodega robbery since they were the new kids on the squad.

As they waited for the vic's boyfriend, Mike Scavi, to arrive, the captain told them that Tommy and Lou would be out for a few more days. Just then, texts started buzzing on Maggie's and Hank's phones. Tommy had the flu, or so he thought, and he would be out. Lou as well. They had called in sick overnight and were just getting around to telling their partners.

"Looks like we're the new A-Team," Hank said to Maggie. Bradshaw nodded his assent and suggested they all wear masks when moving outside before dismissing them with his usual discharge, "Stay alert and be safe out there."

As one of the new young detectives passed by the Brittany case board, he stopped in his tracks as he looked at the young woman's photo which was taped to the white panel.

"Something wrong, McGuinness?" Hank asked the new detective.

"Hey, Detective Flynn, she could be your kid sister!"

There it was, what had been troubling Maggie all night since finding poor Brittany spread like a snow angel but covered in early spring mud.

She couldn't process it now, nor research any possible impact on the case, because Mike Scavi had just arrived, and he brought company.

It was never an easy feeling being questioned by police inside a station house, especially for a Scavi since it was the cops' home turf. The family was well known in New York City, not only for its big yellow construction trucks and equipment rolling across the boroughs, but also for its criminal dustups in the past.

Big Al Scavi inherited the business from his father and grandfather before him. It was no secret that the Italian mob had control of the city's building trades for more than a hundred years until the early nineties. Yet, when the Russians and the Albanians arrived, the Italians seemingly went legit or really, really underground. They appeared to be altar boys now.

"Good morning, Mike," Maggie said, extending her hand to shake his.

"Mr. Scavi," said Hank, greeting the father in the same way. Frank Scavi did not need an introduction. He was just as well known to cops, citywide, as was his big brother Al. The brothers, like most of their family, had a few minor arrests when they first arrived in New York, but the kid was clean. While Mikey Boy worked part time, processing payroll at the construction company, he was one of those tech whiz kids who worked inside most days, stuck at home in their virtual world with little social interaction.

The detectives ushered the pair toward the interrogation room when Mike just stopped, frozen in place like Lot's wife in the Bible, viewing all that was lost behind him. His face went a whiter shade of pale, and he remained breathless as he glimpsed a first look of Brittany's dead body lying in the mud, her photo tacked to the board like a kid's drawing with a refrigerator magnet.

"Oh, Mike, I'm so sorry," said Maggie, directing Detective McGuiness, with a nod of her head, to flip the board around. "We were working this morning and forgot to cover this before you arrived. "I'm so sorry."

The detectives legitimately forgot. Sometimes, however, they used that feigned loss of memory as an investigative tool to observe a suspect's gaze on his handiwork, but not in this case.

"Brittany was a lovely young lady," said Frank Scavi as they entered the interrogation room. Hank brought in two cups of water as they all sat down. He offered to get each a coffee or soda if they preferred.

Mike took a sip immediately to quench his parched throat. He was so dry from nerves and lingering grief that he imagined his tongue must have been coated in white chalk.

Frank hesitated. He knew what it meant to voluntarily give cops your DNA on a cup or a bottle. But he figured that since he was already in the system, what the hell!

"Any chance you have an espresso machine?" he asked.

Maggie smiled a bit, but Hank seemed confused and thought the guy was just a sarcastic wiseass.

"She was so smart and had a great sense of humor," Frank continued with an arm draped around Mike's hunched shoulders. Clearly, Mike was devastated, and this morning's questioning was not going to ease his pain. If anything, *agita*, the acid of anxiety, would bubble in his stomach wanting to push through for air.

"Mike, I won't kid you. This ain't gonna be easy this morning," Maggie said preparing him for the tough questions which had to be asked and answered.

She started with soft questions, asking him to describe how he first met Brittany, the when, where and how. She hoped and expected this would relax him and ease his jitters, at least somewhat. The easy questions usually did just that.

His eyes, which had spent the night crying from the looks of him, brightened as he described the night he met Brittany. She walked into a local bar and grabbed a stool, alone, confident, friendly and with the biggest smile. She wore her chestnut hair in a ponytail to melt the hearts of most men. She was simply, casually beautiful, approachable and a friend of the bartender who introduced them to each other. Mike had gone in for just one beer to catch the last half of the Georgetown-Villanova game as the NCAA teams were heading toward March Madness.

"That was mid-January and we've been together ever since," he said.

"Did you know her last boyfriend?" Maggie asked, taking the lead while Hank's eyes glanced back and forth, first looking at Mike, and then at Frank, and then back again. It was the same dance they had done before but with different partners.

"She was busy in her last year of school," Mike continued. "She hadn't dated anyone in more than a year and neither had I."

All couples, these days, exchange that basic information before they're on a second date or discover each other's favorite pizza, or search it online, scoping out the inside skinny which is no longer hidden from anyone. Mike was the man they needed that info from. Poor Brittany could not speak for herself, and she didn't have much of a social media presence which they had already checked last night. She had not posted anything, not even a silly meme in months, although she seemed to have lots of friends, over a thousand of them.

"Was she having trouble with anyone at work?" Maggie asked.

"Brittany couldn't have trouble with anyone. She saw the best in everyone and could charm or rationalize her way out of any argument."

"I know it was only two months, but did you ever cheat on her?" Hank asked. He had to play bad cop.

Mike and his father gave Hank the death stare, daring him to repeat the ridiculous question before Mike answered with a firm no.

"When was the last time you heard from her Saturday night or early Sunday morning?"

"You saw my phone," he said in frustration after talking with them for nearly two hours.

"Yes, your phone said she texted you around midnight?" Maggie acknowledged what they already knew. "Did you hear from her again after that?"

"No, I thought she'd be at my place shortly after the last text. She had called just before sending it when she was getting ready to clock out.

"I think she used a work phone for that call because the caller ID said Montefiore.

"She said she wanted to walk home in the fresh air to shake off the germs before she kissed me." He smiled wistfully.

Maggie and Hank thanked the father and son for coming in and cooperating and said they would likely have more questions as the investigation proceeded, probably after the funeral.

But Mike had a question of his own before leaving, something close to his heart.

"If it's possible, when this nightmare is all over, can I have the heart necklace I gave her for Valentine's Day?" he asked. "Maybe we can bury her with it."

"Mike, there was no necklace recovered at the scene," Maggie said. "Maybe she left it at home or forgot it at the hospital."

"No, no, no, never happened," he said, shaking his head in disbelief. "You don't know her. She doesn't forget anything, and she *never, ever* took it off. She told me that she even showered with it."

Maggie thanked him for the information and said they would let him know if anything turned up and suggested he ask her mother to look around the house.

As Mike and Frank Scavi were leaving and just about to head downstairs, Hank yelled after them with a seemingly forgotten question, that feigned memory loss technique.

"Hey, Mike, what kind of car do you drive? And you too, Dad?"

Mike said he had a blue 2019 Honda Civic Si and Frank said he had a black 2019 Ford 150-XL for work and also shared a silver Caddy CT-6 with his wife. The detectives had already run their registrations before their arrival but just wanted casual confirmation. The detectives wondered who was driving that beat-up grey Honda Accord, Brittany's last ride to her final destination.

Chapter Fourteen

Since the minutes were ticking away on the crucial, first forty-eight hours following Brittany's death, Maggie and Hank had to hustle to cover a lot of ground in a very short time, so they decided to divide and conquer. They knew the imminent citywide shutdown would simply paralyze their efforts. Since there was no forensic pathology center in The Bronx, the autopsy would be done in Manhattan, causing one of them to go south while the other headed northwest. Hank would cover the autopsy while Maggie went to Riverdale to talk with Brittany's classmates on campus.

Hank made sure he wore a surgical N95 mask before entering the Medical Examiner's office on First Avenue, conveniently located adjacent to the NYU Langone Medical Center, offering a real continuum of after-death care. He was more than a little creeped out since so many bodies had been brought here, dying at home, apparently from the flu, but now thought to be the early victims of Covid. It was simply too close for comfort for him.

The assistant medical examiner at the crime scene had removed Brittany's pashmina and bagged it separately at Indian Field, hoping a careful examination of the scarf and her clothing, would yield the killer's DNA. He had also taken some preliminary blood samples and swabs at the scene, but today's postmortem would be a more thorough examination of the body, inside and out.

When Hank arrived, he was shocked to learn that the city's Chief Medical Examiner, Doctor Emily Johnson, would be doing the postmortem. She was the city's top doc of the dead who had worked her way through the ranks for more than fifteen years, before becoming New York's first female chief ME. And although she supervised a staff of thirty assistant medical examiners, Dr. Johnson did not mind getting her hands dirty with a bone saw when a crisis brought hell to her door. Staffers were not showing up, whether sick or out of fear, while others were overworked because the center had been operating around the clock since at least the end of January. Yeah, this was no ordinary winter flu season.

"We're going to run out of fridge space soon," she said to Hank. "Bodies are piling up and we just don't have the space. It's worse, much worse than 9/11, and this is only just the beginning." Nineteen years ago, the city had opened a makeshift morgue for nearly 3,000 people who died in the terrorist bombings on September 11th and this modern-day plague could potentially have a much higher death toll.

"Between you and me, we're being told, from the higher-ups, to mark all at-home, flu-like deaths as caused by Covid, whether tested or not.

"Then we're getting pushback from funeral directors who are overwhelmed and can't store all of these bodies in their mortuary coolers, nor will they sign off on the death certificates when the death is unknown.

"The Department of Health just reduced its death registration window from nearly twenty-four hours to less than eight," Dr. Johnson continued expressing her frustration. "And, in their infinite wisdom, the DOH also decided to roll out its electronic registration system, expecting funeral directors to get up to speed with the new online process when they can barely handle the onslaught of bodies dropping, hourly not daily.

"This is going to be the winter of our discontent," she predicted.

Frustrated and over-worked, she pulled out the drawer with Brittany's covered body and transferred it to an autopsy table, where she gently cut off her clothing and secured it separately on a nearby table. Her assistant placed it in a marked envelope and labeled it accordingly.

"Yesterday, the on-scene assistant ME took a swab of the jogger's cheek, which he provided voluntarily," Dr. Johnson explained. "We're sending it out for DNA testing just to rule him out as a suspect, as we normally do. But there's nothing routine about how death is being handled right now, so who knows how long it'll take to get those results.

"He also took swabs of the victim's face, her cheeks, her forehead, you know the drill," she assumed the experienced detective had been to more than one death scene and attended his share of autopsies. "But we're unlikely to find the killer's DNA from any of those swabs since the weather washed most of it away and then the officers first on the scene apparently covered her with a nearby trash bag to protect her from the elements, contaminating whatever evidence might have remained.

"I know the patrol officers meant well, but someone should speak with them," she suggested.

Hank understood. His eyes peered over his mask, pressing across the bridge of his nose as the ME moved an ultraviolet light closer to the table in order to scan the body from head to toe looking for anything not easily seen by the naked eye. Dr. Johnson would take some additional blood samples and swabs, including whatever remained of Brittany's saliva inside her cheeks, for eventual drug testing, along with urine and hair samples, to determine the cause of death. Yet, in this case, the fingerprints of murder, around her neck, superseded the mandate to list Covid as the general cause of all inexplicable deaths.

"The pashmina was a weapon of convenience for the killer," the doctor said. "He used it to strangle her as we can see the bruising here under the scarf line and the petechial hemorrhaging just above it," she continued. "We can also see the petechial hemorrhaging in her eyes.

"I'm almost certain that strangulation was the ultimate cause of death, but I won't make that determination until we get the toxicology reports back."

"But look at this," Dr. Johnson continued, using her hand to direct Hank to move from the other side of the table around to where the ultraviolet light was hiding the killer's secret.

Hiding in plain sight was a needle mark carefully administered on Brittany's neck in a spot likely to hit a major artery since the arteries in that part of the neck are larger than in the arms and easier to catch with a syringe. Dr. Johnson guessed it was a paralytic which made her woozy but not necessarily unconscious before death.

"You mean this sick idiot wanted her to know she was dying, and he merely prolonged it?" Hank uttered the reality which often motivated the killers who crossed his path.

"Yes, probably," Dr. Johnson agreed. "It was part of his control, and he likely got off on it."

"You mean sexually?" he asked in disbelief. That thought always troubled Hank no matter how often it appeared in a case or how many times he heard it in an autopsy, at the station house or in a courtroom. He could not imagine strangling someone to get off sexually. He was still a newlywed and fully enjoying the wherever, whenever sexual mindset that was gratification of passion without infliction of pain.

"Sexual satisfaction by dominance and submissiveness is more about control and power than the anger most people relate with homicide," the doctor explained.

"In fact, anger inhibits the physiological effect on sexual functioning," she continued. "So, he can't really get off physically."

"Some argue, therefore, that sex-based serial killers are more sexual offenders than murderers, but this doesn't appear to be that since there's no sign of sexual activity on the body or on her clothing so far."

"Wow, doc, a visit here is never dull or boring," Hank said in surprise and not much surprised a Bronx homicide detective.

"But that's a pretty well-trafficked and well-lit area," Hank explained to the ME. "It would be hard to carry a lifeless body from the car to the field without someone seeing them."

"She might've walked," she replied. "Depending on the dose, she might have been woozy but lucid enough to walk with some support from him, at least for a few minutes.

"The good thing is that her death, whether by the drug or a resultant cause, or from strangulation, would have been painless.

"I'll know the exact drug sooner than I know the DNA identification from the scarf, her body or her clothing, the jogger's swab, or the boyfriend's sample which you brought this morning on his water cup.

"My guess is that the killer used propofol, which is an anesthetic sedative, because it's easier to get than most stronger paralytics, especially if the killer also worked at a hospital. I think I heard you say that she seemed to know the person driving the unidentified car, right?

"Even if the killer worked in another hospital, propofol is still easy to get because it isn't controlled by the feds," Dr. Johnson continued, revealing another Achilles' heel in the world of medicine and death.

"Only three states control the dispensing of propofol within their borders, and New York isn't one of them."

"Then wouldn't the death have been from an overdose, like Michael Jackson?" Hank asked a reasonable question.

"Unlikely," Dr. Johnson said and continued to explain in layman's terms. "It's very difficult to die from a propofol overdose. Propofol is a sedative-hypnotic. It works by depressing certain neurons from working the right way to process information. It can lead to both cardiac arrest and respiratory depression which would be the resultant cause of death but not propofol toxicity *per se*."

Dr. Johnson swabbed the area of bruising on both sides and in the front of Brittany's neck and prepared a slide to view under the magnifying glass. Hank observed quietly. There wasn't even a tattoo on this young woman's body to ruin what God had created.

"By the way, you may want to get a subpoena for the system records from the hospital's drug vending machine," Dr. Johnson suggested while looking through the microscope.

"What drug vending machine?" Hank asked. In five years as an NYPD detective, he had never investigated a hospital-related homicide. In the five boroughs of New York City, most people were killed as a result of old-fashioned crimes like robbery or arson, vendettas, domestic violence or gang-related violence and drugs.

"Hospitals across the country employ a system to dispense drugs, presumably efficiently and expediently," Dr. Johnson said, offering another editorialized version of the facts.

"Each doctor, nurse, physician's assistant or hospitalist, is given a unique code which they must input to dispense prescribed drugs to patients, but the system is quite vulnerable," she revealed.

"Wicked people steal codes to withdraw drugs but can cover their steps by exploiting the machine's vulnerability," she explained. "They physically take it out of the machine but then cancel the withdrawal as a recorded error in the system, all while holding the stolen drugs in their hands.

"It happens more frequently than you can imagine, with some staffers using certain uncontrolled drugs, like propofol, to get a good night's sleep when they've just worked a double shift or amphetamines to stay awake during a long day's journey into night.

"Eugene O'Neill pretty much got addiction right on the money in that play."

The ME then returned to the autopsy table to pry open Brittany's mouth to begin a routine examination of each of her body cavities, while taking additional swabs.

"Well, what do we have here?" she said, grabbing for the tweezers on the adjacent equipment tray.

Hidden inside Brittany's mouth was a folded piece of paper. They never saw it at the scene because they didn't poke around too much in the sleet and the rain and the mud.

Hank started recording a video on his phone as the ME carefully lifted it out of the corpse and unfolded it. Her body stopped producing saliva at the moment of death so the contents of the note did not run as much as they could have if they had been soaking in any liquid for more than twenty-four hours.

"The invisible pain is unbearable #2" was handwritten in pencil on a tiny piece of paper.

The seasoned investigator and the veteran medical examiner just looked at each other in stunned, puzzled silence. Neither could make sense of the cryptic message nor the significance of the number two. This just added a whole new dimension to the investigation, one that would take time which they did not have, and one which must be concealed from everyone, except the investigators and the ME. The killer left a calling card. He wants to be discovered and make a name for himself. They had just entered a new level of this game with an adversary they did not know and could not see.

Brittany never knew she would not make it to graduation or walk down the aisle with her future husband. The killer knew but he did not care. On the surface, her life was as routine as most college kids working their way through school. Yet, under the dark cover of a muddy March night, her death was anything but ordinary.

Chapter Fifteen

"*Call me - 911*" was the emergency text from Hank. Maggie heard her phone signal just as she was about to meet with the dean of the nursing school at Mount Saint Vincent College.

She excused herself from greeting the receptionist and phoned him immediately. Hank explained they found a note, hidden inside the body, and read her its contents. He said it was handwritten, in cursive, and made an educated guess that poor Brittany was forced to write the note because the writing was very shaky and it looked feminine, like Catholic school feminine, cursive but not frilly. He knew Maggie would understand the reference having been educated by Catholic school sisters from a young age. Catholic schools gave special grades just for penmanship.

They would hate having to show the note to Brittany's Mom or boyfriend to have them identify the writing and would definitely need a handwriting expert to analyze the indicative meaning of the killer's signature.

"What does the number two mean? You think he's killed another and is just getting started?" Maggie questioned the note.

"Well, it certainly isn't a quote from scripture," Hank quipped.

"I've already checked department records in every borough and there are no cold, open, or even closed cases, where a similar note was stuffed inside the vic's mouth.

"I'll search NCIC and ViCAP next." Hank was hopeful the National Crime Information Center or the FBI's database, known as the Violent Criminal Apprehension Program, would possibly lead them somewhere which made sense. But right now, it was like searching for the proverbial needle in a haystack until the killer struck again. That was one thing they were sure of because if a killer leaves clues and notes and numbered victims, he will do it again and again, usually until he is eventually caught, otherwise there is no need for a note.

"Listen, I've got the dean here waiting for me," Maggie explained reluctantly. She would much rather spend her time and use her skills to track down the latest clue, which was far more important than speaking with a few friends who had yet to meet the victim's boyfriend.

"Let me get this over with and I'll meet you back at the house to dive in as soon as possible."

Maggie knew she owed it to the dean, and most certainly to Brittany's classmates, to assuage their fears and concerns as best as possible.

The college had already notified the entire student body a day earlier, alerting the campus before the story broke on the Sunday night news. Red alerts were now blasted by college administrators, via email and texts, on most college campuses, nationwide, at the earliest hint of any unrest, criminal activity, or any other threat to their welfare. It was distressing, on so many levels, that colleges now have to operate this way.

The college was a small, close-knit community, now understandably on edge at the thought of a possible killer in their midst. Kids, whether they're six years old or twenty, generally reach for extremes when dealing with anything they don't understand. It is a sad commentary that when someone is murdered, they often defer to serial killers.

The dean had asked Brittany's trio of close friends to meet with a detective in their residential suite. Maggie thought keeping the young women in familiar surroundings might ease the jitters of speaking with a cop about their dead friend. She also requested the dean remain in her office for the same reason.

Maggie was a stranger to this environment and surveyed the scene and took it in as they opened the door to their quad suite. Maggie did not go away to college. She had gone to the John Jay School of Criminal Justice and commuted to and from school and her dad's home in White Plains. There were two desks, arranged catty-corner in the living room, crowded with two laptops and plenty of textbooks neatly stacked. There were flowers and scent diffusers seemingly everywhere, as if the group of close friends fought for scent control of the apartment which merely resulted in the rooms smelling like the soured vintage cologne of an old grandmother. There was a small microwave oven and coffee machine on the counter of the kitchenette area with a tidy collection of neatly labeled canisters seemingly to hold things like tea bags, coffee pods and coffee. That was also unfamiliar to Maggie since she could not imagine espresso, or any coffee, made in a pod. Coffee was only meant to steam in a vintage moka pot or bubble in her nonna's old percolator.

Maggie introduced herself and handed each of them her business card. Their grief was not etched but carved into the lines of their faces. They wore it openly and it appeared they had not slept since first learning of their friend's demise.

They explained they were glued at the hip, wavering only when one or the other got a job or a boyfriend and then the girl-of-the-moment, understandably, had to divide her time and her focus away from the group. They were looking forward to meeting Mike and described Brittany as more in love with him than anyone else she had ever met in the past four years they had known her.

When Maggie asked if there was any indication of trouble in paradise, the girls simply said that Brittany seemed slightly upset last week that she did not have enough time to spend with Mike because of work. They fluffed it off to the unsteady, soft ground of any new relationship, and Maggie appreciated their insight.

She asked if any of them had a handwritten note from Brittany, and they said they had tons because Britt always left postie notes for herself and for them as reminders. They removed an old one stuck to the fridge, still there from when she moved back home a few months ago. Its words of encouragement simply said, *"You've got this, ladies. You're not invisible. I ♥ you!"*

Maggie carefully placed the small note into an evidence bag, sealing it and marking it with the date, time and location before placing her initials on the closed bag. She felt a heavenly sign from Brittany, quite literally, since the self-adhesive note contained one of the words the killer used on the note left inside her body, behind her lips, whispering from beyond. Maggie kept that info close to her chest and told the students to call any time, day or night, if they recalled something or if they simply needed a person to talk to in the middle of the night.

Chapter Sixteen

The day flew by, and Maggie rushed to headquarters to grab Hank for the pre-scheduled meet-and-greet with the night shift at Misericordia. The nursing administrator had requested the night shift come in an hour earlier to meet with police about Brittany's murder.

"The number two must be significant but how?" Maggie asked Hank as they tossed ideas back and forth in the squad car on the short ride from headquarters to the hospital.

"Lucky number? Second victim? Unlucky in love?" Hank juggled the easy choices, the ones which rationale people might consider, not serial killers. "I've spent the better part of the past four hours tracking down each of those possibilities, coupled with a stuffed note in the vic's mouth in nearly every accessible database, but nothing popped," he vented his frustration to Maggie.

They were eager to compare notes before they met with the evening crew. Maggie retrieved the postie note out of her bag and Hank brought up a photo of the note removed from Brittany's mouth on his phone.

"Wow," Hank was surprised. So was Maggie. The notes did not match although they both appeared to have been written by a woman.

"You think this guy's got a helper, maybe a girlfriend helping him?" Maggie wondered.

"It would make his job easier and ours a lot more complicated," Hank answered.

"If he's hunted with the help of anyone, maybe they easily got rid of the bodies who knows where," he guessed. "That could explain why there are no hits on record in any database."

Hank doubted it was a girlfriend, unless she had a fetish for playing with the ultimate bad boy. Yet the handwriting was characteristically female.

"He's got a pattern," Maggie said. "We just need to find out where and when it all started and whether he acted alone."

Brittany's second shift yesterday started at 5:00 p.m. and tonight's crew was the same. Maggie and Hank asked to meet with everyone who worked in the critical care unit, Brittany's last assignment that deadly night, and anyone else she might have interacted with based on hospital records.

People like transporters, orderlies, physicians' assistants, and other workers who float from floor to floor often see more than they admit. Of course, the hospital would pay the staffers overtime for their voluntary attendance, so they expected a full house in the cafeteria, which had been closed off to anyone but those attending the four o'clock meeting.

The buzz of the overhead fluorescent lights was not the soothing sound of a healing, sonic frequency which many believe have calming, spiritually healing powers. Sadly, very few city hospitals were places of healing right now. The aluminum trays of the chow line, usually offering three or four hot entrees served behind a glass barrier like in a prison, were empty to eliminate hovering people spreading all kinds of germs over the food supply. Maggie guessed that anyone in this medical center had likely lost their appetite and a taste for food amid the unsavory sights, scents and sounds of this ungodly purgatory.

The cafeteria doors swung open and shut as about a dozen members of the nightshift ambled in, masked up, making it easy for detectives to focus on their eyes which were the only facial feature not covered. The veteran detectives were well aware that people who looked down and to the left were generally lying or insecure. Body language experts believe that certain people who unknowingly engage in such behavior try to create a memory on the spot rather than recall something or someone from their recent or distant memory bank. That makes all the difference when investigating a homicide, the suitable pretext of their story, masking a lie, in that moment.

"Brittany was great when we left work," said the nurse who saw her get into the grey Honda Accord. "She was excited to be going home to her boyfriend's place, new love and all," she explained to Maggie.

"She was a ray of sunshine in this gloomy place.

"She turned left out of the employee entrance and started walking toward East 233rd Street," she continued. "My car was parked out back, on Carpenter Avenue, so as I phumped to get my key in the car door in the dark, I looked up and saw Maggie getting into the beat-up grey Honda up at the corner.

"I just thought her boyfriend had come to surprise her and pick her up, especially because it had started snowing, not heavy but those messy, wet flakes that quickly turn to slush in The Bronx."

"Had you met the boyfriend before?" Maggie asked.

"No, but she told me that he often came to get her when she worked late. I just assumed it was someone she knew because she got in the car without hesitation."

Hank had gathered a group of six other staffers in a corner. He wanted to weed out those who saw her but had no interaction with her and spend more time in the brief, hour-long meeting with anyone who had something to really contribute to the investigation. He came up empty after a quick *voir dire* of the group.

All city hospitals had been working with a skeleton crew which started just after Christmas and New Year's Eve. The critical care unit had become a flu isolation floor with people getting sick during the holidays and winding up on ventilators. Nothing made sense. So many patients came in and never left except in body bags. Ventilators became as rare as diamonds and needed to be shared between two patients, like stoners fighting to inhale on a hookah pipe, a questionable practice to say the least since hose contamination could easily spread any deadly pathogen.

Frustrated at the lack of progress, Maggie and Hank left Misericordia no further ahead in the hunt than they had been up to that point with less than a dozen workers showing up.

"Well, it sounds like she knew the killer," Hank said. "We didn't need to waste time here to learn that!"

"Well, we can always try to focus on the thousand friends she has on Facebook," Maggie said, also stymied. "How can one young person know so many people? And why would she let them into her little world?"

"You're sounding old, Mags, but I still love you."

"Seriously, I know about a dozen people outside my relatives and some of them I don't even talk to," Maggie said. "I don't want strange acquaintances knowing my business.

"Maybe it's what we do for a living that focuses our radar on the ugly in almost everything," Maggie complained. She was just winding up, or winding down, since the pair was heading home shortly.

"At her age I was walking a beat and carrying a gun, all while fully expecting some villain to be around every corner with a weapon pointed in my direction," she grumbled about their chosen profession.

"Didn't you feel that way?" she asked Hank. "I mean since we're bonding now and all, be honest."

"Yeah, of course I did, and I still do but we chose to do this," he replied. "Most millennials choose an easier career path. They're looking to sit home, get rich and enjoy that work-life balance, whatever the hell that is."

"By the way, some cub reporter for the campus newspaper stopped me at Saint Vincent's this morning on the way to my car," Maggie revealed, wanting to make sure the kid did not blindside Hank if she was not around. "I told her she had to go through the PIO. I hope that's the end of it. I just wanted you to have a heads up. Her name is Christy Maxwell, a communications major, obviously," she said rolling her eyes and wagging her head like a dashboard bobblehead doll.

"Obviously," Hank shared her sarcasm. "If you need to talk tonight, or any time at all, just call me," he said, fist-bumping her as he exited the squad car, each heading home in their own cars to find a tiny slice of solace in this crazy mess.

These two could never phone it in. You couldn't as a homicide detective in the NYPD, the nation's largest police force. Phoning it in could kill you.

Chapter Seventeen

It had been two days since Brittany's body was found at home plate much too close to home, both hers and his. He thought their relationship was off to a good start, but that bitch had to ruin everything with a boyfriend. Dare she turn down his advances in the car!

Rejection is not in his vocabulary. It had not been since that girl in seventh grade first turned him down. He only tried to get to second base and cop a feel. That's what seventh-grade boys do but she was not having it. She was just a stupid girl who deserved to be pushed off the curb. The bus flying down the street was just a bonus when it crushed the life right out of her a few blocks away from Indian Field. It was such a rush and killing Brittany brought it all back, front and center. He loved the surge of adrenaline and desperately craved recognition for crushing any form of rejection. There was a swelling in his groin just thinking about his exploits in his own backyard.

This neighborhood was home. It had been off and on since he was a kid, since his mother could not spend time with him and his sister the way other mothers in the neighborhood did with their kids. It was the Irish moms who baked the cookies and led scouting troops while most of their husbands walked a beat or fought fires. His Italian Mom was too busy working out of the house and when she was home, she slept. No flipping pancakes on the weekend or coming to watch his after-school pick-up games. It did not matter that no one ever picked him for a basketball team until they stretched for the second-string. He was just too short at thirteen years old. Still, his mother should have been there. Someone should have been there, but they never showed up.

He and Brittany had seen each other nearly every day for three months since she first started on the job. Their nights were spent commiserating about the growing darkness blanketing the city while The Bronx seemed to be getting hit the hardest. They supported each other, encouraged each other to keep pushing through, at least for the patients who could not help themselves. This was what friends did for each other, and he was hoping for more than friendship. He hoped that she wanted that as well, but he guessed wrong. And oh, how he hated being wrong.

He gazed at his view in the mirror as he shaved. Shoulders back, chin high, he admired his reflection. It was noon, because he rose much later than many people who had already worked most of the day. He didn't get home from work most nights until the next morning, usually between two and three o'clock. He moved about under the cloak of darkness much like the deadly vampire he had become, draining the very life from the people he was supposed to help or sucking it from the people who emasculated his ego. Either way they had to go.

This afternoon, the man who looked back at him in the mirror was unchanged from the day before, or the year before when he left the last place under the veil of jet-black desert skies. His surroundings were always spartan, always the same wherever he settled, even if only for a short time. There were no family photos hung as memories since he had none. There was no designer after-shave in the medicine cabinet to allow any ignorant cop to track down his specialty purchases. There was nothing to tie him to the past or to project his tomorrow to allow anyone to enter his space today.

He operated without a checking or savings account and received an actual paycheck each week, which he brought to a check-cashing store up north on White Plains Road, where it terminated at the city line in Mount Vernon. It was a different city in a different county. It was close enough for him to get there by bus, yet far enough from the hospital and his apartment. He didn't own a car. He borrowed them or stole them as needed.

It was always time for him to move on when his urges began to spiral out of control, usually revolving around some spirited, ignorant girl who thought she was better than him. She never was and he took care of her, eliminated the insult, before moving on to the next place.

He was hoping the move east, back home, would offer him solace in this crazy world where his internal compass always spun faster than his Kafkaesque mind could process. He simply did not have the mental or emotional capacity to distinguish deliverance from evil versus evil itself. He really did like helping people and truly believed that his compassionate hand assisted many in making the transition from this world to the next.

He resented the weak survivors of his patients, the so-called relatives, those insensitive to a suffering person's plight or just too indifferent to actually care about anyone other than themselves. They often misplaced reliance on easy street and doctors and were comfortable to have machines or other people decide how long to prolong life rather than rely on God. He, on the other hand, was quite comfortable being God's helper because that is how he envisioned himself when he looked in the mirror. Only the strong survive because only the strong can take care of themselves and this new job offered him the opportunity to help more than he could have ever imagined.

There was nothing ordinary about what was happening in the world despite global health officials trying to minimize the impact of this deadly scourge, using labels such as the novel Corona virus. The only thing novel about it, he thought, was that it started with a thumb-sized bat more than two months ago.

They've already locked down Italy. Yet, the United States, in its infinite arrogance, thinks what? We're America and it won't head this way. He knew better, and so did every first responder in the city, that catching whatever this deadly virus was could have him checking out before he checked in for his next shift, which could be his last.

A new year, a new job, with new adventures. He was just getting started.

Chapter Eighteen

The old adage of the first forty-eight hours being the most important did not add up to much. Maggie and Hank had nothing to punt across the finish line to bring this case to a quick close. The commissioner was breathing down the captain's neck and he, in turn, was on top of his squad to put this case to bed, make an arrest, get it off the news and move on.

Not even the victim's boyfriend looked good for this one. Or was he just too helpful?

The Scavi family had offered to pay for Brittany's funeral. There is nothing the mob likes more than throwing a good wake. They had to wait for the girl's distant relatives to arrive, but the clock was ticking toward a citywide shutdown, so they would hold the wake on Saturday and the funeral on Monday and pray the city would hang on just long enough to say goodbye to poor Brittany Jenkins.

Hank and Maggie realized they had to cast a wider net quickly and returned to Misericordia by late morning, this time hosting anyone and everyone who wanted to talk to them in the cafeteria.

The scene was starkly different from yesterday. This morning a long line of people flowed in and out of the dining room. Word was spreading fast around the hospital, and many others had seen the news reports. The curious, typically, just wanted to vent their own concerns. Others searched for information as to exactly what happened. Some were hanging off to the side hoping to learn something, anything, while others eagerly jumped to the head of the line so as not to miss the start of their shift.

"Are we in danger here?" one nurse asked.

"Did she know who killed her?" a transporter wondered.

"Is the hospital beefing up security?" an intern grilled the detectives as if they had control over administration of the hospital.

Right now, they were all operating on autopilot with a common refrain of *danger dead ahead* floating through their incestuous world, looking like the masked aides of a war zone field hospital, exhausted and disheveled, hiding the misery under their scrubs. The uniform served as a shield so the walking wounded could easily move through the community which they were almost too tired to serve. It also placed investigators at a great disadvantage, not being able to see the people they were speaking to about the heinous act which silenced one of their own.

They have no idea who I am, he thought, as he joined the long line of his colleagues, now standing six feet apart, out the door and down the hallway, waiting patiently for a turn to see the detectives. He had no intention of actually speaking to them. Silence is golden on his mission. He merely listened as he neared the table so he could hear the babble of what the detectives were telling his ignorant co-workers.

"Yes, we're keeping the hospital informed of any developments," Hank assured two nurses standing in front of him. He could see the anxious masked man standing just behind the pair of nurses. Hank was taken aback, surprised, when that same man smiled at him through dark, piercing eyes above his mask and then abruptly turned, away and off the line, just as he neared the table.

The masked employee carefully retreated, stepping back into the hall to disappear to his workstation, quite sure the cops had nothing on him based on the cafeteria chatter. He was confident that he was not in danger but cautious because he had made it this far. He did not want to be caught just yet when there was so much more for him to do amid the organized chaos and the unremitting noise.

He struggled to quiet his mind, to silence the racket inside his own head, so that he could do what he was meant to do, to help patients. He was focused on the mission at hand, and he knew that dear old Thelma Ondrovich was waiting for him in room 602. The poor woman was barely hanging on and had been connected to life support for nearly a week. There was no point in prolonging the inevitable.

"How ya doin', sweetheart?" he asked as he entered the room. He didn't expect an answer, but he believed she could still hear him in her semi-sedated state. She was lying there in isolation, like dozens of others elsewhere throughout the hospital, wheeled in on stretchers and barely able to breathe. The ventilator was the only way they had a chance of survival and that was slim at best.

He approached her bed calmly, gently holding her hand and telling her about Saturday night's first snowfall of the season. His voice was the first she had heard in what seemed like forever. Her eyes were closed but she was not restful. She was stuck in the twilight where one loses all sense of time and space and prays for relief from the pain and the monotony of nescience. It is only the doctors, the nurses, the staff and whatever family connects through a mobile phone who comfort themselves with the fiction that she feels no pain and is unaware of her surroundings.

He was all too familiar with the shadows of the gloaming that exist between pain and death, as well as the narrative he told himself to ease his pain watching his sister die day by day. It is that monologue which we all have with ourselves in our darkest hour. We give voice to regrets in an effort to ease our conscience and trust that the unaware soul can hear us. We hold onto the belief that they are unaware of their pain while simultaneously cognizant of our prayers and confessions to relieve it, because without those feeble beliefs the effort to anesthetize our own pain would be futile.

He always deferred to trying to connect, seeking permission for what would be the most important decision of the life they had lived – when to end their own story!

"Thelma, can you hear me? Squeeze my hand if you can," he directed her. He had learned from experience that semi-sedated patients respond quicker to being called by their first name and not their surname. Formalities fall by the wayside when your life is on the line.

She squeezed his hand. It was weak, more like a gentle compression than a binding constriction, but still strong enough to indicate that poor Thelma was still in there, in the grey zone between knowing and unknowing, mindful enough to know that she was still Thelma.

"Thelma, would you like me to help make it all better? Squeeze again if it's a yes." He directed her once more and she complied.

He held her intravenous tube in one hand and the syringe in the other hand. It was not his usual drug choice, but it would be just as quick, and she would absolutely feel no pain.

"Who are you and what are you doing there?" A doctor startled him as he entered the room.

Dr. Scott Levy generally worked in the emergency room and was not familiar with all of the ancillary personnel who seemed to aimlessly roam the halls these days. He did not see that the man at the woman's bedside was actually holding a syringe in his hand but was more concerned that he was too close to the bed of a Covid patient and could catch the deadly bug himself.

"I was just talking to her," he answered the doctor's question without hesitation. "It's what we all do on this floor. We help them make the transition easier." He was firm in his conviction, having just pushed the drug into poor Thelma's IV port.

Levy was puzzled. He dealt with life and death on an hourly basis in the ER and had distanced himself emotionally from everyone who came through its doors on a stretcher, whether that patient was a non-responsive accident victim or a child who had fallen to his death from a sixth-floor window. Learning to compartmentalize his emotions and his reactions was a coping mechanism which left him questioning how and why non-professional volunteers and low-level employees could pour so much of themselves into handling the death of strangers.

He quickly approached the doctor to offer a fist bump, the new greeting of the Covid era, but instead gave him a dose of his own medicine. Levy's hesitancy was just long enough to throw off his internal compass, the one which questioned the authenticity of this worker's empathy.

Within seconds the doctor had fallen to his knees, sliding his hand down the patient's bedside, grasping for anything to hold onto as he lost all control of his own body. The doctor's gut feeling was right, but his fatal mistake was not acting fast enough on his hunch.

He caught the water pitcher precariously left on the bedside table to keep it from hitting the floor along with the doctor, causing any sound to make an attentive, sensitive staff come running.

With the doctor out of the way, he was free to administer last rites, his way, to poor Mrs. Ondrovich and held her hand as she took her last breath.

He was out the door before anyone answered Thelma's death alarm, finding a two-for-one mess on their hands.

"We're losing them," Hank whispered to Maggie. He noticed many workers drifting into the hall to go about their day, while others remained off to the side to commiserate with each other as distant friends often do at a wake.

Maggie could see the stress of the workers in their bloodshot eyes, eyes which had seen more than their fair share of death in the last month, more than most others had seen in their entire career or lifetime.

The accomplished detectives knew that without a major development soon, Brittany's murder map, outlined on the white board back in the squad room, would be photographed for posterity and then erased, joining the list of other cold cases in the city's backlog. While New York's murder rate was rising, the homicide clearance rate was sharply declining. Brittany's body would be buried in one box on Monday, while her murder book would be stored in another box if Maggie and Hank did not identify the killer, make an arrest, and charge that person with murder before turning them over to the court. They needed to clear the case quickly but agreed to keep this query session open for at least another two hours until the start of the next shift change.

A patrol officer was brought in to assist with taking down the names and numbers of doctors, nurses, administrators, clerks and even volunteers, basically anyone who showed up to ask questions or voice concerns. Not one of them offered a viable lead or clue worth pursuing.

"They're numb and just plain exhausted," Maggie said, pulling Hank aside. She was just as tired and knew the group interrogation was not useful.

"They're war-weary," Hank agreed. "How could they not be? It's like sound torture in here."

The incessant clamor of sirens and alarms was suddenly elevated as pagers and text alerts went off from every direction, sending most personnel running to their stations.

"I'm sorry but we're now dealing with the loss of one of our own," the nursing administrator said after reading an urgent text on her phone.

"I have to go. A doctor just dropped dead in a patient's room."

Chapter Nineteen

Maggie and Hank shared the same thought for a nano-second, that the killer was not only on staff but on duty and active at that very moment.

"Nah, can't be," said Hank. "We can't get that lucky."

Luck had nothing to do with it and the facts sometimes speak for themselves. Maggie chased the administrator down the hall, suggesting they follow her to the floor to investigate, but that idea fell on deaf ears.

The hospital needed to function and if any more staff were killed on the job, or even worse that one of their own was killing their own, the already depleted workforce would continue its hiatus, leaving very few first responders to handle the growing caseload.

Maggie and Hank were reluctant to leave but they were guests without a warrant. They had no authority to go traipsing through the hospital investigating every death. If anything was out of the ordinary in the doctor's demise, they were confident the hospital would call them to report it.

"Let's stay on this," said Hank as he jumped into the driver's seat. "We'll grab a couple of pies at Louie's and head back to the house. We've got other leads we can check in the meantime while waiting to reconnect with the hospital."

"You're right," Maggie agreed. "People are dropping dead, left and right, even doctors. It doesn't mean they were murdered."

This new coupling for the law enforcement pair was working well. They were laser-focused like the pilots of an F-22 ready to take down the target as soon as he was in their crosshairs. They picked up the dinner of champions, two honey pepperoni and garlic pizzas, knowing it would carry them for the long night ahead. Maybe, they hoped, just maybe, that if they could corral other detectives in the squad room to look at the murder map with fresh eyes, then they would move the case off the dime.

They had to plot and revise the timeline, based on all of the staff interviews, while the scant information they received was still fresh in their heads and not buried in their notebooks. Unfortunately, the squad room was as quiet as a school library on a Friday night. All they could hear was the heavy snoring of Captain Bradshaw emanating from his office. The captain had also been working around the clock and must have run out of steam.

He rustled awake as the smell of spicy pepperoni and garlic wafted back toward and through his open door.

"You guys are working late," he said. "Thanks for picking up dinner. Cholesterol be damned," he proclaimed, grabbing a slice and his coat before heading home.

Maggie never saw her father stop to eat while he was working on anything, whether a case or building her treehouse in the backyard. She was like him in so many ways but needed to refuel to make her grey cells function properly.

Maggie jotted new notes and plotted on the board while Hank got a chance to make a few follow-up calls to see if any beat-up, grey Honda Accords had been reported missing in the past week or so.

"Bingo," he shouted while returning the old black desk phone to its cradle base. He schkeeved holding the dirty earpiece which someone forgot to wash with alcohol after holding it too close to their lunch.

Someone set a grey Accord on fire at the Jerome Avenue station late Saturday night into early Sunday morning just a few blocks from where Brittany Jenkin's body was found. The area was well-trafficked by kids in cars just hanging out, booming salsa and hip-hop music from sound systems worth more than their cars. Drug dealers also sold their wares to many of those same young people. They favored the spot knowing there were no cameras in the darkened dead zone behind the west side of Woodlawn Cemetery and the dense black southern edge of the woods behind Van Cortlandt Park just behind the golf course. It behooved the dealers to know their turf well, empowering them to thwart possible competition from sneaking in while avoiding the attention of the cops.

The only eyes on the well-known hangout for rogues were the eyes of the souls buried long ago across the street, and they were not talking. The security cameras at the elevated subway stop were also broken, conveniently on purpose.

Hank explained to Maggie that the car had been stolen from New Mexico about a year ago while the New York tags were reported stolen or lost only about ten months ago.

Things just got a lot more complicated. A car stolen more than halfway across the country winds up in The Bronx with New York license plates stolen less than a year ago. The car must have been driven across the country with old New Mexico plates, from the Land of Enchantment to the Empire State, before the thief needed to fit in with Bronx locals while not catching the eye of the local NYPD.

It was only four o'clock in the afternoon in New Mexico. Hank crossed his fingers that someone would still be hanging around for the day at the Guadalupe County Sheriff's office where the car had been reported stolen.

"The car was taken after a young girl went missing about a year ago," the sheriff's deputy told Hank. "The girl was never found, and the car was never recovered. We chalked it up to her being a runaway since that happens a lot in this backwater.

"It's possible that she was kidnapped by a drifter or went with him voluntarily," the deputy explained. "Unfortunately, kids here are always looking for a way out of Nowheresville."

Hank also learned that the car had belonged to the missing girl's family who lived on a nearby reservation. He thanked the deputy for that information and so much more unnecessary data on the county's demographics.

"There are less than 4,500 people in Guadalupe, New Mexico," Hank told Maggie after he hung up the phone. "The girl had been working nights at a gas station near Interstate 40, the old Route 66, and she just vanished, never to be seen again, along with her family's car."

"That car was probably someone's ride to New York, whether back home or for that first visit to the promised land," Maggie said.

"Simple as that, huh?" Hank questioned her guestimate at best. "Why didn't they bring it to a chop shop and make a few bucks?"

"Well, maybe they were using it for dark and nefarious purposes, and it was getting too hot to handle, so they just torched it."

Chapter Twenty

Hank and Maggie regretted the visit they had to pay Friday morning to the man who reported his plates lost or stolen ten months ago. He lived in the Pelham Bay area, and they grit their teeth with each pothole they hit along the way.

They had called ahead, so Vinnie LoCascio was waiting at his front door, like a sentry waiting for the troops to arrive, when they pulled up in front of his 1940s two-story, red brick house. This mini fortress looked like every other red brick house on the block except for the ten-by-two-foot strip of lawn, which ran parallel to the well-maintained driveway, crowned by a shrine of the Madonna. Vinnie came from Palermo and thanked God every day for his new life in America. Yet, he had nothing but criticism for Mayor DeBlasio's failure to fix the potholes which plagued the borough and the crime which necessitated iron bars across all of the windows on each and every house in the neighborhood.

"*Ma, tu sai. Capisci?*" he asked Maggie if she understood in Italian because she had spoken a bit with him in his mother tongue on the phone when she called earlier.

"*Si, si,*" Maggie said, recognizing when it was best to use the mother tongue. She was bilingual from the moment she was born, living with and listening to her Irish American father and the Sicilian grandmother who raised her after her own mother died in childbirth.

"The mayor, he is uh from Napoli, whadda you expect?" Signore LoCascio, spoke with his hands and shrugged his shoulders, speaking English directly to Hank who didn't understand the man's disdain of people from Naples in the south of the boot.

"I guess I lost, uh, dee plates when I hit uh dee crater as big as uh dee moon," LoCascio said, holding his hands wider than his shoulders to exaggerate the size of the pothole.

Hank had to look down or he'd burst into laughter. New Yorkers, when speaking to cops, either bashed them with verbal barbs or spoke to them like they had a direct hotline to the mayor's office for complaints, with the ensuing power to wave a magic wand and cure all of their troubles, like fixing potholes. If only it were true, Hank would have called DeBlasio a year ago with his own complaints and questions about working without a contract and no pay hikes for cops for several years.

It was back to the drawing board with a much-needed chinwag in the squad car, just the way she used to discuss cases with Tommy before the world turned upside down.

"So, before we go down that road, what's with the Sicilian-Naples rivalry?" Hank asked.

"Oh, that goes back centuries, and we don't have enough time today," Maggie laughed. "Northerners dislike anyone south of Rome. Sicilians are not looked at as true Italians because they only unified with Italy after the king of the two Sicilies was overthrown by Garibaldi in 1860. And Naples, well, that's a whole other story but largely now because the Napoli Ultra soccer fans are rued the world over as boorish." She spit out the script faster than an old-school tickertape machine because she had repeated it so many times to so many non-Italian-American people.

"What the? I thought you were Irish, Flynn?" Hank sat behind the wheel as puzzled as ever.

"Don't let my deceased Sicilian nonna hear you say that," Maggie said. "She raised me when my mom died, and my Irish dad wholeheartedly embraced her deep love for her favorite and only granddaughter."

"*Begosh and begorrah,*" Hank snickered back in a bad Irish brogue.

"Yeah, Tommy tells everyone that I had the Irish drummed out of me long ago.

"So, do you buy that story from the New Mexico deputy that the drifter was just walking along a desolate stretch of Route 66 without a plan, and without a car, and figured he'd kidnap a girl and hitch a ride at the same time?" Maggie shifted gears. She questioned the deputy's unsubstantiated guess.

"That plot just sounds like a bad TV movie where a slasher hides a chainsaw in a garage deep in the woods of the Appalachians."

"You're a Bronx girl and you ask why and immediately jump to a slasher in the woods?" Hank said, shaking his head in astonishment. He looked dead ahead while driving back to the house to steer clear of the numerous crater-like potholes, but his words were pointed directly at Maggie in the passenger's seat.

"Maybe he had no plan but was loaded with cash and chatted up the girl just to get the car," he hypothesized.

"And maybe tumbleweed blows across Bronx Boulevard in the spring," Maggie snapped back. "All we have are guesses and that's not good enough for Brittany."

"We don't know whether the girl in New Mexico is dead," Maggie said. "She just may be living anywhere between here and there, but it may require a visit to the southwest."

Captain Bradshaw ixnayed a road-trip and adamantly reminded them that New York was on the verge of collapse, the magnitude of which he compared to a nuclear winter. He needed them to hunker down rather than pack their bags and escape to warmer climates where the novel Corona virus had yet to rear its head.

They pivoted sharply, as adept New York detectives could turn on a dime in the right direction. Instead, they arranged an online virtual meeting with Sheriff Mitchell E. Gallup later in the afternoon. He explained there was no surveillance footage and no records of any purchases at the time the girl vanished with the family's car. She was a Native American who lived on a reservation, and they don't give up their secrets easily, if at all.

"It could've been a kidnapping," the Sheriff suggested. "It could've been an escape. Whatever the reason, alone or with someone, they likely jumped on I-40 and never looked back."

He explained the disappearance was reported first by a customer who wanted to buy gas in the middle of the night, but there was no one inside the station. The lights were on at the gas-mart and the door was unlocked, but no one was home.

"The girl left her belongings behind, including her purse and phone. The only thing missing was her driver's license," the sheriff added. "She vanished without a trace, or she didn't want to be found."

Gallup also shared with his New York counterparts that there were a few drops of blood on the floor by the cash register, which turned out to be hers, along with the torn wrapping of a prepaid phone card and the plastic container of the phone she also took.

"She could have known how to do a work-around to validate the card without registering the sale," Gallup suggested. Yet, that was just another shot in the dark and he suggested there wasn't enough blood on the floor to mean anything more than she probably cut her finger trying to open the damn blister pack which formerly held a new burner phone.

"Santa Rosa is only about three hundred miles from the Mexican border," the sheriff continued. "If there was a perp, he could've been an illegal, someone from the rez or someone just passing through, but we'll never know. We have too many alleged kidnappings out here, so we solve the ones we can solve, and we keep moving forward. It's a sad reality."

"So, maybe the Guadalupe vic wasn't a vic at all and she just wanted to start a new life," Hank said after they ended their online meeting with Sheriff Gallup.

"So, why torch the car unless you're hiding something?" Maggie asked. "And so close to where Brittany was found? There's no such thing as coincidence.

"You know what Einstein said about coincidence?" she asked Hank.

"No, but enlighten me, please." He could barely silence his sarcasm.

"Coincidence is God's way of remaining anonymous," she said. "You can take the girl out of the Catholic school, but you can't take the Catholic school out of the girl."

"In this case, the killer is only unknown until we find him," she asserted confidently.

"Unless he dies of Covid first and then it's lights out, permanently," Hank quipped only to receive a roll of the eyes from his temp partner. He also reminded her to add a note to the murder map that the doctor who died the other night at the hospital was just a tragic casualty of the pandemic. He had called Debra Feingold earlier just to wrap up that possible lead.

Maggie continued typing notes from their virtual consultation with the sheriff and taped them to the whiteboard for reference and placed a copy in the murder book as well.

Everything was backed up twice. Double everything would make a difference if the case went cold and needed to be reinvestigated years later. The clock never runs out on murder.

Chapter Twenty-One

Brittany's wake, at the funeral parlor on McLean Avenue in Yonkers, started much earlier than the usual 2:00 p.m. afternoon session. The funeral director knew her mother from the church and squeezed in Brittany's wake as soon as he buried another Covid victim that Saturday morning. By one o'clock, mourners, mostly colleagues from the hospital and fellow students from Mount Saint Vincent, had formed a long line winding down the avenue and along the side street which reached back into The Bronx.

Maggie and Hank had arrived earlier to speak with Mrs. Jenkins and to offer their condolences. Mike Scavi was already there, offering her the support of a son, sitting next to Brittany's mother in the front row, facing the casket which held her only child. The funeral director had to open an adjacent flower room because of the large number of arrangements which had been sent in sympathy. Someone had sent a large spray of Brittany's favorite flower, pink Gerber daisies draped with a stethoscope. Maggie carefully spied the note clipped to the ribbon and noticed it was from her friends and former roommates. Of course, one of them had shared their loss and expression of shared grief on a pink postie note in her honor. Mike's heart-shaped pink roses stood on the other side of the casket while a rosary of white roses was pinned to the lid of the casket, identifying its sender with the simple gold-foil letter garland, *Loving Daughter*.

Hank asked the funeral director if there were security cameras at the front door and was advised the home would fully cooperate in turning over the video files to police without a subpoena. Death may be big business to funeral directors, but it was in the best interests of everyone in the neighborhood to get a killer off their streets.

The detectives knew that killers often show up at a wake or funeral to view their handiwork, so Maggie took a seat in the back corner while Hank wandered around the very crowded vestibule and inner hall. Mourners walked through in a steady stream but very few lingered to chat or share memories. Maggie lost count after a hundred and that was an hour ago.

Why do dozens, sometimes hundreds, of mourners show up when a young person dies? Maggie wondered. She knew from personal experience that less than a handful sometimes show up when an older person dies. She hoped it was the shock of the loss, tinted by the element of curiosity when the death was caused by the homicide of a young victim. Whereas the mourners for senior citizens are often limited to their surviving relatives and a few close friends while death is anticipated as the human body ages. It was a grim thought, but she tried to keep her brain active as the monotony of the ceremonies of death was never easy to sit through no matter the individual's role.

Mike's mobbed-up relatives showed up in dribs and drabs, while some straggler wannabes smoked feverishly, chatting like old crones on the sidewalk. Many were known to Maggie or Hank or both of them. Cops know their turf and who brings trouble. Some of these guys lived scattered throughout The Bronx and Yonkers, while others were on Staten Island or in Brooklyn, each in their own corners playing nice. They came to pay their respects to Mikey Boy more than to Brittany's mother, whom they never met until that afternoon. There's nothing quite like a good wake to bring out the mob in large numbers, or to send lots of big showy floral arrangements. And each member of the Scavi crew knew Maggie and Hank, maybe not personally, but detectives can't blend in, no matter how hard they try. They just stand out in a crowd!

During the afternoon wake-break everyone, including relatives, friends, the media and Maggie and Hank, seemed to gravitate toward Rory Dolan's just down the street, to grab a bite or a drink. It was the largest eatery and pub near the funeral home and the funeral director had a printed sign with directions to Rory's posted near the guest sign-in book to keep people from repeatedly asking the staff the same question as to the location of the nearest restaurant or bar.

Maggie and Hank grabbed burgers but mostly listened to the whispers and gossip which permeated the pub-like dining room. Some talked about avoiding the area around the New Rochelle temple which seemed to be ground zero for the new Covid assault on New York. Others recalled bad memories of the Son of Sam killings by David Berkowitz forty years earlier. The young college kids, guzzling down midday beers like camels drinking water, wondered who would do such a thing to Brittany and selfishly imagined whether they could be next. Their inexperienced scope of reference had not yet expanded enough to make them think anything could happen to anyone other than themselves. Yet, the death of a random young person never made sense in anyone's world.

Someone dies, anyone, and others are affected in ways they could never have imagined until the eternal absence of that person becomes the ever-present constant in their lives.

Chapter Twenty-Two

Lying mixed with empathy in his world, atypical for a sociopath. While he empathized with those who were suffering, either from illness or societal isolation, he easily lied to himself and to anyone who crossed his path that his actions to alleviate their pain and suffering were acceptable and without consequence. Earlier today he was able to shake Mrs. Jenkins' hand and express his sorrow for her loss. Yet, in a strange way, while he lied to the woman, he did feel sorry for her, losing her only child, all the while still believing that Brittany was a bitch who deserved to die. On the one hand, rejection left a sour taste on his tongue worth killing for, while on the flip side, empathy and sorrow served up savory, if not unusual complements, mutually satisfying his unusual palate.

He avoided eye contact with police and returned to the hospital for his evening shift. Those who hadn't attended the wake in the afternoon would surely pay their respects tonight, while he worked and plotted and helped. He loved the night shift. He thrived in it, out of the daylight, slithering through hospital halls and roaming around neighbors' homes to do as he saw fit, dispensing death as he deemed necessary. He could move freely in the hospital with fewer people around. He was relaxed at night and that made his job so much easier.

The number of people dying was tripling daily, putting everyone on edge. So much pain was overwhelming. He had to help by weeding out the weak so the strong could survive. Nurses and doctors took oaths, but he did not.

For more than 1,600 years, doctors, under the Hippocratic Oath, have pledged to minimize suffering while understanding that a dignified death is an important goal. Nurses, likewise, under the Nightingale Pledge, have promised to themselves *and* to God that they will not administer any harmful drug. Fortunately, he never made promises he couldn't keep. He was not bound by either constraint and thrived under his liberal interpretation of professional responsibility.

He had been stealing vials of propofol and vecuronium like candy from a baby for some time, in many places and for many reasons. The unregulated drugs left him unleashed to administer death under his terms and according to his covenant with the devil. He was on a mission to rid the world of rejection and to help the neediest in making their transition to a better place. If a body was rejecting life, who was he to help prolong it?

He was like an obsessed video gamer playing with the drug dispensing machine. It had become his favorite toy a few years back when he first became a hospital transporter. He became a master of its operation and manipulation in very short order. Watching from the corners while waiting to take patients to and from the imaging center, operating rooms, discharge or eventually, the morgue, he learned how passcodes could be manipulated and the drugs dispensed in error.

No one ever suspects him, they never do. They are always too busy to notice those who blend into the sterile surroundings of the hospital's hierarchal culture. They look at him every day but never see him. He is unimportant in their world, just a necessary element always on standby, always in the shadows. The professional staff ignore those they don't see as necessary to patient care, but they won't for long. Soon, everyone will know his name and rejection will be in his rearview.

In this moment, amid the surging death toll, he needed to live in his new power and craved recognition on a grand scale with someone, anyone to acknowledge his contributions before his time ran out. He was cunning, strategic, well-organized and cautious when necessary but not hesitant to act. He had been getting away with it for years. His patients needed him, while those other women were dispensable. Who were they to say no to his advances? No one would ever say no to him, not ever again.

Confident, strong, smart – that's how he saw himself, catching his reflection as he passed a window of the ICU, his nod was a self-serving pat on the back but like Narcissus it could also be his downfall. Whether helping those deadly ill with a virus or those who made him sick to his stomach, it didn't matter to him. He expressed his personal duality in a singular hell. After Brittany's funeral on Monday, this chapter would be done and dusted and onto the next.

Chapter Twenty-Three

Maggie slept late this Sunday morning, or at least she didn't wake until seven o'clock, which is her idea of getting a late start on the day. Jax stayed at his place in the city, and she was happy to have the bed to herself. As much as she loved the safe space between his ripped biceps, she also appreciated, and needed, her time alone.

She took full advantage of her free day for a mental health break with a morning massage at the nearby day spa and a stop at Boiano's to grab Uncle Bobby's cookies before heading to his place for Sunday dinner. They had a packed agenda for their weekly get-together. Of course, she needed his insight on the Jenkins' murder through a verbal game of Clue, but she didn't want to guess any longer on his opinion of Jax, the most important relationship that she's had as a grown-up.

When she arrived, he was just finishing up a quick *Spaghetti all'Arrabbiata*, after tossing a garden salad with a balsamic vinaigrette dressing. She set the table as he finished in the kitchen, his happy space. This was home. He was family. This was a safe place to be her true self, safe enough for her to let her guard down or put her walls up and not be judged either way.

Bobby knew better than to push her about the case after dinner. She'd speak when she was ready, so he carried over a bottle of merlot to the spacious yet comfy sofa pit where they could talk over something he knew she was dying to hear.

"You've found a good one, Mags," he said, refilling her near empty glass.

She breathed easier. She hoped Jax would stick around, or that she would as well. Either way, it was so much better to do the relationship thing with Uncle Bobby in her corner.

He held off advising her against the usual self-sabotaging behavior which was endemic to the profession. Cops, as a rule, tend to put up walls, internalizing the job's stress and eventually pushing their partners, friends and family away. He had done it himself much too often and remained a bachelor as a result.

"Why didn't you bring him tonight?" he asked.

"You knowww," she whined like she did when she was sixteen and not too sweet. "It's been a week of fifteen-hour days. I'm exhausted," she said, offering a pat excuse.

"Uh, what I do know, young lady, is that even a good one will leave if the relationship is built on texts or voicemails."

"Noted," she said dismissively to force him onto the deadly subject of murder. She wasn't the first cop to struggle with the work-life balance and she wouldn't be the last.

"First, Captain Bradshaw gave me his blessing to consult with you," she advised him. "He also noted that in the murder book as an official consultation." Her honesty served her well, on the job and in life. She knew better than to discuss the details of an ongoing investigation with anyone outside the inner circle of investigators, and while Uncle Bobby was a sanctioned consultant because of his legacy on the job, Jax did not fit that role.

"We know the victim, the what, where, when and the how, but we don't know the who or the why," she said, starting to fill in the blanks for him which had not been released to the media, including the possibility that he took a souvenir from Brittany Jenkins.

"We've also ruled out Brittany's new boyfriend or his mobbed-up family, and the victim herself seems squeaky clean, loved by all.

"Weird, though, she looks like she could be my kid sister, so it's crawled under my skin just a little bit."

"Okay, so whaddya need me for?" he asked, sipping on his second glass of wine.

"Murder is predictable," he reminded her.

"Murder always has a pattern. You've known that since I bought you your favorite board game for your tenth birthday.

"Your attention to and retention of detail was astonishing for a kid whose mind changed on an hourly basis. And your analytical skills constantly surprised me and scared your father," he said, smiling a bit with a nod of his head as he remembered his longtime partner and best friend.

"I guess the acorn doesn't fall far from the tree."

"Walk me through it, the who, what, where, when and how and we'll figure out the why and build a profile of the who together," the probing retiree said to his favorite, and only, godchild and mentee.

Maggie ran down the basic facts that Brittany Jenkins, a young nursing student was murdered at Indian Field, just blocks from her home on Saturday night into early Sunday morning. She was strangled with her own scarf and sedated with a drug, most likely propofol, which the ME is testing.

"We know that strangulation is a crime of passion or sexual release where the killer needs to control or dominate the victim, so it must be a man," Maggie said. She offered only an educated guess, surmising that most women would not have the physical strength to drag the semi-sedated dead weight of anyone from the street to the field.

"Our problem is that he also drugged her and then strangled her in a well-lit area, albeit at night.

"And here's the kicker – he left a calling card, which we haven't told anyone yet, not outside of me, Hank, Tommy, Lou, the captain, the ME, and now you.

"He left a handwritten note inside her mouth, and it looks as though it was written by a woman," she said. "And yes, we compared it to a sample of Brittany's handwriting, and it's definitely not hers, even if she was under duress.

"But he may have an accomplice," Maggie tossed out a clue she had only just thrown around the empty space of her own mind when she couldn't sleep.

"While the words seem to be written by a female, the number is heavier and appears to be written by someone different, perhaps a man," Maggie surmised. "I'm no handwriting expert but the words and the number were definitely written by two different people."

"Can I assume you and Hank checked all of the state and national databases for similar crimes?"

She assured him they had, for open, closed and cold cases, and all came up empty.

"The note said, *"The invisible pain is unbearable #2."*

"We're not sure if Brittany was his second victim or two is his lucky number. We also think that he borrowed or stole a car that was reported missing in New Mexico a year ago when a gas station attendant vanished without a trace. We think he torched the car just under the Jerome Avenue station after leaving Brittany's body at home plate.

"We have no physical evidence linking the car to her murder because most of it was destroyed in the fire except for a New York license plate which was reported lost or stolen in The Bronx just under a year ago," she summed up the key issues for her favorite sleuth.

"So, linking the scarce clues, the question is who did it in the park with a pashmina in the rain? It certainly wasn't Colonel Mustard," Maggie said in frustration. It had been just about a week since Brittany's body was discovered, and they were no closer to finding the man who took her life.

"If Brittany had a boyfriend, she likely rejected this guy and that's his stressor," Bobby said. "Rejection doesn't sit well with him, but you know that. It's Murder 101."

"He lacks societal restraint and craves control, so he asserts his dominance where he can, not in the bedroom or sexually anywhere else, but by physically subduing them," Maggie agreed.

"And since the co-worker saw her voluntarily get into the car on a cold, wet, snowy night, then she must have known him," Maggie added. "She didn't feel threatened."

"Exactly!" Bobby agreed. "And most likely she worked with him.

"I mean who else is driving around on a slushy night near a hospital these days?" He also noted that the young victim did not have much of a social life outside her hectic schedule and her new relationship, limiting her connections.

"Her friends told you that her schedule was work – boyfriend – home, repeat and that wasn't likely to change until she graduated," Bobby punctuated the obvious.

"Focus. You and Hank, plot it step by step and recognize that you already have more than you know."

She knew he was right, as always, but all they had were educated guesses based on their joint experiences.

She hugged him goodnight and called Jax from the car. They could both sleep better knowing each other was safe, at least for now, in this crazy new world.

Chapter Twenty-Four

As expected, not as many people attended the funeral mass for Brittany on Monday morning. New Yorkers, who are usually fearless-to-a-flaw, were now too scared to leave their homes. Many were visibly shaken and worried by whatever this bug was that was killing people in droves, while younger millennials were more concerned with how to spot a killer in a crowd since they might be his next victim and wanted to avoid possible extinction at all costs.

Maggie and Hank had arrived early and grabbed a legitimate parking spot on McLean Avenue a few blocks away from Saint Barnabas Church. It was weird for Maggie each time she came here on a case, like four years ago when the Binky Killer was murdering priests at the start of her career as a detective. This was the church where she was baptized in the arms of Uncle Bobby, where she received First Communion and Confirmation and where she had attended funeral masses for both her nonna and her dad, bittersweet memories, reverence mixed with traumatic and unforgettable memories. There was so much life and death inside this one parish church. The century-old Neo-Romanesque building looked like a block of warm, melted butter with its yellow stone exterior balancing the extremes of life, the darkness of the world outside with the light inside the walls of this holy sanctum.

The burial service at Woodlawn Cemetery followed the morning mass and was quite brief, attended by only a handful of relatives to offer support to Mrs. Jenkins and Mike. Most people now bypassed crowded gatherings, even if held outside in the fresh air. If the killer lurked around the nearest mausoleum, no one saw him since everyone now routinely wore surgical masks everywhere.

Maggie missed Tommy, still out with Covid for nearly a week. They had often used the squad car as their think tank to brainstorm the theories of any case. Maggie was a strong, independent woman, an energetic, acrobatic thinker who often suggested ideas outside the box. Tommy, on the other hand, was the wise sage, tempering his young partner's enthusiasm and wild hypotheticals as more appropriate for a crime fiction novel, or a game of Clue, than the reality of solving a Bronx homicide.

Her relationship with Hank, while easy, was tenuous on uncertain ground since neither of them knew when, or if, their assigned senior partners would return to duty. She was not sure whether to dive deep with Hank and she certainly was not comfortable enough to start a verbal game of who did it on the baseball field with a scarf, as she often did with Uncle Bobby or Tommy, or both. She was the only woman on the Bronx homicide squad, so she played it cool, on the down-low, forcing herself into that uneasy position of not being in control.

Their discussion was probing and insightful to the extent it could be with the lack of leads. They had their marching orders from Captain Bradshaw. If a trail grows cold quickly, move on. If a trail is hot, chase it down and make the arrest.

They grabbed a Crave Case at the White Castle on Allerton Avenue before heading back to headquarters. She was a Yankees girl and Hank was a Mets fanatic but the two at least agreed on their favorite fast-food burgers. Their temp pairing was working better than anticipated in light of his prior squad room antics and sarcasm.

"Are you kidding me?" Hank asked.

"What?" Maggie answered with a question when she already knew that she had solved the mystery seconds earlier. She was driving but knew quite well that she had just reached and fiddled around in the box to grab the last cheese slider in the Case.

"Girl, there were thirty burgers in that box."

"And you ate twenty of them, Detective Summers."

"I'm glad I'm not your boyfriend. I'd rather dress you and buy you gifts than feed you."

"I'm glad too," she said, pausing for a second before adding, "that you're not my boyfriend." She released the pent-up weeklong stress of the case in a good five minutes of uncontrollable laughter. Hank was reticent to join in as the subject of her witty comeback but the more she laughed, the harder he found it to resist. They were both snort-laughing by the time they were in front of the Simpson Street building, ready to call it a day but knowing they could not with all of the work facing them.

By noon Tuesday, Governor Cuomo was announcing the one-mile containment zone around New Rochelle, setting up the first Covid testing sight for people in the area or anyone who attended that super-spreader funeral in February.

"This is the nuclear winter I told you about last week," said Captain Bradshaw as he addressed the daily squad call slightly later than usual this afternoon. It seemed the whole world was unusually tilted off its norm in every way.

"Listen up," he addressed the only four people he could, Maggie and Hank, along with new detectives Sean McGuiness and Trey Fuller.

"Chiefs and Captains met with brass over the weekend and told us what we on the streets have already known for two months, the so-called flu is likely Covid, but they don't have enough tests for first responders, or personal protective equipment, the PPEs, which they'll be rationing soon.

"And everything the state has is going north to New Rochelle."

Patrol had been seeing a huge spike in emergency calls, substantially higher than last year with lots of people dying at home, in their sleep, for no apparent reason. While the state mandated masks for anyone out in public, the NYPD battled the frontline troops trying to enforce the mask mandate when its own officers waffled on adherence.

"We have masks, at least for now," Bradshaw said. "I was able to buy a case on the streets, the good kind, the N95s, and they're in my office.

"I urge you to be mindful of tossing them out at the end of your shift. Try getting one of your own that can be washed out at night so that we can limit the use of the disposable ones," he continued. "On the other hand, I've been told by paramedics that you can disinfect a used N95 by placing it in a brown paper bag in a dry place for forty-eight hours and then re-using it.

"The paper ones won't last long, so be prudent.

"And please, wipe down your cars with disinfectant before and after your shift. Again, there's a case of disinfectant in my office. We can't be too careful right now.

"We're down six detectives and now it's affecting the rank and file," he vented to the people he relied on, the best in the city, in his eyes.

"Look, I can't tell you what to do personally but I'd get a flu shot, if I were you, and pray, a lot. There's no sure way to prevent this thing and the availability of the Covid vaccine is on the distant horizon.

"There's a cold wind blowing and we have to face it dead on," the captain continued. "That's what we do. So, stay alert and be safe out there," he said, dismissing them into the unknown.

In his thirty-seven years on the force, on the streets, as a detective and now as a captain, Ernest Bradshaw had never felt so behind the eight ball when chasing down anything.

This grey cloud was about to rain down a torrent of hurt and death on the Big Apple, soon, very, very, very soon.

Chapter Twenty-Five

Brittany's friends and Mike Scavi had formed an alliance based on their shared grief and decided to toast her with a drink at a Friday the Thirteenth party. It seemed like the entire neighborhood joined what could be a last bash at The Squealing Pig Pub on Katonah Avenue. The Irish barkeep had stocked up on beer and chicken wings in advance of a planned Saint Patrick's Day celebration, but everyone now was living in the moment. With the annual parade up Fifth Avenue already cancelled, he realized that no one might be partying on the seventeenth if the city went into full lockdown and his pigs in a blanket would be floating in stale Irish beer for who knows how long.

So, while some were avoiding crowds in cramped spaces and others thought the night was unlucky, tonight The Squealing Pig was offering two-for-one green beers, half-price wings and squealing pigs in a blanket, which had college kids and locals lining up outside the door and onto a busy sidewalk. Yet the atmosphere was more grab and go than stay and hang out, but you could not beat a bargain with a fearless drinking crowd.

It was midnight when he left work and heard about the craziness up on Katonah Avenue from a colleague, which piqued his curiosity. Maybe he could grab a beer and get lucky, all in the same gulp. Surely, he could find at least one drunk girl to give him a tumble by the end of the night. He sized up the crowd and thought he would play the funny Covid card, "*do me now before death and destruction kill us all tomorrow,*" he laughed inside his twisted mind.

Within ten minutes of arriving at The Pig he spotted her leaving alone, barely able to wobble much less walk herself to a car or her house. He was attracted to her cheap green feather boa, falling carelessly off her shoulders and imagined it could be very useful later tonight.

"Leaving so soon?" he asked. "I've been looking for you all night," he said, turning up the charisma and charm with an overused bad one-liner.

She smiled. What girl wouldn't at least laugh when any guy hit on her with such a cheesy line? Toss in half-priced green beer and lots of people were going to get lucky tonight.

"I'm trying to get home to feed my cat," she slurred each syllable of each word, annunciating as best as she could, overcompensating for her less than elegant speech pattern since she had drowned herself, chugging four green Boilermakers in too short a time.

"I, I, I'm Heather," she finally uttered politely. "What's your name?" she asked, unable to barely utter her own.

"Beautiful Heather," he used her name to endear himself. "What kind of a man would I be if I let you walk home alone?"

He ignored responding to her request for his name and continued the mindless bar banter usually encountered among Millennials and Gen Z. It didn't take much coaxing from him to garner an invitation from poor Heather after discovering that she lived alone and just round the corner. He might not even need to knock her out to have his way with her. And who said Friday the thirteenth was unlucky?

"Shh," she said to him, pursing her lips with a finger across them, as she fumbled with the key to her apartment door. He voluntarily held her purse so she could open the door, grant access and invite him inside, a legal technicality if it ever came to that. He always planned ahead.

"You're not gonna kill me, are you?" she laughed. "They all turn down their hearing aids in this building. They'll never hear me scream anyway!"

"Oh, this night is getting better and better, he thought, stepping in and immediately tripping over her midnight black cat which she introduced as Nero. *I might not even have to drug her. She just may be the girl of my dreams.*

She plopped down on her worn sofa like a sack of potatoes and her head fell back, landing on the armrest. She closed her eyes in that moment and her mouth hung open like the gaping hole left behind by a manhole cover moved off its berth and then she simply nodded out. He took the time to double up her boa with another one he found lying on the coffee table. He tied the knot quite securely, extending its total length to about eleven feet. She had quite the collection of cheap and tawdry paraphernalia.

She was jostled awake as he carried her to the bedroom and tied her securely to the headboard with her feathered accessories.

"You're not gonna kill me, are you?" she slurred again with a weak chuckle, this time with her eyes closed.

This was foreplay to him. He did not need hugs or cuddles or blow jobs to realize his fantasy. He would be satisfied with absolute power and control and might even entertain the possibility of a return performance.

Since she was snoring, he finished off in no time, avoiding the awkward goodbyes of a onesie with a wham, bam, thank you, ma'am. Leave no man, or no condom behind, no easy to find DNA. Anyway, this was consensual. He was an invited guest or at least that is what he would tell the cops if this bitch didn't take his future call for another trip around his maypole.

He did the nice thing and untied her before leaving, hopeful he would have an encore soon, very soon. He was living the dream now and she was in a nightmare that she would never remember tomorrow.

Chapter Twenty-Six

He slid down the long corridor, hugging the railed walls as nurses and doctors came running from every direction on the critical care unit. The ear-piercing shrill of the death alarms, the flash of monitors counting down the life of too many and the incredibly cold air which blasted the stink of a high school gym locker, swallowed spirits and bodies with reckless abandon. The cries of the sirens' doleful lullaby rattled even the most experienced nurses and aides. They ran toward the mounting Covid death chambers which now housed the lifeless body of the pathogen's latest victim. They always knew before arriving, when those alarms sounded, what waited for them, but they mounted a valiant revival effort, each time, to no avail.

He was smarter than them with their advanced college degrees. He watched from the sidelines. He liked to help but you would never get him to straddle a body contaminated with a deadly virus to jumpstart a heart placing his own life in final jeopardy.

Poor Mrs. Rodriguez, he thought to himself.

He rarely worked seven days in a row, but he had a job to do. He had to help those ready to meet their god, whoever or whatever that was to them. He remembered praying to his God as a child to save his sister who had childhood leukemia. God didn't show up for him then, as he thought he should have, so now he believed his only answer was to help those who could not help themselves because in his eyes, God, any god, was missing in action.

Each death fueled his survival, multiplying his courage and strength. He was in his power now, the strongest he had ever been. He was no longer the restless kid, always serving detention in school and never having a purpose, or the short, lean man with the limp handshake and the nervous eye tick that fluttered the more he spoke to strangers. Now he was the pillar of strength who held the hands of patients as they took their final breaths. Death was seized as an opportunity for those without a conscience.

"Don't worry, Mrs. Rodriguez," he said comforting her, rubbing her hand as he held it gently. "Soon, it'll be all better."

It's what his mother used to say to him before she would slap him with her large flipper of a paw, telling him to suck it up and be a man. "Big boys don't cry," she would always say.

"Yes, I know that nose tube isn't comfortable," he continued talking to the semi-conscious patient. "This will make it all better," he consoled her as he injected her intravenous line with his liquid helper, all this while grasping her hand for a final goodbye.

He had quickly developed the skill set to use the hospital's drug vending system to complete his mission, and he was faster than a jackrabbit crossing the desert in front of a tractor-trailer hauling down the highway. He was much smarter than he was given credit for, probably more intelligent than his humble job warranted. He conveniently walked the floors at the times that nurses commonly dispensed drugs to patients, day or night, when he was scheduled, or on his days off when he would simply pay a visit. He also roamed other floors and gathered as many helpful codes as he could in very short order. He knew from his earlier work experience and the mistakes he made at other facilities that the codes had to be random, and they needed to be the codes of nurses and doctors with whom he never worked, which would be especially helpful in slowing down investigators if he ever became a suspect. He was quite cunning and clever for someone with only a high school diploma. He had street smarts which no amount of old school money could buy!

The entire staff was also dead on its feet, so no one was doing inventory checks of the drugs which were randomly disappearing. The medical infrastructure was at critical mass and getting ready to implode while he was just revving up at the starting line.

Chapter Twenty-Seven

Maggie had not seen Jax in nearly three weeks since the case first broke and the world tilted off its axis. Jax said they needed a sleepover date last night, and she wasn't one to argue. She lowered the volume on the TV that morning. She didn't want to rattle him at the crack of dawn, but he was already in the shower. She forced herself to watch the morning news, even though it was more depressing than most days before the pandemic altered reality.

"Do you know the lady on the second floor, the one who is 107 years old?" she asked, as he came out wrapped below the waist in only a towel, dripping wet hair all across the oak hardwood floors. Maggie didn't care. Little things no longer mattered.

"Oh, good morning," she said smiling as he reached behind her dripping all over her to kiss her on the top of her head.

"What about her? She got Covid?" Jax asked.

"No, that's just it," Maggie said. "She didn't get it. She's already survived three pandemics in her lifetime, the Spanish Flu, diphtheria and polio, and now her fourth, Covid.

"And she still has all her marbles and some great DNA."

"By the way, would you like a taste of my DNA for breakfast?" he asked, jumping over the back of the sofa and onto the couch next to her.

"Oh my God, seriously?" She loved his playfulness, which often forced her into relaxed submission, which she desperately needed in her life.

They sat in numbed silence as the networks rattled on about the growing death toll in Europe and the fact that New York

State now had more confirmed Covid cases than any other country outside of the United States. When the headlines were over and the network broke for a commercial, Jax just grabbed her in a warm hug. She had grown used to his bear hugs as the safe place she could return to after battling the demons on the streets of The Bronx. It was the no-questions-asked, no judgment zone which she had been searching for in every other relationship which generally wilted after the first few dates. Jax was secure enough in his masculine energy to appreciate that while his girlfriend packed heat, she could easily navigate her many roles from vulnerable feminine to femme fatale with a simple click of her cuffs, way more powerful than ruby slippers.

It was Saint Patrick's Day, but the city had already cancelled its annual parade and closed schools which would start remotely next week. Lockdown was coming in just days. Jax worried but didn't tell Maggie. How could he, when being a cop was not just what she did but who she was and right now her stress level was on uber steroids?

She worried also but never told him why. She knew that catching Covid on the streets was a real possibility for her, which could jeopardize both Jax and Uncle Bobby. She texted her godfather and told him that he would be having company for dinner tonight. The three of them needed a powwow to develop an action plan. Three households, with one of them working the streets, placed all kinds of obstacles in their way and posed health risks which could be fatal to any one of them or all of them.

It was about seven o'clock by the time she finished her shift and headed to Uncle Bobby's apartment where he'd been hanging out with Jax most of the afternoon. Even Sotheby's business came to a halt, so their general counsel suddenly had a lot of free time on his hands.

Her hands were full as she managed to ring the doorbell. She made six loaves of Irish soda bread and brought three of them with her tonight. It was her tradition. It was her annual nod to her

Irish heritage, a shamrock coming out party every March but then right back to her Sicilian nonna's cooking roots.

Jax opened the door and grabbed them from her. The TV was oddly on mute since he and Uncle Bobby were yacking like two old ladies in the kitchen while they cooked, and no one wanted to hear the same headline over and over and over again. Maggie loved this. It centered her soul in the world of crazy people eating bats and countries closing borders.

Her lifelong friend, Lauren, had become unrecognizable, just one eggroll short of a combo plate during this crisis. Her anxious, worried friend bombarded her phone with numerous texts that Armageddon was not just coming but that it had arrived! While she appreciated Lauren's concern, it was not something that supported her difficult task of going to work every day and placing her life on the line so that all of the crazy people, like Lauren, could stay safe at home.

This, Uncle Bobby and Jax cooking together, this was food for her soul and her knackered spirit. There was no place else she would rather be.

"Hey, kiddo, you're just in time," said Bobby Stonestreet, as he stirred a huge pot of Irish lamb stew and a smaller one full of creamy *colcannon*, the Irish mashed potatoes and cabbage dish was a rich buttery side to the oozy goodness of a stew basted in dark, creamy stout. She could also spy a tray of corned beef and more cabbage on the top of the stove. No one does potatoes and cabbage quite like the Irish.

"What, no lasagna?" Maggie laughed.

"It could be worse," Jax said. "There are people eating bats tonight."

She laughed out loud and so did Bobby. She loved that Jax got their twisted sense of humor.

They didn't rush dinner. They never did. Bobby learned that from Maggie's dad who never answered the phone while eating dinner. Jax learned not to rush from Maggie and no longer carried his phone everywhere. There is work and then there is family and never the twain shall meet.

Maggie drifted in and out of their conversation. Both men could read her, as her jade green eyes, usually so full of life and adrenaline, were now exhausted and staring blankly straight ahead, out the window to the river and its mesmerizing lights, periodically drifting back to rejoin the table chatter.

Jax had to choose whether to stay at his apartment in Manhattan and not see Maggie or nest with her in the northern suburbs, while Uncle Bobby would be on his own, which was never an option in Maggie's mind.

"I'll choose her every time," Jax said, "That is if she'll have me as a roommate."

"As long as you clean and do laundry, oh, and cook, you have to cook," she added to her list, "then we're good."

It was settled, Jax was moving up to Westchester and would work remotely. They didn't want Uncle Bobby mixing in public, so Jax would do his grocery shopping and drop it at his apartment door once a week. Maggie promised that no day would pass without her stopping by to visit her godfather, yet he knew all too well what Maggie would face on the streets when the city went into lockdown. It was not a matter of if but when that would happen. He loved her impractical thought but needed to dissuade her gently.

"Do I look like I'm gonna starve?" Bobby asked while rubbing his bloated belly. The man had the girth and the fortitude of a Notre Dame linebacker, but he was as squishy and loveable as a teddy bear.

"Besides, you've got Clarence Darrow over here delivering my groceries," he said with a smirk and a bit of side-eye in Jax's direction.

"I mean, how long can this last, right?" Maggie asked. They all knew the answer but chose to ignore it.

"Here, keep these in a safe place," Bobby said handing her a case of N95 surgical masks.

"I know a guy," he said, as if reading her mind. He smiled before she could ask where he got the hot commodity.

"They fell off a truck," he said assuredly.

Uncle Bobby suggested she wear a mask if she was out and about, especially if she was at the hospital. Yet, Maggie was young and seemingly invincible. She will be thirty-four in three months, if she survives.

With logistics worked out and their action plan in place, Jax headed south to grab clothes, along with his laptop and his plants. Maggie headed home and Uncle Bobby said a prayer of thanks that they were both in his life and that they had found each other at just the right time.

Chapter Twenty-Eight

It had been a week since New York City went into lockdown and the city's nightly ritual of banging pots rattled even the most jaded paramedics. New York neighbors, having seen Italians on balconies applauding and singing to health care workers, aped the loving gesture with the loud way that only New Yorkers can, ramp up the volume. Yet when mixed with the screeching ambulance sirens passing at a record pace, it was more of a Covid cacophony than a welcome symphony of gratitude. And the closer you lived or worked to a hospital, the louder the sound was amplified, reverberating through and between and around the granite corridors of tall buildings and apartment dwellings. The echo was the discordant expression of a city's fear on the verge of collapse. It was a hell the rest of the country could not imagine. It was not music to soothe the soul but the soundtrack to New York City's worst nightmare, including him.

It sounded like jackhammers drilling inside his head, the auditory distractions, the sirens, the banging pots, the ICU monitors and alarms, and the wails and cries of the dying who were still able to barely breathe. It was all too much. He needed to focus amid the sonic boom in a city on tenterhooks waiting for the next body to drop. He had a job to do. In the last week, he had sat with at least three patients taking their last breaths while he held their hands, comforting them during their transition.

"It's gonna be all better," was the only message he could deliver while holding their hands, leading them into the afterlife.

And with the death of Brittany Jenkins no longer headline news, he could be thankful to Covid at least for that.

He returned for another go on the lobster shift tonight, 11 p.m. to 11 a.m., although twelve-hour shifts barely covered the staffing needs of the dead and dying. These poor souls were the casualties of an invisible war, with an enemy the United States could not see and could not reach.

Yet, the reduced night shift crew made it easy for him to visit those in need without getting noticed. He was just the transporter guy, and the exhausted, overworked staff stopped seeing much long before he entered the room, or so he thought.

"What a great guy," the staff would say to each other but never to him, never acknowledging or validating his efforts.

New York City had ordered dozens of refrigerator trucks to help with the bodies piling up here, there, and everywhere. They should arrive in days, just like 9/11 but that death toll was going to be much lower than the lethal tsunami rolling toward them. More than a third of hospitalized patients in The Bronx, Queens and Brooklyn were dying. Some of those deaths were attributed to a seasonal flu back in December and January. Still others, dying in their sleep at home, remained unattributed to the foreign pestilence while new people dying at home were automatically labeled as Covid victims, sparing the ME a flood of unwarranted autopsies. He could not have asked for a better time to offer his able-bodied help.

"You've been so good with the patients," the lovely young nurse said to him. The first in a long while to give him kudos. "Would you mind sitting with Arthur Goldberg while I get his family on the phone? It won't be long now."

"Would he mind?" This was what he lived for. This was his time to shine. Of course, he would oblige. Mr. Goldberg would be gone before she returned, and the family would sadly miss out on their final goodbye.

He was methodical, organized and always planned ahead, carrying a spare vial in his pocket to serve in emergencies just like tonight. While propofol was used to keep the vented patients moderately sedated to limit them from gagging or yanking the tubes out of their mouths, one too many hits of propofol could cause sudden cardiac arrest and then it was lights out for good.

Mr. Goldberg had been one of the lucky ones. He had his own ventilator, the tube precariously taped to his mouth to hold it in place. He was not breathing. The machine was pumping air but that was not living. He pitied this bedded stranger who inspired his rush to assist tonight, coaxing him to move the needle forward on the agonizing process of a slow death.

"Hey, Arthur, how you doin' tonight?" He always asked and he always received the same reply, silence, deadly silence.

"This is going to make it all better really fast. Don't you worry. You won't feel a thing," he said aloud as if the poor guy could actually hear him.

He gave him a double dose just to be certain it happened quickly. Then he broke the news to the night nurse who was already running toward the alarms which had exploded at her station, signaling Mr. Goldberg's demise.

Death was a process, The victims had to be examined to make sure they were dead as if the lack of breathing and no pulse were not enough to alert his medically educated colleagues. First a physician had to determine the cause of death and sign all kinds of documents in triplicate while nurses disconnected machines and the orderlies cleaned up the body, eventually bagging and tagging poor Mr. Goldberg. It was then up to him to relocate the patient to the jam-packed morgue in the basement or the trucks outside.

He had taken a spare body bag each night while moving through the gallery of death, folding it tightly and tucking it into his pants under the back of his shirt. The zippered bags were pretty thin and barely caused a bulge, so no one gave him any notice under his hefty winter jacket. They had too much else to manage. The extra bags were for his disposal needs, neighbors helping neighbors, that sort of thing.

Chapter Twenty-Nine

Jax let her sleep late this Sunday morning, two weeks into lockdown but nearly six weeks since the Covid pandemic had taken its first acknowledged bite out of the Big Apple. He could not imagine the stress that she was under. A Bronx homicide detective deflects stress like a superhero, all in a day's work, but he was seeing his wonder woman slowly melt into a dark place when she returned home. It was taking her longer and longer each night to unwind and fall asleep. Some nights, sleep was not even on the agenda. When the alarm rang this morning, he quickly turned it off even though he knew she heard it and just rolled over, her eyes wide open.

Days faded into each other for both of them. He knew he needed to exert one thousand percent more effort to hold up one hundred percent of their relationship but that's how mature individuals manage life, and it was something which came naturally to him in her moment of need. They usually took turns carrying that extra fifty percent to make any relationship work when your significant other can barely carry themselves, but he was holding up more than the full load now and he did not mind, not for a second.

His only escape these days was a jog along the harbor, or a quick run to the supermarket for their own groceries and then to drop off food supplies for Uncle Bobby. He knew the guy was sneaking out to grab a cup of coffee or a beer at a private social club run out of the garage of another retired detective from Yonkers. He only wished he'd been invited to join for the laughter and the stories which he imagined they shared. The streets were empty except for other zombies making food runs just like him. New Yorkers were losing their internal fortitude, the one characteristic which makes them stand out all over the world, except maybe north in Boston where rough and tumble was in their bones.

He heard her rustle from the kitchen. The condo was compact so it is not like either of them could get lost in the cozy space. Boiano Bakery had closed for a week to do deep cleaning, but he knew what his girl liked for breakfast from the supermarket, and elsewhere, and was always so accommodating. He had her latte and *panettone* French toast waiting for her on the granite island and her Sunday morning playlist already piping through her sound system, which was quite impressive, *for a girl*, he smiled to himself before she entered the room wearing her Jeter t-shirt. The Yankees' retired legendary shortstop was his favorite player as well, so he could hardly be jealous of the love she showed him.

"*Come away with me,*" was the soundtrack to their morning.

"*And I'll never stop loving you,*" Maggie was singing to him, on key, happy to be in this moment, with her man and nowhere else, singing one of her favorite songs by Nora Jones and stretching on her tippy toes to kiss him on the cheek before slumping onto a stool at the island.

"Please, don't look at the headlines," he begged her as she was about to grab the newspaper which had been delivered earlier, tossed inside the lobby door like supermarket flyers for anyone to take. He made the mistake of placing the bulky Sunday paper on the island right next to where he set her dish for breakfast.

"Maybe you could meditate instead," he suggested, fully expecting her reaction.

She leered at him over her coffee mug without saying a word. The cup was true blue in color and stated "Keep Calm and Hug a Cop" on the one side which she had turned toward him as a silent signal.

He knew her look all too well, the "*go fuck yourself, but I love you*" look. The look to slay most men with her piercing eyes, as green as the Emerald Grotto of the Amalfi Coast, dark, deep and magically luminescent if you dare to hold on for the ride.

"I'll tell you the headline, how about that?" It was more of his plan than a question or a suggestion as he grabbed the paper out of her hand.

"Tigers, and lions, and bats, oh my!

"A Zookeeper infected animals with the 'Rona at The Bronx Zoo," he explained it in a nutshell.

"Get out," she said in disgusted disbelief.

He held up the front page of The Daily News to show her that his mind was not as creative in real life as it often was in the bedroom.

"And there it is, a full circle moment in the animal kingdom," Jax said. "Now eat up and then go forth and save the world, my beautiful crime fighter, and stay safe out there."

Chapter Thirty

Samantha Gallo, Sammy as her friends and family called her, was fortunate enough to have a job at a supermarket when lockdown began. New York kept food stores open as essential to life, from big chains to small mom and pop shops like Boiano Bakery because they made bread and *sfogliatelle*. After all, what is life without fresh bread and Italian pastry which are both necessary and essential.

Sammy had to work if she was going to help pay her college tuition next year. She was not born with a trust fund or a silver spoon in her mouth and gladly helped her parents in planning ahead. Yet the job did more than just feather her college fund, it helped her develop social skills while most of her friends hardly left their bedrooms, studying online and texting or video-chatting with friends. Sammy was out there, interacting with the brave souls who visited the supermarket, but it was quiet this Sunday night. It was a damp April evening, and she would be going home soon enough, as she waited and watched the digital clock on her cash register countdown toward the 7:00 p.m. closing time.

She grabbed for her phone to get a ride home because the clouds outside the front window looked ready to burst.

Damn! She thought to herself, realizing that she forgot to charge her device last night. There was no juice left, and she reluctantly decided to walk the short eight blocks to the home she shared with her parents and younger sister rather than have her father come get her.

"Closing time?" the customer asked as he grabbed his groceries from her lane, the lane where he always checked out. She was clearly his favorite.

"It's getting nasty out there," he said. "I can give you a lift if you'd like."

She just smiled, nodded and politely declined his offer of a ride home. She was no dope. She was born and bred in The Bronx. She had the deadly combination of street chops and common sense and knew better than to get in a car with a stranger. Just because you may know someone in passing does not mean you know them.

She was the last one to leave, as the store manager locked the door behind her. He was staying behind to close down and balance the registers and secure the little cash they had taken in with most people now using debit or credit cards for all purchases. Cash was hardly king these days.

The clouds parted and the heavens opened as she stepped onto the sidewalk. It was pouring down as if Thor himself was angry about the global state of affairs, but not even the hammer-wielding god could knock this bug out of the kingdom.

With her phone secured inside the pocket of her stylish anorak, she pulled it tighter around her, secured the drawstring on the hood snug around her head, over her knit skull cap, and started walking south without the umbrella which her mother always told her to carry for emergencies. As hard as she tried, it was a losing battle, her clothes growing heavier with every step. At this rate she would be soaked to the bone by the time she got home.

He had been lurking for shelter, as much as for cover from her view, in the doorway of the closed Italian *bonboniere* shop next door. The little gifts for wedding guests or parties for baptisms and first communions were big business in the Italian culture and this Wakefield neighborhood used to be more Italian than Irish. Wakefield, like much of The Bronx, was now a blend of everything and nothing in particular to distinguish one neighborhood from another.

This was Sammy's neighborhood too and she usually did not hesitate to walk home in the early evening. She did not feel threatened until tonight, until this moment. She did not notice him in the recessed doorway until he stepped up next to her, as if invited for company to take a leisurely walk in the rain.

"Are you sure I can't drop you at home?" he asked once more, firmly grabbing her right arm.

She screamed for help, but the streets were empty, as barren and bleak as a Bronx high school in the middle of July. He clutched her arm tighter, forcefully ushering her to his waiting car, all while holding something pointy, scratching at the nape of her neck.

He always carried the sharpest blade for the cleanest, quickest cut across the throat and right into the carotid artery, cutting the blood supply and silencing her screams with one strong stroke. He was like a surgical sponge walking around the hospital, slopping up information for his personal knowledge and execution.

He learned early on his twisted journey that one deep, oblique cut from the bottom of either ear, pressing firmly as he pulled the blade up and across the throat, could easily sever one of four carotid arteries in the neck. It was a certain, quick death, and silent as well. So far, he never had to resort to it but there was a first time for everything, and he did not hesitate to snatch and grab a supermarket bagger who turned down his kind gesture.

He locked the doors after forcing her into the bench seat, tying her to the skeletal door frame which remained after he had ripped off the handle to keep anyone from escaping. It was an old shebang of a car that had been parked forever at the end of his street for weeks. The elderly owner lived on the block and had not moved it in a month or more. Those old cars were the easiest to hotwire since the newer models had all kinds of anti-theft features and split seats in the front, but the owner actually hid a spare key on this piece of junk, making it easy to grab. He had watched the idiot hide it in plain sight so many times after parking it on the street. This one was not getting away tonight.

She begged for release, and he snickered.

"You, stupid, young bitch, the next time say yes, although there won't be a next time for you," he prepared her, as if anyone could prepare for their own death at a moment's notice. He thought he had already prevailed on his mission this wet, miserable night, the kind of night where you wonder why you're even out and about. He knew, however, that he had a purpose, to absolve her disrespect and take control of the situation.

The El seemed to amplify the rain's strength and his power as the water trapped in the overhead tracks pummeled anyone unlucky enough to be caught below in its downpour. It was the one overhead canopy which did absolutely nothing to provide shelter to anyone, dark or light, good or evil, all equally exposed to the elements.

Sammy was too scared to say a word amid his constant rambling which was muted by the thunderous rain. She remained alert, her breathing heavy but muffled under the scarf which she had tied low around her chin and up to her nose. She tried to remain calm and kept her focus on one goal, escaping when she could, as soon as she could. The skills they taught her in that self-defense class last semester were finally being put to use. Fortunately, this was her 'hood and she knew every nook and cranny. She watched as he headed south on White Plains Road, turning right onto East 220th Street. They caught the red light at the corner of Bronx Boulevard where he turned right again, heading back north, as if making a big U-turn. She was unsure whether he was lost or confused or that he didn't know where he was going. Maybe he had a clear plan known only to him.

He slowed down and eventually pulled up to park along the curb, almost parallel to the Bronx River Parkway. The curb was directly adjacent to a row of multi-story apartment buildings, decorated with rusty metal fire escapes down the side and across the front, whether providing emergency access to occupants or easy access to thieves was always a guess in this neighborhood. In this moment the rickety iron rungs were not staging those who took part in the nightly pot-banging ritual which had ended a short while ago. This street, which was generally well-traveled even during the pandemic, was a dark, desolate bypass, any street noise silenced by the sonorous sound of God's deluge.

It was not late, only about 7:30 p.m. What could he possibly hope to do in this very public stretch, she wondered. She knew there was a playground somewhere along the parkway, nearby. The last cross street she noticed before he slowed down to park was East 216th Street. Being shrouded in fear and wet to the bone, she was slightly disoriented when he came to grab her out of the front seat.

It was equally difficult for cars to see them in the grey dusk of the heavy evening deluge. The white box truck slammed on its brakes just inches from them as they tried to cross the street to the unlit park. It was the jolt she needed to break free from this monster and she ran straight toward the truck, frantically waving her hands to get the delivery driver's attention on his side of the cab.

He was spooked. He had never come this close to being seen or caught in the act before, not ever, and there he was now caught in the spotlight of the truck's headlights!

The driver was spooked too. He had never come this close to turning two humans into roadkill or apparently rescuing a runaway, or whatever this was. No matter what it was, he had kids of his own and he saw the sheer terror on the girl's face as she froze in the middle of the street. He waved her toward the passenger side door and Sammy jumped right into the truck's cab without saying a thing, while the killer got away, running into the muddy blackness of the park's weeded foliage.

All Sammy wanted to do was get home to her parents and curl up in her bed with a cup of hot chocolate and pretend it didn't happen. The truck driver had waited with her after she called her parents on his cellphone. Her dad thanked the trucker profusely, realizing his kid could have jumped from the proverbial frying pan into the fire getting into the cab of a random truck with another stranger on a bone-chilling night. He stopped short of yelling at her and just let her vent inside the safety of his big dad hug and the security of his car. He told Sammy that reporting this to the police would be first thing on their agenda tomorrow morning, but for now he just needed to get her home.

He waited in the wooded mess, like a sniper scoping out the turf. He waited there in the wet slop around him, augmenting his level of disdain for this girl, this night, this unfortunate fumble. He waited quite impatiently until he was sure the truck and the girl's ride home were clear. The longer he waited, the wetter he got, drop by horrible drop. He was soaked to the bone and angered to his core when he finally drove off into the night, heading north, straight to the Metro-North rail yard, where The Bronx meets the city of Mount Vernon. He would torch another hot car which was sure to be lost in the jurisdictional nightmare where The Bronx crosses paths with its suburban neighbor in Westchester County. Even as a kid he recalled seeing the body of an electrocuted rail worker dangle from the lines over these very yards while the NYPD, local and transit police decided whether the poor guy died in The Bronx or Westchester.

You put your left foot in, you put your left foot out. His twisted sense of humor started singing the senseless lyrics of the 200-year-old Hokey Pokey at the thought of the poor victim's fate. He imagined that with all the junk strewn across the tracks being sloshed about by tonight's torrential downpour, it would be a few days, at least, before anyone discovered the battered vehicle's charred skeleton. It would then be longer than a New York minute while the NYPD debated with the rest of them to control the investigation of a torched car. He just bought himself some time to pivot and plan his next steps.

With the glow of the flaming car behind him, he walked quickly uphill toward the Wakefield-241st Station, the northern terminus for the Number 2 train, which afforded him a straight shot home to Allerton Avenue. This was really getting old, and it could easily get him caught. He needed to pace himself. He would help those who needed him and forget about useless, ungrateful women for now.

Chapter Thirty-One

"So, here's where we're at," Captain Bradshaw said, addressing his squad for the routine morning call, hoping to rally their morale as much as his own. When you spend twenty-four hours a day, seven days a week, with your squad, they are not like family, they are your family.

"Chinese bats gave this crap to humans and now an American zookeeper has given it to Asian cats. You can't make this stuff up.

"God does have a sense of humor, doesn't he?" Bradshaw asked rhetorically.

"You mean she, right, Captain?" Maggie questioned pointedly, waking from a bored slumber with a quick retort.

"Yeah, Flynn, of course, she has a sense of humor!"

They had slammed right into the proverbial brick wall on the Jenkins homicide and were now doing whatever task they were assigned to do, just like every other detective citywide. Covid had consumed the NYPD in more ways than one.

"Are any of you detectives awake up there," the desk sergeant boomed over the internal speaker, mounted into the formerly white ceiling which had greyed over the decades. The popular but trashy-looking drop ceiling tiles served as a dart board for various writing instruments stuck into the tiles' random cracks and corners, precariously waiting to plop on the head of an unsuspecting victim below. It's all fun and games until someone gets a poke in the eye.

Tommy had picked up the phone to speak with the sergeant. He and Lou had just returned to the job today and he was the closest to the desk.

A teenager had come in downstairs to report that she was kidnapped last night on her way home from work. The captain asked Tommy and Lou to meet with her as everyone else had already been paired up and assigned to other cases or tasks.

"Get a sketch artist, if there's one on call, and get a description from her and then let her go," Bradshaw ordered. "Let her go. That kid shouldn't even be out."

The two highest-ranking members of the homicide squad didn't even question why veteran homicide detectives were now fielding reports from possible kidnap victims. The reluctant team just rolled with it and realized that squad management had changed in their absence, just like everything else in life.

Detective Sergeants Tom Martin and Lou Lopez greeted the sixteen-year-old victim, Samantha Gallo, with her father, Enzo Gallo, in the lobby before inviting them up to an interrogation room to take down her report. Sammy, as she asked to be called, had requested that her father remain in the room and the detectives did not mind. It might have been different had Sammy been a suspect in a crime or the victim of a rape, but fortunately, this was neither of those scenarios. They did, however, ask the father to remain quiet and allow his daughter to answer all questions without interference.

"Sammy, we're going to take this nice and slow this morning, okay?" Tommy said to put her young nerves at ease. He had a seventeen-year-old daughter at home and could only imagine what she would be like and how jittery she would be in this situation and her father was a detective.

Whether someone was a victim or a suspect, their nerves came into full bloom when asked to sit down in a windowless interrogation room, devoid of anything remotely considered to be décor, to answer questions from New York City detectives. It kept everyone's focus in check and on each other, but for very different reasons.

Tommy asked her to start at the beginning once he began the recording. Lou stepped out for a moment to call down to the sergeant to see if a sketch artist was available to come over and meet with the girl. Resources were being pulled every which way to plug gaps in coverage on the street, so the availability of a sketch artist might be wishful thinking.

"The supermarket's been closing early, at seven o'clock every night since the pandemic began," she explained. She told them that it had just started pouring outside when she left work last night, and her phone had died earlier, so she couldn't call her father for a ride home.

A customer had asked her if she wanted a ride home as he left the store, but she declined not thinking anything more than she did not take rides from strangers.

"He was all masked and wore a hoodie because it was raining," she explained. "It was difficult to see anything more than his eyes.

"But his voice sounded really familiar, like I'd heard it before," she continued.

"I was waiting for the light to change at 233rd Street when he came up behind me and forced me into his car which had been parked right there on the Avenue, right under the El," she said emphatically, tossing her hands in the air, as if the coincidence did not escape her recognition in retrospect.

Locals had long called the heavily congested main shopping drag of White Plains Road the Avenue and affectionately referred to the elevated subway train tracks, which ran above and parallel to it, as the El. Everything happened on the Avenue and anything really important happened under the corroded fretwork of the El. The noise of the subway cars on the tired old tracks above actually drowned out the din of life for most residents struggling to get by day to day.

"It felt like he had a knife, or something held to my neck," Sammy said, gesturing with her hand, pointing to where she thought he held the blade under her ponytail. "I couldn't really see it, but I definitely felt the point of whatever it was pinching my neck."

Tommy waited to jump in with another question. He knew the rhythm of a teenager's chatter and marveled at how they barely came up for air before carrying on with a seemingly breathless diatribe.

"Did it pierce your skin?" Tommy asked her. "The knife or whatever?"

"No, it was like he was holding it there as a threat," she replied.

"He had pulled down my hood when he pushed me into the car and that's when I first felt it.

"But I grabbed for his mask when he shoved me into the seat, and I managed to pull it down before he tied me to the door with my own scarf."

"That's my girl," Enzo Gallo said proudly, nodding his head up and down and tilting it a bit toward her in admiration.

"He was one of our regular customers," Sammy added. "I think from Misericordia because he usually wore scrubs, or at least a scrubs top."

She explained how grateful she was that a trucker almost hit them as they crossed the street to the woods.

"It could've been a very different story this morning if that driver hadn't done the right thing when he saw her last night," Enzo added. He was still shaken this morning thinking he could have lost his oldest child to a crazy person all because he did not pick her up at work. He gave Lou the driver's contact info which they had exchanged last night.

Tommy and Lou asked Sammy if she could return tomorrow to sit and work with a sketch artist. She agreed and so did her father who was itching to get the kidnapper in a dark alley all by himself and deal with this guy, old-school, Bronx-style.

The senior detectives had more than sixty years between them on the job. Despite their recent absence due to Covid, neither of them needed to be hit in the head with a two-by-four to realize they might have just stumbled onto the same perpetrator as in the Brittany Jenkins case.

Hank and Maggie were still in the squad room when their old partners came rushing in, beaming with confident smiles like the old guys who still had razor-sharp tools in their chest.

"You guys look like the cats who ate the canary," Hank said. "What's up?"

"The kidnapping vic says the guy who grabbed her last night was wearing scrubs," Tommy said.

"Yeah, and he tied her up with her own scarf," Lou chimed in.

The pair were in sync as if they had rehearsed a victory speech. Captain Bradshaw, whose door was wide open, heard their proclamation as well, and came out to listen and learn.

"Basically, the kid says one of the supermarket's regular customers forcibly grabbed her after she turned him down for a ride home," Lou explained, continuing with the short version of her statement. "He tied her to the door frame of a dark-colored, older sedan, which was banged up, and then drove her toward Shoelace Park.

"He got her out of the car and was dragging her across the street when a delivery driver nearly hit them with his box truck.

"It gave the sassy kid her chance to escape, and the perp must have jumped back in his car and drove off."

"Must have?" Hank questioned him.

"Well, the driver was focused on the kid and calling her father," Tommy said. "Neither one of them really saw where the guy escaped to in the darkness."

Hank, Maggie and the captain sat in rapt attention.

"This is the kind of scenario where generally, you're never found until your body drops," Tommy suggested. "First-degree kidnapping turned possible homicide, but she was lucky, very lucky." He still couldn't shake off the fatherly anger of a papa bear in protective mode, knowing full well what he would do if it was any one of his five kids.

"Either way the doer is fucked," he paused. "Excuse me, captain."

"Never mind, continue," Bradshaw directed him with a forgiving eye. Tommy and Bradshaw had come out of the police academy together, so the formalities of professionalism often yielded to the colloquialism and street sense of two seasoned investigators who respected each other outside of their rank.

"Either way, the perp is going to jail," Tommy smiled, correcting himself. "That kid last night had gumption. She fought back and got lucky, and we might've caught a big break in two cases.

"The sketch artist couldn't get here today but the kid's coming back tomorrow morning to sit down with him."

Captain Bradshaw reiterated the sad reality that right now, both the NYPD and hospitals were severely understaffed. He did not have enough investigators to delve into serious crime and the hospital administrator could hardly take a bio-break without someone else dying from Covid.

"They have the National Guard on their doorstep," Bradshaw said. "We cannot sit on this, but if we even hint at the possibility of a killer on staff, or someone killing more staff, the hospital administrator might just have a meltdown. Not to mention the mayor and the governor."

He directed the four detectives to work the two cases together, as a team, searching for similarities such as where did the perp get a car, a second time, and where did he leave it, a second time. He urged them to lock it up as tight as possible before they sounded the alarm at headquarters and the mayor's office or the hospital.

"By the way, this guy's gotta have some connection to this area, something more than just working here," Bradshaw proclaimed. "Who else would know about Shoelace Park unless he was from here?"

Chapter Thirty-Two

Days were flowing into nights and into a daze for everyone. New Yorkers were forced to work from home, kids were forced to take classes online and criminals and the homeless alike were forced off the streets, and surprisingly not hiding in the subways. The trains were sanitized every night by humans in white hazmat suits. The veil of death shadowed the whole metro area with an odd moribund atmosphere inhabited by zombielike creatures. The vibrant city, which never slept until Covid, had devolved into a comatose metropolis.

Uncle Bobby never left the house except for a daily, masked walk along Broadway, up to Untermyer Park and back again, or to grab coffee with his secret society in the nearby garage. Jax did the same thing except up and around Harbor Island. They each pitied the people who were too scared to leave their homes but wound up dying in bed anyway. Life is meant to be lived amid its dangers and its pitfalls, to do anything else is merely existing into a slow death anyway.

Yet even Maggie was losing all sense of time, and she was hitting the streets every day, sometimes every night, for weeks at a time. The governor's daily televised briefings were used to mark the passage of time, as the death toll grew and supplies were depleted. The screenshots of real life in 2020 looked like scenes from every sci-fi movie of the last fifty years.

Sunday dinner at Uncle Bobby's happened on Monday night this week. She was champing at the bit to share the latest break in the case but couldn't with Jax in the room. He wasn't

NYPD and they weren't married, and she had to protect the integrity of the investigation. It was one of the only disadvantages to having him around all the time, while in her heart, she knew the benefits outweighed the inconveniences a thousand times over.

Her godfather had made Italian comfort food, lasagna, to make them all feel better. Cooking for anyone is a true expression of love, feeding their body, heart and soul all in one bite.

"Oh my God, how did you get this so creamy, even with the chopped meat in here?" Jax asked.

Uncle Bobby looked at Maggie with a side glance as if he needed her permission to let Jax in on a family secret.

"Should we tell him?"

"Ah, I think it's safe, go ahead," Maggie said. "I think I'll keep him around for a while. And if not, we can just kill him," she deadpanned while lifting her fork to taste a mouthful of the velvety Italian food staple.

Jax was too busy savoring every forkful to notice their repartee.

"It's our secret recipe from nonna and you must make a Sicilian blood promise right here, right now, to never reveal it to anyone," Bobby said sternly as if requesting an *omertà*, the Mafia's pledge of silence. Maggie's tough, old Irish brawny built godfather fixated on Jax, leaning into him across the table, eye to eye, man to man, finger pointed at his face from a taught bent elbow resting as if to arm-wrestle a new opponent.

Jax instantly crossed his heart and pricked his finger with his knife, intimidated by his relatively new foodie opponent.

Maggie couldn't stop laughing.

"He meant it figuratively," she was choking on her wine which nearly came through her nostrils.

Uncle Bobby maintained his composure, not blinking, the weight of his solid persona leaning closer to Jax across the table, his finger still pointed. He had stared down death more than once on the job, so this was kids' play.

Maggie reached for Jax's hand and kissed away the trickle of blood, still laughing as she did.

"You people are crazy," Jax said realizing he'd been the foil for their set-up. Yet, laughter was getting the sane people through it all at the end of the day.

The dinner table cleared, Bobby and Jax sat down for a night of penny polka and more wine while Uncle Bobby's 1960s R & B music blared from his old sound system, wired to a classic turntable and receiver. Maggie made her way back from the kitchen with a plate of chopped pepperoni and sharp provolone stabbed with colorful toothpicks. This was her weekend night as a kid, with her dad and Uncle Bobby, and now Jax. This was the port in the storm.

"You don't have to worry 'cause you have no money,
"People on the river are happy to give."

Maggie sang "Proud Mary" as it blasted through the speakers, which seemed to be everywhere. She yelled the lyrics, pointedly in Jax's direction, to warn him that they came to play, dancing toward him as she placed the tray of edible delights in front of him.

One card shark, at this closed-door game, was smarter than the next in this trio. There was the retired detective with a photographic memory; the lawyer with keen analytical skills; and the girl who was a double threat. Maggie had the analytical mind of a young, experienced detective, coupled with a lethal but alluring look to disarm even the most guarded of sharks. There was nothing artificially intelligent at this table.

Uncle Bobby mentioned crime was down at least thirty percent since Covid. He did it to throw his two adversaries off their game. There was big money on the table, at least fifty cents.

"Even the criminals are scared of Covid," Bobby suggested.

Jax was now focused and playing too, but he could also multi-task. He was a commercial litigator before moving to easy street as inside general counsel for one of the world's leading auction houses. He mentioned Émile Durkehim's hypothesis that if society is sick, criminality is the response, as the realized manifestation of the disease.

"Oh, here we go," Bobby understood that he was now a target at this table, but Jax underestimated the old guy's repertoire.

"I think Durkheim was suggesting that if society lost its moral compass, then crime was the inevitable result," Maggie jumped in. "A sick society naturally forces a reexamination of the morals and laws which got them there so that changes could be made globally."

"Oh, geeze!" Bobby uttered in exasperation. "I thought we were playing cards tonight.

"There isn't enough wine for this discussion. You two are a perfect match," he said, rising from the game table to get a few bottles of water in the kitchen. He did not want either of them driving home on a stomach full of wine.

"Let me know when we can get back to playing five-card stud instead of a discussion on nineteenth century French sociology.

"I'll be in the kitchen grabbing some *macarons*. I'm out." he said facetiously, turning over his hand on the table and walking away.

"What the hell?" Jax looked at Maggie, questioning how detectives knew of Durkheim.

"OK, pretty boy with your juris doctorate, I love you but we both went to John Jay, and it's taught in sociology," she instantly corrected his implicit bias.

Jax called the hand and upped the ante with a pair of kings but still had not learned to never underestimate his queen.

"Oh, pretty boy, read 'em and weep," Maggie said, placing her full house, three aces and a pair of jacks, on the table for all to see, while sweeping the instant dollar pot in her direction.

"Look, it's a pair of jacks," she said to her man, demurely, with a bat of her alluring eyes and a tilt of her head. Jax just shook his head in his hands.

"You've got it tough, kids," Bobby said to Jax and Maggie, recognizing they each confronted different obstacles, his in their relationship and hers on the city's streets.

"Crime used to be more predictable, a jilted lover, an abused wife, a good old-fashioned mob hit but now it's more random and more violent," he added to the discussion.

"So, if you can't spot the bad guys, then how do you catch them?" Jax questioned what the two detectives had assimilated internally after years on the job.

"Good old-fashioned police work and this young lady is the best!" Bobby was a very proud godfather.

After a few more hands, they called it a night, but she was not about to get away easily.

She started walking toward the door, since she had been avoiding physical contact, not wanting to pass along any bat bugs from the outside world to Uncle Bobby.

"Get over here kiddo," he grabbed her in a bear hug. "Stop worrying about me. If I die tonight, I want it to be after hugging you. Stay safe out there and you too, card shark," Bobby said to Jax, pulling him in for an oversized man hug.

Chapter Thirty-Three

It was barely 6:30 a.m. when Maggie was called out of bed, again, just as Hank received a similar call at home. Another jogger found a woman's body on the dock inside Shoelace Park.

Patrol was already on the scene when the two detectives pulled up separately about forty minutes after getting their respective calls. The simple things in life, a morning shower, clean clothes, and breakfast were now vague memories for both of them. Maggie had fully embraced her nightly bubble baths just to hedge her bets against uncertain mornings and both detectives now kept not one but two sets of clothing changes in the go-bags which they each stored in their trunks.

While many people, including lifelong Bronx natives, passed this stretch of parkland between the Bronx River Parkway and Bronx Boulevard on a daily basis, very few of them, if any, knew about Shoelace Park. The small park was created when the city diverted a portion of the old, outdated parkway in the 1950s and officials thought the city could use more greenspace. The small wooden boat launch was more of a platform for kayakers than a true dock hidden among the tumbled woodlands which smelled like a cross between a Bronx sewer and the decomposing bodies of small creatures hidden in the bramble underfoot.

"Sitting by the dock of the bay, eh?" Hank said as they came upon the woman's body which had been propped up against a log, her legs dangling off the platform like she was sitting there catching some rays with a good mystery novel.

Maggie rolled her eyes and knew exactly why Hank was called the ham to Lou's cheese by the other members of the squad. Ham and Cheese both shared corny humor and were loyal to a fault.

The victim's body and the log teetered near the edge of the well-worn platform, strewn with dead leaves, moss, cigarette butts and assorted other small bits of life caught between the boards of the deck. The faded and knotty planks had seen better days. If anyone fell into the river, they'd be easy to pull out since it wasn't deep, maybe knee-depth at most. Actually, anyone who fell in could probably walk right out. You could actually see the garbage on the riverbed, old bicycle tires and other things which did not float. Two patrol officers hovering overhead could have inadvertently tipped the body into the water with one sneeze above the victim's precarious perch.

She was clearly staged. She could have been reading a book except for her slumped head. Nearby fallen trees mimicked her pose, looking like fallen drunks who couldn't make it back up the hill to return to their own beds last night. The first two officers on the scene did not touch the body, waiting for detectives and the crime scene unit to arrive, so her name remained a mystery.

After CSU had taken preliminary photos of the scene, Maggie grabbed the victim's knapsack, took out her wallet to search for identification and sealed everything into a zipped evidence bag, dating and signing it in order to preserve the chain of custody. Obviously, this was not a robbery since her wallet was untouched with just over a hundred dollars inside.

The team continued rummaging through the muddy, grassy, wooded area searching for other evidence, while careful to avoid grabbing the abundant skunkweed which carpeted the area near the river's embankment. As a Bronx kid, Maggie knew better than to grab at the benign-looking plant which resembled large heads of romaine lettuce but smelled worse than any dead rodent entombed in a tenement wall. She was looking for clues as to the woman's identity while Hank ushered the jogger to the side to get a statement. The man had remained on the scene after calling 911 and as requested by patrol.

Her driver's license was issued in Arizona but the lanyard ID card, still draped around her neck said she was Susan Robbins, a "Travel Nurse" who worked at nearby Montefiore Hospital, just south of Misericordia.

She had a pashmina around her neck, which the assistant medical examiner bagged and tagged in order to start his inspection. He had arrived shortly after the detectives to complete the on-scene team of crime fighters. The death grip of strangulation was obvious. And after Jenkins' autopsy, he fully expected to find a syringe mark somewhere along this victim's neck as well.

"She's a fresh one," said the assistant ME. He had done a liver probe at the scene to determine the time of death, but his educated eye could tell she hadn't been there long. "The time of death was about midnight last night."

He went on to explain that her liver indicated her core temperature was 86.6 degrees, and rigor was only just starting in her face. The post-death muscular rigidity had not yet settled throughout her body which helped narrow the window for the time she took her last breath.

"So, follow me," the ME addressed the detectives. "If the body loses approximately 1.5 degrees per hour, after it ceases to function, and then continues to lose heat until it reaches the environmental temperature, she hasn't been here that long because the coldest it got last night was forty-five degrees." He explained the science in terms easy to understand for a medical examiner or a math major but not for two detectives without a calculator at the ready.

Everything in life is science and numbers don't lie. Death is merely a calculated reality when it comes to murder.

No one ventured a guess on whether she was killed on the dock or elsewhere but due to the remoteness of the scene and the steep decline from the street down to the river, it would have been difficult for even a strong man to carry her from the car and down the hill with no one seeing them. The killer would have had a difficult time lugging a body that weighed about one hundred thirty pounds that distance without a struggle in the dark.

The assistant ME then asked Hank and Maggie to form a guarded perimeter around the body and asked everyone else to move away. No one present thought anything of it since there are often discussions at a scene which must be had away from the ears of others not central to the investigation.

"I want to check her mouth," he mentioned to them. "Dr. Johnson filled me in on the Jenkins' clue and told me to check before we took the body from the scene.

"Bodies are piling up and we can't promise this autopsy will be done in my lifetime," he added with sarcasm singed by the new world order of forensics in New York.

He directed the detectives to grab the plastic tarp he had carried with him, and they held it up to shield the body from any eyes which might inadvertently want a glimpse.

Sure enough, there was a folded postie note stuck inside the victim's mouth.

"The invisible pain is unbearable #10"

All three were now pretty certain that Susan Robbins was indeed the killer's tenth victim, but since they only had two bodies, so far, where were the other eight?

There were too many similarities to the murder of Brittany Jenkins. Two nurses killed in parks which were frequented by joggers, who worked at affiliated hospitals less than two miles apart, who were strangled and staged for others to conveniently discover and whose bodies held a secret message from the killer. There's no coincidence in crime, just hard facts and they needed to tie these two cases together to catch a killer and a kidnapper because if his numbered notes indicated anything, they meant they were already behind the eight ball with eight other victims.

"You thinkin' what I'm thinkin'?" Maggie asked Hank as they headed back to their respective cars.

"Yeah, our killer didn't get off with feisty Sammy and had to find another woman to satisfy his itch," Hank answered.

"He's escalating rapidly," Hank suggested. "Sammy got very lucky. It was just a matter of homicidus interruptus."

Chapter Thirty-Four

It was noon as they headed back to headquarters. They had called ahead to see if Tommy and Lou could meet them since the loose ends of the two murder cases were now forming a Gordian knot. Hank asked Lou if he would mind calling Montefiore to see where and when the travel nurse had worked before coming to The Bronx. It would give them a jump on plotting out the murder boards.

"She came from Seattle by way of Arizona and New Mexico," Lou said as Maggie and Hank arrived carrying deli sandwiches for all of them.

"She came here to help with the Covid crisis and was sharing an apartment with several other travel nurses in Wakefield." Lou continued speaking while updating the whiteboard with the new information he had quickly jotted down during his phone chat with Montefiore's nursing administrator. It was written in a code only he could understand. So, it took him a bit longer to decipher and print it neatly for the team on a new adjacent murder board.

There were actually three boards now dividing the small room, one for Brittany, one for Susan and a third to list all of the common elements. They would plot them out while eating because there was no time to waste, and Captain Bradshaw had directed them to work both cases as a team.

Lou explained that travel nurses often worked through an agency and went where the need was the greatest. That is why so many of them headed to New York this month from all across the country.

"They usually work on the assignment for about thirteen to twenty-four weeks and then move on," he said. "But they never knew what hell they were coming to when they signed up for this."

Killers can easily hide during this kind of a crisis where the focus is on anything but crime, and the devil himself is ordered to hide behind a mask. Yet, sometimes, a demon's misplaced reliance on the cloak of commonality can expose the darkest of secrets with the slightest error in judgment or misstep away from the bedraggled path. The dormant dots of Brittany Jenkins' murder were not only connecting but were converging at an accelerated rate with those of Susan Robbins' homicide.

Bodies on top of bodies on top of bodies were piling up at hospitals in trucks, at morgues in cold storage trailers, while funeral directors were turning away bodies since the death toll had quadrupled from last week. The ME's office advised them that they would examine the Robbins' body today for needle marks and draw blood for a complete toxicology screen to determine the type and approximate amount of both legal and illegal drugs in her system, if any. However, a full autopsy would have to wait for an undetermined time. The detectives understood but at least the needle mark, if it was there, and an eventual, predictable match on the killer's death drug of choice, would provide a strong foundation to connect the clues in both cases.

The core four of the homicide squad were so engrossed with their team skull session and tossing around theories between the two homicides, that they nearly forgot that Samantha Gallo was sitting in a room down the hall with a sketch artist. The buzzer on Lou's phone alerted them via a text from the artist to come down to view the final sketch.

"That's him," she said as Lou came in the room.

"It's him," she repeated in excitement. "It looks just like that customer Rob. The one I was telling you about yesterday.

"He would always hit on me or flirt with me before Covid, but I ignored him.

"It creeped me out, so I told the manager.

"We didn't see him much in the past month or so."

Lou was happy that she was happy, but his mind did not give it too much weight. He knew that a victim, in their anxiety, would often easily describe the image of someone they thought it could be just to put a face to their fear and pain. Sammy said she had pulled off the kidnapper's mask and was able to get a good look, but they would need a bit more to identify him. It was dark and raining and Sammy Gallo was in survival mode with fear and panic looking for any way to escape that night.

It was four o'clock before it all started coming together. Lou thanked Sammy and made his way back to the squad room to let everyone, including Captain Bradshaw, know that they had a definite identification from the kidnapping victim. She thought he worked at Misericordia Hospital because it was closest to the supermarket, but she never imagined that he was a doctor or a nurse even though he wore scrubs. She described him as kind of schlumpy.

They decided to divvy up the hospitals, with Lou and Tommy heading over to Montefiore with a copy of the "Rob" sketch, while Hank and Maggie headed to Misericordia, having already established relationships there.

Chapter Thirty-Five

Hospitals citywide had enforced a no visitors policy. They had to in order to minimize the viral spread and death toll. It did not matter if it was a new father waiting to see his new baby for the first time or if it was a daughter struggling to kiss her mother one last time before she took her final breath. Absolutely no one was allowed entry unless they were carried in on a stretcher or they came in as a walkie talkie who arrived in the emergency room, on their own, exhibiting Covid symptoms.

That meant Tommy and Lou had to meet with a hospital administrator outside Montefiore, on busy Gun Hill Road, not the best place to ask anyone about a possible serial killer. The deathless shrill of ambulance sirens yielded oh so briefly to the deafening silence of hospital workers dragging deeply on cigarettes, desperate to escape death inside yielding to another fatal habit outside.

Tommy and Lou did not mind. They were used to questioning anyone, anywhere on city streets and they were in no hurry to enter a hospital having only just returned to the job from their bout of Covid. One visit from the deadly bug was enough and they did not want to carry it home to their wives and kids, or even their dogs, now knowing humans could pass it to animals.

The hospital administrator understood the detectives' urgency but said the best she could do would be to ask if anyone in human resources could identify him from the sketch and their database of hundreds of employee photos. She would call them back, either way, when they could get around to it.

Yet perhaps she didn't really understand the urgency because she was in crisis mode. There was a dead travel nurse on her watch, not through her fault, but her management barometer should have been a bit more elevated. You would think! When the devil strikes from the left, his one-two punch will knock you down from the blind side every single time.

Chapter Thirty-Six

Hank and Maggie were working the relationships they had already established at Misericordia a month ago when Brittany was murdered. They were recognized at first sight by the hospital's rent-a-cop security force who allowed them to wait in the vestibule to get out of the chill while waiting for the nursing administrator to come down.

Sometimes the toughest part of being a detective was getting people to speak to you in New York's very misplaced anti-cop environment. Then mix in the isolating effects of a global pandemic to the poisoned stew and it can handcuff all efforts to get reticent New Yorkers to trust anyone enough to speak about anything, let alone chat with detectives.

"Something's bothering me about this sketch," Hank said to Maggie while they waited. "I'm not sure what it is. Do you recognize him?" He asked his partner just as Debra Feingold greeted them.

"Sorry about meeting like this," Feingold apologized as she opened the lobby's front glass door which was to remain ajar during their discussion. "You think you have a lead?" she asked hopefully, all while keeping an eye on her pager which beeped constantly. Beeps, sirens, alarms, ventilators, all contributing to the facility's sound torture on a new level.

She had been pulled in a hundred different directions since the start of the year and her focus was certainly not on the detectives in front of her.

"We had a victim in another case identify a person of interest she believes works here at the hospital," said Maggie.

Hank handed her a copy of the sketch and watched as her mouth dropped open.

"That's Robbie Campbell," she gasped. "No doubt about it. You think *he's* Brittany's killer?" she asked. Her disbelief filled up the tiny ante lobby.

"It can't be him," she said. "He's a patient transporter. That's all he does. And he loves the patients. He sits with them sometimes until they take their last breath."

She accessed his personnel file on the small tablet which was now glued to her hip by a bungee tether hanging precariously from a carabiner. It was always at the ready, along with her cellphone, so she could call employees to fill in shifts on short notice.

She explained that Robert Nathan Campbell had been working at the medical center for nearly a year without a blemish on his record.

"This sketch is nearly a mirror image of his personnel photo. Just look at it," she said showing the photo on her tablet to Hank and Maggie.

"In fact, the nursing staff tells me that Robbie's been exemplary during this crisis, staying late, helping them to sit with patients as the end nears," she continued, her brow wrinkled not from exhaustion but the skepticism of the cops' hunch. "You must be mistaken." Her words were brimming with incredulity.

"Robbie? I just can't believe it," she said again. "He actually assisted with a patient who was dying when the doctor at her bedside dropped dead of a heart attack in the room.

"Remember? You were here speaking with the staff about Brittany's murder a month ago and I had to run?"

"Was there an autopsy done on either that doctor, I think his name was Levy, or the patient in that room?" Hank asked.

"No, doctors are signing off on deaths which are obviously Covid or Covid-related and Dr. Levy had a history of heart failure and a triple bypass just a year ago, so his death was attributed to sudden cardiac arrest," she replied. "Everyone's on edge here and the stress is off the charts, so a sudden cardiac event did not seem out of the ordinary for him."

"Have they both been buried?" Maggie wondered if they would need to request an autopsy, or if that was even possible at this late date without first asking the district attorney's office to seek an exhumation order.

"That was a month ago," Feingold said. "Dr. Levy was cremated. I went to his funeral. As for the patient, I think her name was Ondrovich. Let me review her record, but I would imagine she was buried since that was before the lockdown.

"Oh, Mrs. Ondrovich only had one surviving son who lived in Seattle," she advised them as she continued reading the file on her tablet. "It says here that he waived having an autopsy done and had a funeral director pick up the body and arrange for cremation."

"God, another dead end," Hank mumbled under his breath, exasperated by their futile attempts to push this case over the finish line, instead feeling like Sisyphus forever pushing that boulder uphill only to have it roll back down as he neared the hilltop.

"No pun intended," he backpedaled, realizing his audience of two was silent at the inuendo clouding the moribund atmosphere.

The administrator emailed them the contact info for the funeral directors and surviving relatives of Mrs. Ondrovich and Dr. Levy, along with Campbell's contact info and personnel photo. She understood their directive to keep this information from anyone other than her superior, the overall hospital director who was the chief executive officer of the medical center. She also advised them that the hospital would agree to voluntarily cooperate in granting access to Campbell's work locker.

"All employees sign a waiver upon hire, granting the hospital full access to their lockers, with or without their consent, at any time and for any reason, left solely to the discretion of the hospital," she explained. "But I'd still have to get the official okay from the CEO."

They all waited in the vestibule while she called him.

Bolt cutters were not necessary as the administration kept control of all locker combinations from an app. Even if an employee tried to circumvent the hospital's access by frequently changing his locker combo, an administrator could easily override and reset it. There was no one in the employees' locker room when the three of them entered and Campbell was off that day, so there was no need to worry about being caught in the act, although they had his written authorization. Hank videotaped the process on his cellphone as the administrator opened Campbell's locker and stepped aside.

Maggie, who had already been masked, as was Hank, was now wearing surgical gloves so as not to contaminate anything they might find inside Campbell's locker. At best, they would knock it out of the park if Campbell stored souvenirs from his victims where he worked. At worst, they would find nothing.

His locker was unusually empty, nothing, *niente*, *nada*. Not even an extra shirt or hat or toothbrush, something, anything he might need if overtime was required during this health crisis.

Another dead end but at least now they were able to put a name with a face. They would have to ask Sammy Gallo to come back to view a proper photo array to see if she could still pick out her kidnapper from actual photographs. That would at least nail Campbell's coffin on the kidnapping charge.

"We'll be in touch soon," Hank advised her. "In the meantime, mum's the word.

"Oh, by the way, where did Campbell work before coming here a year ago?" he asked, as though he had forgotten something. It was a pattern he used a lot, something he found quite useful as a kid watching vintage 1980s police dramas on television. The lead detective always comes up short and then pulls a rabbit out of the hat at the eleventh hour to solve the case.

"He relocated back to New York, his home," Feingold said. "He came from a hospital in New Mexico, but he was only there a short while. I guess he got homesick."

Ding, ding, ding! This silent alarm rang simultaneously in the minds of Hank and Maggie. Brittany's case just got a lot more interesting.

Chapter Thirty-Seven

It was nearly eight o'clock by the time the two teams returned to the station. Each pair carrying two large pizzas offered a moment of levity as the four detectives enjoyed a good laugh together. Two pizzas too many or great minds thinking alike? Either way, a cop's gotta eat!

Four whiteboards now stood side by side, two murders and a kidnapping each laid out on separate boards, while the fourth board was a clean slate to connect the dots from the other three cases and quite possibly the deaths of Thelma Ondrovich and Dr. Scott Levy.

Lou called Samantha Gallo and asked her to return first thing in the morning to identify their lead suspect from the photo array. Slow and steady wins the race. If she confirmed Campbell was their man, at least for the kidnapping, they could get a warrant and search his apartment while arresting him on kidnapping, unlawful imprisonment, and assault.

If Campbell kept any of the victims' souvenirs at home, they would amend the warrant to include the Jenkins' and Robbins' homicides, doing everything by the book to avoid Satan's spawn from going free on a technicality. Slowly, methodically, they'd reel in the big fish now that they had him on the line.

They diagrammed the info in the only way they knew how, going old school with a Venn diagram, overlapping circles to show the logical relationship between two or more sets of facts. The method had been around for 140 years and lasted this long for a good reason. It was dummy-proof. They made the largest circle in the middle because there were enough intersecting facts to flush out the commonality among the cases.

The two murders had the most in common – dead nurses; working at affiliated hospitals less than two miles apart; killed and staged with their own scarves around their necks; syringe marks near the carotid artery to maximize the drug's absorption at a faster rate; the killer's note stuffed in their mouths indicating non-consecutive numbers which were eight digits apart; and the bodies placed in locations frequented by morning joggers. The ME had called, confirming the syringe mark in Susan Robbins' neck but could not yet confirm the presence of propofol since tox screens were backlogged for months. Still, there was already a lot in common between the two murders, and Sammy Gallo's ID of her attacker just might lead to arrests in the two homicides as well.

The kidnapping could have been another homicide, but spunky Sammy got very lucky. Her fighting Bronx spirit came out and she made a break for it. Her only apparent connection was the most important one. She identified the suspect as a hospital worker who tried to drag her into Shoelace Park the day before the body of Susan Robbins was dumped in that very park, killed in the same fashion as Brittany Jenkins.

The good old Venn diagram had finally made sense of the one board which had previously looked all higgledy piggledy with very few connections. Even the link to the missing girl in New Mexico was completing their puzzle. They would be sure to ask Campbell about that girl once they caught him and then pass on their knowledge to the sheriff in Guadalupe County to follow up.

The detectives all lived in Westchester, north to south, east to west. Their adrenaline was pumping, waiting like a kid for Christmas morning, as they anticipated Gallo's photo ID of Campbell in the morning. In pre-pandemic times they all would have grabbed a drink on the way home but that was not happening now. The state shut down bars and restaurants, and all non-essential businesses, three weeks ago, modifying laws to allow bars to deliver liquor to individuals at home. Nothing like staying home alone and drinking yourself into a stupor. Anti-social deviants all liquored up at home – what could possibly go wrong?

So, the core four headed out the door, in separate cars to separate homes, and would likely spend most of the night awake, too pumped on life, and death, to fall asleep.

Chapter Thirty-Eight

He jumped the Number 2 train and headed north, seven stops to the Mount Vernon border. It was about eleven o'clock and he needed a car if he was going to move Mrs. DeLeon later tonight. She was still breathing yesterday, just barely, when he last checked on her. She was a petite woman. He guessed that she weighed less than a hundred pounds, but dead weight would be cumbersome to carry downstairs in a body bag without being noticed. Fortunately, the bags were black, so he hoped to move her easily, in the darkness of the wee hours of the morning, nary a pot-banger in sight.

At least the trains were clean. The hazmat crews scrubbed and disinfected them each night, making them almost attractive for a late-night ride. The city held off closing the 24-hour transit mainstay because so many overnight hospital workers used the subways to commute. The seats were a lot cleaner, and the trains and stations smelled a lot nicer than hospitals where the vile stench of death, mixed with disinfectant, could prompt retching from even those with an iron gut. If this was hell on Earth, then heaven must be at the next stop. All aboard!

He stepped off the El and headed down the stairs, walking east at a quick pace toward the transit rail yards. He laughed to himself that he would probably get busted for stealing cars or torching them before he was nabbed for murder.

He hotwired a car near the row of warehouses which overspread the landscape near and around the yards. The area known for drug dealers and the occasional hooker looking to score some coke or meth, or whatever the cookers had stewing in the 'hood, was eerily vacant and void of any outdoor security cameras. He spied two cars which had already been dumped and torched and not yet cleared off the streets by the cops. The procedural delay was probably a combo of more jurisdictional border questions with the two departments arguing whether the front bumper was in The Bronx and the rear tires were in Mount Vernon. Or just blame it on Covid. That was the tendency nowadays for everything wickedly vile or just plain crazy to blame it on Covid.

It really was his lucky night. He found an old 1995 Impala with a manual transmission just calling his name. He sighed at the condition of this black beauty with its V8 engine and four-speed stick shift. In its heyday it could fly. Tonight, all dented and peeling paint, he just needed it to get him home for the sake of Mrs. DeLeon. He found himself back on Allerton Avenue by midnight, but time was irrelevant to senior citizens who lived alone, isolated, and often too frail to go to the toilet on their own. It didn't matter how late he checked in on Mrs. DeLeon. She wouldn't know if it was day or night anyway. That is if she was still breathing.

All of his elderly neighbors trusted him, and most had given him keys to their homes or apartments when he first moved into the neighborhood. He ingratiated himself by running their errands while their distant kids often left them to fend for themselves. Family dynamics are a mixed bag. He knew firsthand that the goodie bag could be salty and full of nuts and leave a bitter taste in your mouth, but rarely was it full of sweet lollipops and gelato.

He stepped quietly into Mrs. DeLeon's apartment, using his key to open her door. It looked as though she had not left her bed since he checked on her less than twenty-four hours ago. She was slumped like a sack of potatoes and smelled like she had wet herself.

"Mrs. DeLeon, can you hear me? Squeeze my hand," he directed her and felt her weak grasp.

"Squeeze my hand again if you want me to help make it all better."

All he needed was her consent and her pain would be gone. This one had no family and no one to check on her. In that moment, she consented in the only way possible for her with a feeble squeeze of his index finger and he assisted in the easiest way for him with a prick in the neck and Mrs. DeLeon went to meet her maker.

He stripped the bed and wrapped her neatly in a clean sheet, placing her thin, frail body into a new body bag. He stopped for a brief second to look at her limp bones and veins visible under her crepey skin, looking like a grid map to the afterlife. He zipped her up and carried her out in one trip. He carried her out to the waiting car at the end of the dark alley where he deposited the dirty sheets and trash into the nearest dumpster, under the shroud of darkness and empty streets, while he checked on Mr. Ortiz one floor down in the old walk-up apartment building.

Mr. Ortiz was a widower and his only real friend. His wife died years ago, and his two kids headed south and never returned. He would often stop in and shoot the breeze with him while they puffed away on stogies that he would pick up at the corner bodega. They would share a beer and tell dirty jokes, mainly about hookers. Ortiz was Haitian and barely spoke English, but they had their own language and got by, usually over a game of chess which he let Ortiz win most of the time.

He had called him earlier in the day and the old man could barely whisper his name because his time was near. And by the time he arrived tonight, Mr. Ortiz was already gone, as cold as ice. There was not much he could do to help his old friend right now, and he was not about to call the cops to help remove the body. Mr. Ortiz would not want that, and neither would he right now. He knew that the rancid smell of death would soon be in full bloom in the heated apartment because the landlord was legally obligated to keep it toasty for another month. Neighbors would eventually call 911 and Mr. Ortiz would be marked up and attributed as another victim of Covid, dead at home, no autopsy or investigation, just another statistic.

He was grateful because it was one less body that he would have to move to cold storage. He was also grateful the pot-bangers were not hanging out on their fire escapes like dirty laundry. Dirty because life in the 'hood was anything but clean. Life was messy. That's the reality no matter your economic bracket. Money might make it easier for some, but for others it's a day-to-day struggle from the moment they wake up to the moment they go to sleep, sometimes exhausted by life and weakened from hunger during the moments in between.

They gazed out of cloudy windows from behind sheer curtains, trying not to appear callous and curious while straining to hold their own lives together. Even the churches were closed, leaving everyone at home in cloistered prayer and reflection. The brave souls ventured out to their fire escapes, fearful of a trip to the streets below, scared they may catch who-knows-what if they mingled with anyone anywhere.

Poor Mrs. DeLeon had spent about an hour locked in the trunk of his new ride while he tended to Mr. Ortiz. She was okay. It was in the mid-forties outside so she wouldn't bake. He had managed to find an illegal space for his classic Impala just outside the building's rear door which led from the laundry room to the side alley where trash cans lined the adjacent cinder block retaining wall. Neighborhood kids had long ago broken the outdoor overhead lightbulbs, once hidden behind their protective wire mesh shield. It gave them a place to sneak home past curfew in the dark or smoke some weed without nosy neighbors seeing them. Put a Bronx kid under the spotlight and they'll know just how to avoid it, every single time. No one knew better than him what a slippery, imaginative group they could be.

He was not expected at work since it was his night off. It was a good thing because he could not delay hiding Mrs. DeLeon's body in plain sight. While most unexplained, at-home deaths were being marked as Covid victims, he could not risk the chance of an eventual autopsy finding a needle mark on her body or a note in her mouth, so while she was his eleventh victim, that would be his secret for now.

He had emptied the kitchen trash and the wet sheets while he took her out the back to delay any musty smell from emanating from her apartment, prompting complaints from the neighbors. It was a short ride back to the hospital where he was easily able to load her up into one of the morgue trailers parked alongside the hospital.

He drove directly to the hospital's loading ramp and backed into it, down a slight incline, where he spied a nearby dumpster and a valuable waiting gurney in his rearview mirror. He was dressed in his scrubs to look the part and peered up at the apartment windows across the street. They were all dark, no signs of life to interfere with his plans for the dead.

All he had to do was wheel her from the trunk a short distance down the block to one of the waiting forklifts manned by hospital workers assigned the unsavory task of cleaning up what the pathogen left behind, assisted by the eager-to-help National Guard, living up to their motto, *"Always Ready, Always There!"*

"I've got another one here for you," he said to one of the orderlies donned in a white moon suit, looking very much like an escapee from another planet. The guy was spent, sitting on top of a nearby stack of crates, downtrodden, exhausted with life. He had opened the facial hatch of his suit just long enough to take a few drags on a cigarette.

"Rough night?" he asked the suited figure who replied with nothing more than a nod, a shrug and barely a willingness to rise from his makeshift seat.

"No worries. "I've got this," he directed the guy with hand gestures to continue seated.

"I can manage this one," he said, stretching out his hand and gesturing for the guy's tablet, which held the log for all bodies in and none taken out of the ice boxes.

Date, name, body count number, in sequential order, and toe tag ID. It was all there, along with death by Covid listed as the cause of death for each and every entry in the digitized record.

He could not really enter the truck without the correct personal protective equipment. He did not have his own hazmat suit, and he would raise all kinds of protocol alarms if he tried to sneak into the truck. So, he completed the log entry, confirmed the information on the toe tag which he had counterfeited in his car and placed the body bag on the forklift.

"Thanks, I appreciate it," said the young orderly who rose after finishing his smoke. "It's a bit rough out here some nights.

"I'll move her in now," he said, pushing the button on the lift and watching the body rise, eventually relocating her to the furthest slot on an available shelf away from the trailer's door. They had orders to pack them in back to front and work their way out the door without having to revisit the patients who had been interred inside for a few days.

And just like that, poor Mrs. DeLeon just disappeared into the night, and no one was the wiser.

Chapter Thirty-Nine

Sammy Gallo bounced into the station house right on time as the clock struck ten o'clock. She wanted her kidnapper caught as much as the cops did so she could sleep easier and so they could get a likely killer off the streets.

The photo array was solid. Tommy and Lou had quite a selection of snapshots, twelve in all for Sammy's consideration. Robert Nathan Campbell was as white and plain as a bag of microwave rice and as indistinctive as was every other man in the photographic line-up. They all had floppy brown hair, trimmed but barely combed, and dark eyes. They were a bit crusty around the edges, not one of them polished in any manner and all wore a white button-down shirt. They were not the kind to stand out in a crowd but oh could they draw attention one at a time, at least one of them in particular.

Sammy gave the photos the once over and it did not take her long, less than a minute, to place her finger on the target.

"That's him," she said emphatically, pointing to Campbell's hospital employment photo in the array before her. Her enthusiasm for catching her bad guy was echoed in the music of her frenetic tapping on his picture. "That's the guy who grabbed me and he's the same person as our customer, Rob, at the supermarket."

"You gonna arrest him?" she asked eagerly.

"That's the plan, we hope," Lou assured her as best he could. Cops never make promises. How could they in a world of half-truths and bail reform where the guilty often lie, and the bad guys are returned to the streets time and time again?

"But don't go saying anything to anybody," Tommy reminded her as if telling his own kids who would require more than one, or two, or three reminders on anything important. He repeated the instructions to her again in front of her father who was waiting in the hall to take her home.

She zipped her lips closed with her thumb and pointer finger pressed together at the corner of her mouth as quietly as a mime and then tossed the imaginary key behind her back before waving goodbye to the detectives and bouncing down the stairs.

The four detectives, now working together on two homicides and Sammy Gallo's kidnapping, waited in the squad room for the warrants to be signed, to search Campbell's apartment and arrest him on charges of kidnapping, unlawful imprisonment, and assault. They hoped murder would be next and quite possibly grand larceny if they could tie him to the auto theft. They wanted the bigger get with this guy – double murder, dead to rights, no procedural mistakes which could get any one of these cases kicked out of court on a technicality or worse yet, cop error.

It was a bit early in New Mexico, but Maggie reached out to Campbell's former employer, the hospital in Guadalupe County, which was listed in his personnel file from Misericordia.

"Really? Uh huh!" Maggie said, repeatedly, and generally in disbelief as the rest of the squad listened only to her end of the conversation. Apparently, Maggie didn't need to say more after she asked the hospital administrator about Robbie Campbell's performance as a hospital transporter in the small desert facility.

She ended the brief call by thanking the woman for her time and explained they might reach out again since the investigation was ongoing.

"You really can't make this stuff up," she said, turning to look at Hank, Tommy and Lou after hanging up the phone. Captain Bradshaw had also arrived and sat at the corner of Hank's desk waiting to hear the latest.

"The guy worked at this small community hospital, just off Route 66 where the girl disappeared from the gas station.

"He was never absent and did his job until one day he just left and never came back," Maggie said.

"The administrator was reluctant to say more and sounded somewhat dismissive," Maggie continued. "I think she was reluctant to talk about a short-term employee whom she didn't know personally because she didn't work there at the time."

"Now that we have a name and a time period, call your friend, the sheriff," the captain directed Hank while they sat round waiting for the search warrants to be signed. "Find out why the hospital was so sketchy just now."

Sheriff Gallup explained to Hank that he recalled the guy's name and some concern at the hospital that some pharmaceuticals were missing but there was nothing to tie Robert Nathan Campbell to the missing drugs. "There was no evidence of tampering with the drug storage system and no real cause for alarm," the sheriff said. "It just happened while he was there, and since he was the most recent hire after the drugs randomly started disappearing, the hospital looked to blame someone, but it could've just been an inventory snafu and nothing more. I mean we never even opened an investigation beyond the initial report by the hospital.

"The administration let him go under layoffs and I guess he moved on," the sheriff added. Hank asked the sheriff to keep the query under his hat for now, as Maggie had done earlier with the hospital administrator.

"Just spitballing here," Lou chimed in seeking group input. "Why would a health care worker kill other health care workers when they're all in a universal fight right now?"

"Just a guess but maybe it's as simple as the same old thing – a schlumpy guy can't get the girl and can't handle rejection," said Tommy. "It's a psychosexual thing."

"We're all working 24/7 and I don't have time to think about sex, much less have sex, and you think this guy is busy hitting up nurses?" Lou asked rhetorically. "I think I'm getting too old for this job."

"Every New York City health care worker is living on the edge unlike anything they've ever experienced before and people need release in different ways," said Hank.

"Spoken like a newlywed who probably gets it every night," Tommy rolled his eyes at Hank. "By the way, I hear congrats are in order."

Hank gave Maggie a bit of friendly side-eye for letting the cat out of the bag before he announced his recent Vegas wedding to his co-workers.

"Here we have a guy from nowhere with no one and it sounds like he snapped," Maggie said. "It's not too complicated. It's scary as hell out there with masked zombies walking the streets like the night of the living dead."

"Aren't you a ray of sunshine!" Hank said.

"While I was on hold, waiting for the sheriff, his clerk asked what it's like here," Hank relayed to the group. "They're extremely fearful of it coming west. The clerk made it sound like the four horsemen of the apocalypse were charging in their direction, across the deserts and the plains, faster than a dust devil swirls on the horizon, ramping up anxiety and blinding rational thought along the way."

"Hell, it is the apocalypse," Tommy proclaimed. "In what real world does New York City clear the homeless from their mobile homes every night to sanitize the subway?

"Such a monumental cleanse had to be preceded by the total destruction of society as we knew it."

Maggie had been perusing video surveillance files from the funeral home while Hank and Lou tried to catch up on paperwork. They were each great at multi-tasking and multi-level analytical thinking, releasing their own anxieties while simultaneously focusing on the investigation at hand.

"Ah, here he is at the wake," she said as though solving the case when all she did was satisfy Hank's itch, the feeling that he had seen Robbie Campbell somewhere before Sammy Gallo's identification of her attacker.

"So what?" Hank asked.

"You've now said several times that his eyes in his employee photo reminded you of someone, right?" Maggie replied.

"We all know that the killer often shows up at the victim's funeral," she continued. "That must be where you remember seeing him."

"Nah, that's not it," Hank said, shaking his head in the negative, while his eyes lit up with a lightbulb moment.

"I remember now that we have a photo and not just a sketch," he said taking an extra face mask from the box he had on his desk.

"Look," he pointed to Maggie as he walked to the Brittany murder board and held the mask across the nose and mouth of Campbell's photo, now enlarged front and center as a person of interest.

"He approached us at the last meet and greet with the hospital staff, but he slithered away just as he neared the table to talk to us.

"I thought it was off then, and I still do now," Hank reflected. "I mean why wait on a line only to cut and run when it's your turn?

"It was as if he just wanted to hear what we had on the killer and then he backed off without asking any questions.

"It happened that second day we met with staff a short while before the doctor died and everyone went running."

Chapter Forty

It was late afternoon by the time the arrest and search warrants came through. They had requested them to be issued to search Campbell's apartment and Misericordia, not knowing where they would find him this late in the day, in the middle of the week. One call to the hospital and they knew Robbie Campbell was expected at work within the hour. Their day just kept getting better and better.

Teams of officers, the four detectives, with patrol officers as backup, manned each entrance of the hospital with Campbell's photo sent to their phones for confirmation. They didn't want sketchy Campbell to slip through a door unnoticed, unmasked or masked. It would be better to stop everyone and request they pull their face masks down momentarily rather than risk losing a kidnapper and a suspected serial killer who just walks away.

While Hank and Maggie waited in the ante room of the front lobby, Debra Feingold tried to discover Campbell's location at the medical center. Their cellphones were virtually tethered with a common goal. It was difficult because Campbell, as a transporter, was like a moving target, always shifting here and there, in and out, back and forth from patient rooms to the mobile morgue trucks outside and back again. Texting and earbuds locked on the same frequency kept the cops on the same page as the hospital administrator. Bottom line – don't let Campbell get away!

Lou and Tommy positioned themselves at the employee entrance just in case Campbell stepped outside for a break. The two veterans were not eager to enter the mouth of the dragon at any hospital having just survived a serious bout of Covid, but they had to do what was necessary if the job called for it. Yet their egos and obligations aside, their life was more important than nabbing a collar for another criminal in two careers lauded for catching social deviants.

"Detective, Detective, are you there?" Feingold whispered in Hank's earbud.

"The care coordinator on the Covid floor, up on six, thinks Campbell went to the cafeteria after moving a patient," she said. "The coordinator said he looked a bit frazzled, so she told him to take a short break and go get something cold to drink downstairs.

"But the desk nurse in that unit said Campbell just rolled out a body, a short time ago, because the woman didn't make it. So, she thought he'd be out near the trucks," Feingold added. She was frustrated, annoyed at the conflicting reports from hospital staffers on the same floor. Her bedraggled hair was now uncharacteristically pushed up in a banana hair clip and the muscle between her eyebrows had furrowed into a unibrow in frustration. The man of the hour was missing in action, and she could not tell the police whether Campbell went up or down, in or out!

Hank grabbed a patrol officer standing nearby to ride one elevator down to the cafeteria, while Maggie waited for the next ride up to the sixth floor where Campbell was last seen.

Maggie tried calling Hank as she grabbed the next elevator up, but her signal cut out inside the car just as it slowed to a stop three floors up. Based on the unreliability of inconsistent reports, Maggie wanted to be certain that Hank had radioed patrol officers stationed outside near the trucks to keep an eye out for Campbell.

He was wearing a mask as he stepped inside Maggie's elevator as it bounced to a gentle stop on the fourth floor, his lanyard completely flipped over to hide his identity. Maggie did not recognize him under his routine disguise, but she instantly felt the tension in her core. Her gut tightened, forcing her shoulders back, angling her body toward this stranger in a constricted space where time was not on her side. Fight or flight was not an option for a homicide cop. She was now combat-ready. It was that feeling every cop knows, that little voice inside their head which every cop pays attention to, "*danger, danger, danger dead ahead.*" To not pay attention and ignore that voice is to risk losing everything, including your life.

She was also masked as she stepped aside, to the left, to allow him inside the spacious car. Her skin crawled and her spine crunched as he got a bit too close before stepping across from her and to her right. Her jacket swayed open casually, giving him a glimpse of her gold detective shield which was always pinned to her left waistband just under her shoulder holster. The ballast in the overhead light flickered and buzzed, singeing the energetically charged atmosphere which suddenly felt cramped. While it was deep enough to hold the length of a gurney, right now it was tighter than a small jockstrap on a college football quarterback, squeezing the air right out of their lungs, both of them, but for very different reasons.

She cautiously typed *911* into a text message for Hank. She had been holding the phone in her left hand, keeping her shooting hand free just in case she met up with Campbell. She prayed the text could be sent as soon as the doors opened again to allow the signal to connect. Campbell had repositioned himself, taking a slight step back, just to her rear to keep an eye on her gun and possible trigger finger on the hand closest to him. He had seen her push the elevator button with her right hand and never assumed she was ambidextrous. She did not need to be an expert southpaw, just resourceful enough with her left thumb to push the send button on her phone. She had her thumb at the ready to send the cry for help as soon as the doors parted. Sooner rather than later!

"How are you. Detective?" he asked, trying to intimidate her from his misplaced position of self-importance.

The caustic tone of his voice cinched the already tense knot at the back of her neck. She could feel her veins throbbing as the adrenaline surged through her body. It was a controlled fear but fear, nonetheless. Facing it dead-on didn't make it any less terrifying, just more manageable because to face fear is to conquer it. She inhaled deeply, not audibly, that would only empower him.

Instead, she composed and fortified herself, stealth-like, because that's all a true warrior needs when going into battle, the inner knowing that she has the strength to conquer anything in that moment.

"Fine, thank you, and you?" she replied with a polite, prim response, letting him think he was in control.

"Have we met?" she asked another question to keep him talking, now staring at him from a position of power having turned about ninety degrees to face him, all while keeping a side view of the elevator doors and the button panel which was tucked next to her left shoulder.

"We've been like two ships in the night," he replied sarcastically.

She spied a scalpel in his right hand and assessed the threat, knowing he could lunge at her the moment she tried to grab her gun. She was a fast draw, but he was already armed, and she was not willing to play the odds with her own life on the line.

Why isn't anyone getting on this elevator? She prayed someone's button call would make it stop but there was no traffic on the generally busy elevators, as the car eased its way up to the sixth floor.

The doors are not opening. She was tossing every variable around inside her head which felt like a vice squeezing all survival skills to the front with such pressure and pain in an effort to safely escape and neutralize the threat.

"Oops, false alarm," he said, as the car stopped momentarily on the sixth floor just quickly enough for the doors to open briefly, but no one was there.

A voice coming from down the hall asked anyone inside to "hold it," as most New Yorkers would, but the individual seemed to forget that new hospital protocols required that only one patient and one transporter at a time could occupy the same elevator. Seeing Robbie's profile from her angle as she neared the elevator, the woman recognized him and apologized for the slight error and waved him on, unseeing and unaware that there was an officer in need of assistance inside the cab rather than the usual cloth-draped body on a gurney.

Maggie seized the opportunity to immediately hit the send button on her phone when the doors opened, while her masked nemesis flipped the elevator's bypass switch, giving him control, allowing him to reverse the lift's direction. The car descended straight to the depths of hell in the bowels of the massive building where death resided, and no one got out alive.

"Oh, I missed my floor," she said as the door's quickly closed with his touch.

"No, no, no, you didn't," he said, having now moved within inches of her. "You're coming with me."

He had slowly moved to within inches of her, staring her down, controlling his rage in an effort to manipulate his imagined captor. This was uneasy for both of them, yet each of them fought to control the situation with the skillful moves of a samurai.

"Where are we going, Robbie?" Maggie used his name to distract him.

"Oh, so you do know who I am," he said. He wasn't surprised. He expected that her feeble chatter seconds ago was a lame survival skill she picked up in some detective bootcamp.

"I'm leaving and you're gonna help get me past the officers outside," he advised her with a gleam of confidence in his eyes.

All Maggie saw was the madness of his soul. She swore she could see the devil's darkness inside, although she had never been this close to pure evil and its simmering rage. Yet even his penetrating gaze could not unnerve her internal fortitude. It was a mental tango. He pushed. She resisted. The more he advanced the less she yielded.

Yet his words oddly gave her comfort. She knew that if she could get him outside of the hospital and away from other people, like staff and patients, reducing a wider threat, there would definitely be officers ready to take him down once they saw the scalpel he was holding at the nape of her neck.

"Ladies first," he said, waving his left hand as he directed Maggie to exit the car ahead of him as it bumped to a landing in the basement. It could not go any lower.

The doors opened to the netherworld of the hospital, normally a place of healing and birth and now a repository of annihilation and death, where you enter but never leave. Her heart dropped for a quick second as she surveyed the scene before her and grasped the transient reality with the immediate goal of rushing to the world outside through the exit door dead ahead.

This most certainly was Dante's seventh circle of hell. A complex labyrinth of constricted corridors stretched in every direction. Gurneys lined both sides of the long, dark hallways, with a measured path between the rows of shrouded patients, just wide enough to push another body through, ushering these poor souls from the hell inside to cold storage outside. The rows of covered bodies, hidden in plain sight, appeared like a runway at rush hour at a crowded New York airport, waiting for liftoff to the great beyond. Limbs dangled from beneath sheets while toe tags peeked out of others. It was musty and the rancid odor was unbearable, causing bile to rise in Maggie's throat. Nothing could block this image, this stench, this taste which would be etched on both of their souls forever.

The exit door seemed like a football field away but was actually less than fifty feet from the elevator. She kept her eye on that prize, that exit where the last glimmer of twilight through the small window on the door pierced the blackness of this morbid space. She could feel his breath on her neck and cringed at the thought of the devil crawling under her skin. She prayed for her life and hoped the officers were stationed at the doors outside, where they should be and would be keenly aware of the first signs of a fellow officer in distress and in serious need of assistance. She was trapped like a rat but even those furry creatures outside could scurry along the Bronx River Parkway to escape fleeting cars. Here, in this moment, she could not reach for her gun before he would slice her throat. There is nothing that cuts through human skin as cleanly as the sharp stainless-steel blade of a surgeon's scalpel, not even a bullet.

She could not believe how he callously passed the bodies, unfeeling, non-reactive to the death before him and the pernicious virus which festered in the dark, dank environment, unknowingly mutating. All she could see through the window on the door which was dead ahead was the twilight stealing the last light of the day as night arrived, an almost welcome relief to blanket the ugliness before them.

They were closer now, inching toward relief and freedom, she hoped. She saw the patrol officers standing just beyond in the fading light where the streetlights had come on as she pushed the silver release bar to open the metal door.

"Drop it, Campbell," Hank yelled out emphatically. "There's no way out of here alive for you," he advised the prime suspect. Hank had been hiding beneath a gurney, sheltered by a dangling sheet overhead, waiting for Maggie to get close enough to the exit and for Campbell to pass close enough so he could feel Hank's breath and sense the gun which directly placed him in jeopardy. The sharp detective had eyes on the pair the entire time, from the moment they left the elevator. He was crouched on the floor, protected by his shroud above but free enough to jump when the moment was right.

"Mags, you good?" he asked her casually, although his chest was pounding like a freight train barreling off a cliff until he could guarantee his partner was out of the devil's claws.

"I got your text," he said smiling at her. "Wanna do the honors?" he asked, dangling handcuffs loosely from his left hand while his right hand held the gun steady, point-blank on Campbell, the tip of his gun now touching Campbell at one of his favorite spots, the nape of his neck.

"You feel that buddy, don't you?" Hank said nudging the muzzle closer to Campbell just to make his point known. The suspect dropped the scalpel hoping this was not his day to die. He was not ready for that. He had a story to tell and oh, what a story it would be.

"Robert Nathan Campbell you are under arrest for the kidnapping, unlawful imprisonment and assault of Samantha Gallo and the kidnapping, unlawful imprisonment and assault of a police officer," Maggie said grabbing Campbell's hands behind his back and slapping on the cuffs faster than she had ever done before with any other suspect.

"You have the right to remain silent," she began reading Campbell the requisite Miranda warning. "Anything you say can and will be used against you in a court of law. You have the right to an attorney before and during questioning. If you cannot afford a lawyer, one will be appointed for you.

"Do you understand these rights as I've read them to you?" she asked him.

Campbell nodded his assent and mumbled yes.

"We wanna hear you, asshole," Hank directed him using the gun's muzzle to prompt a louder vocal response. "Oh, excuse me, Sir Asshole!"

"Yes, I understand," Campbell said aloud.

If they only knew, was all he could think with a Cheshire grin as wide as a wedge of spring lemons.

Campbell went without protest. How could he? He had no choice. He was trapped in his lair and there was no way out, at least for now.

Chapter Forty-One

Outside, the streets were relatively quiet for an arrest this big. The Covid lockdown had pretty much silenced media coverage of anything not related to the pandemic and there were no visitors allowed in the hospital, minimizing foot traffic in the area. Oddly, even the wearied National Guard and hospital workers barely noticed as police ushered Campbell outside in cuffs.

"What, no cameras?" Campbell joked, as they shoved him into Tommy and Lou's squad car. It was a team effort, and while they would all share credit for the arrest, the kidnapping was officially the senior detectives' case from the start.

It was just about 6:30 p.m. by the time they arrived back at Simpson Street. They hoped to get him inside the building before the seven o'clock pot-bangers hung out of their windows and took to their fire escapes. Let Campbell's arrest stew anonymously in processing until after the eleven o'clock news tonight. Then they could all catch at least forty winks before tomorrow when New Yorkers would hear the headlines and realize Covid is not the only killer out there.

Maggie took thirty seconds to text Jax and Uncle Bobby before they heard about the arrest from either Uncle Bobby's officer buddies or a police scanner which her godfather still kept on his kitchen counter. Hank did the same with his bride. Checking in with significant others went a long way toward easing nerves during long days which turn into even longer nights and make headlines.

"Hey, how did you know I was in the basement?" Maggie finally asked Hank after they both had time to settle from the rush of adrenaline which was part of any high-stakes arrest.

"I have that app, remember?"

"What app?" she asked and looked at him quizzically, but the puzzle was soon solved as she remembered the answer. "Ah, yeah, that app!"

The four detectives had installed a family tracking app during the Binky Killer case four years ago. They were all fortunate and never had to use it until today. Maggie was grateful she had the lucky lifeline.

"Well, thanks," she said. "I mean it, really."

"All in a day's work," he acknowledged her with a slight nod of his head.

"Did you text the little woman?" Maggie followed up teasingly without missing a beat.

"Yeah, I had to. She's pregnant," Hank said matter-of-factly, sensing his recognized duty but without a grand announcement. All kidding aside, sometimes a cop's life evolves around them while they observe from the sidelines.

Chapter Forty-Two

Getting Campbell into the system was a tedious process. All four detectives escorted Campbell from the squad car outside into the tiny staging area for bookings inside the precinct.

"It's like we're in an alternate universe without the press hanging around here like turkey vultures," Lou whispered to Tommy, certain that their attention-seeking suspect could not hear them as Hank ushered him inside.

"Impressive," Campbell commented as they made their way toward the precinct's dramatic façade with the five arched openings that served as windows and entry points into the infamous structure.

The desk sergeant observed from his high perch over the lobby at the front desk while Hank uncuffed Campbell to allow them access for taking his digital fingerprints. His mug shot was taken in front of the standard height measurement chart, and his pedigree information, name, address and birth date were entered into the system.

"Did you get my good angle, Detective?" Campbell directed his comments toward Maggie. "And make sure you mark my height on the chart. Mom never did that for me," he laughed while mocking most parents who noted their child's growth milestones on the wall or door jamb. He was in the thick of it now, but Campbell still held some cards up his sleeve and he was nowhere near ready to reveal his hand.

His arraignment was unlikely tonight. Detainees are supposed to be in front of a judge within twenty-four hours but the whole world had shifted course in just two months and most routine tasks were taking a whole lot longer, especially in The Bronx. It had been nearly three weeks since Governor Cuomo signed an Executive Order suspending all time frames in civil and criminal proceedings, handcuffing prosecutions until the suspension was lifted. He never anticipated the problems caused by keeping so many criminals behind bars in jails already over-congested and now plagued with widespread Covid outbreaks.

Tommy and Lou had invited Hank and Maggie to sit in on Campbell's interrogation, but they had a search warrant to execute at his apartment and they were dying to start hunting for clues that could lead to additional charges against him for the Jenkins and Robbins homicides.

For now, Campbell had been arrested on multiple charges including the kidnapping and assault of someone under the age of seventeen and the kidnapping, assault and menacing of a police officer, all felonies, which meant the custodial interrogation had to be recorded. It needed to be memorialized for police to defend themselves against criticism from overly aggressive defense attorneys trying to get a case tossed out of court on technicalities, while knowing their clients were absolutely guilty.

Tommy started the recording while Lou read Robert Nathan Campbell his Miranda rights, a second time, from a printed card.

"Have you been read these rights today since we arrested you?" Lou asked.

"Yes, this is the second time now," Campbell confirmed. "I do understand them. I know how the game is played from watching police crime dramas," he continued.

"I don't want a lawyer. Just ask me your questions."

Lou placed the Miranda card which he had just read on the table in front of Campbell and asked him to sign and date it. They were making absolutely sure that when or if this guy lawyered up, that they had a clean record before asking him anything. Now they had a recording and his autograph on a Miranda card for posterity.

They started the questioning with the easy pedigree information, name, address, birthdate, social security information, all of which they already had from his hospital personnel file and just now from his booking. Yet, this case had the potential to expand to double homicides in The Bronx and possibly across the country to charges in New Mexico. Wouldn't the feds love that, snatching their case before they could offer Campbell a plea deal or get him convicted? Captain Bradshaw had reminded them earlier to triple check everything and to periodically check the recording so that there were no digital hiccups, and it continued without a lapse.

Now that he had their attention, he wanted to tell his story, every detail, every kill, every time he wanted attention and didn't get it. Now it was his time to shine and just get on with it, telling his story.

"How do you know Samantha Gallo?" Lou started with the easiest of questions.

"Samantha who?" Campbell honestly did not know her name, at least her last name. "Oh, you mean Sammy from the supermarket?" His surprised realization in that moment was legit.

"Yes, Sammy from the supermarket," Lou said, acknowledging they were discussing the same person.

Campbell said he had been food shopping there since he returned to New York and that he liked her fiery spirit. "A no-nonsense Bronx chick. You know the type, right, detective?"

It was slow-going. Campbell ran hot and cold with his level of cooperation. His answers were measured like he was playing chess with the fictional private eye, Philip Marlowe, trying to outwit the analytical, tough detectives on the other side of the table. His goal tonight was to simply toy with them, playing the line between cooperation and avoidance, dodging questions, trying to delay his arraignment and likely relocation to the city's penal black hole known as Rikers Island. The antiquated, overcrowded jail was not designed for social distancing, enabling Covid to mete out death sentences to inmates and correction workers alike. Campbell ironically saw the old Fort Apache as a lifesaver, quite literally.

The air in the small interrogation room was pregnant with mistrust. Lou and Tommy were skeptical that Campbell knew the meaning of the word truthful as his cunning responses indicated this was a game to him. Campbell doubted the police could link him to killing the two nurses, or anyone else, and he carefully watered down his replies, being polite and respectful as a cooperative illusion.

"So, we're trying to find out what happened with Samantha on Sunday after work," Tommy said, setting the stage for the long night ahead. They planned to drag out the questioning on the current kidnapping, unlawful imprisonment and assault charges until they heard back from Maggie and Hank on what, if anything, they found at Campbell's apartment.

"Did something happen to her after she left work?" Campbell asked. "Young girls can't be too careful these days."

"That's not how this is gonna go tonight," Tommy said, hovering over the table, one foot now propped on the chair which he had occupied a few short minutes ago.

"We're gonna ask the questions and you're gonna answer them, one at a time. Get it?" Tommy advised him with a rhetorical question, not expecting a response.

"How did she wind up in your car?" Lou asked, grabbing the lead from Tommy to mollify the tension building in the small room, slightly larger than the average jail cell at Rikers. It was much too early to rev up the pressure on Campbell. They had to coast for a while and play by his rules, finding mutual ground like the first tenuous steps of a new romance but this was anything but enjoyable.

"I don't own a car," Campbell responded with nothing more. They were double-teaming him now, so he needed to update his strategy to duck and pivot, keeping his answers short. He knew that if he admitted stealing the car off the block, the felony charges against him would start piling up faster than a squirrel stacks acorns in an oak tree.

Lou mustered every ounce of patience he had in revising his question, understanding this was no ordinary brain-dead suspect scared to be in cuffs or scared of his momma back at home. This guy was sophisticated. If he was the serial killer they had been hunting, he was sharp, strategic, analytical when planning his next move and he could ride this night into the next morning like an Italian sports car on rails, smooth, slick, unwavering and unrattled.

"You were driving a car Sunday night on White Plains Road, correct?"

"Yes."

"Samantha Gallo was a passenger in that car, correct?"

"Yes. It was raining, and the kid needed a lift home," Campbell replied quickly. "No big deal."

"You invited her into your car?" Lou asked reluctantly, continuing the basic probative questioning, elementary and tedious but necessary.

"I just told you, I don't own a car," Campbell reminded them, emphasizing each word slowly, one word at a time, to make sure they heard every single word and so would the people who would eventually listen to the recording.

"Oh, yes. You invited her into that car?" Lou rephrased his question. His backhanded effort to trick Campbell into admitting whether the car was his or that he had stolen it would not fly with this guy.

"She saw me outside when she left work, and the car was parked right under the El.

"It sorta just happened, like that," Campbell said casually. He had already relaxed in the hard chair, hunkering down for the long game.

"Well, whose car were you using that night?"

"It was a neighbor's car."

"What neighbor?" Lou continued, also asking one question at a time to draw out the narrative and each element of the charges Campbell now faced and elements of additional charges they had waiting in the wings.

"Some local guy on the street," Campbell said. The voice inside his head knew he was painting himself into a proverbial corner with his vague response.

"I know him, but I don't know him, you know what I mean?"

"No, I don't know," Lou said. "Tell me what you know, so I'll know."

"It sounds like there's a guy on your street that you know but you don't know, and he lets you use his car to pick up young women, you know?" Lou's delivery sounded like a comedy classic.

"I don't know's on third," Campbell joked. "It's not like that, detective," Campbell responded while drafting a better response silently in his head.

"Then please, enlighten us," Tommy asked, irritated but non-reactive to Campbell's wit. The interrogation was progressing as slowly as expected while the suspect stalled for time, coming to the realization that their tomorrow was not looking too bright tonight.

Campbell knew the secrets he was hiding and there were so many of them. He imagined they could guess some of them, but he wanted them to work for the rest.

"We're friends from the 'hood," Campbell offered. "We say hello to each other with a Bronx chin lift," Campbell started providing details while demonstrating with a lift of his own chin and a shrug of his shoulders. "That doesn't mean we know each other's names."

"But he lets you use his car?" Lou asked again. "Sounds like a pretty stupid neighbor, albeit maybe a nice guy, you know?"

"Did he actually loan you the car and give you the keys?" Tommy asked him. The weary detective stood tall to stretch and walk around the room after ninety minutes of questioning, He stopped suddenly just to the rear of Campbell's left shoulder, looming over him, as if to scare a truthful answer out of the guy.

"I know where he hides the spare key," Campbell said convincingly, probably the most truthful thing he would say all evening. In that moment, he was quickly creating a story with a suitable pretext, or at least one that he believed to be suitable.

"Oh, do tell us more, please, Robbie," Tommy implored him. "May I call you Robbie?" Tommy asked, bowing over Campbell's shoulder to look him dead in the eye but Campbell didn't flinch.

"Yes, of course you may, detective," Campbell said. "The guy's so cheap, he has a broken steering wheel club lock which doesn't lock and neither does the driver's side door," Campbell said, starting down the road and a game of self-incriminating grand theft auto.

"So, he always parks the car in about the same spot on the block and then hides a spare key under the passenger side rear wheel well."

"It's like an open invitation," Campbell suggested. "I'm here, come borrow me." Campbell had developed a skill for hot-wiring cars in high school. Tinkering with electronics and wires served him well in life, a skill he picked up at Bronx Science, the specialized high school fostered his analytical interests in everything from electrical engineering to neuroscience and forensic science, his favorite courses.

"So, you took the car without the owner's express permission?" Lou asked to illicit a clean admission from a guy who was playing his hand quite well.

"Of course I took it. I borrowed it," Campbell insisted. "I was gonna bring it back before the guy had his morning coffee."

There it was, an admission to car theft. They chalked up another felony charge as they meandered toward him making a bigger criminal reveal, hopefully murder.

Lou restrained himself from asking about the status of the car and kept it in his back pocket to randomly clarify later in the interrogation. Campbell was slick but these detectives were slicker. Three could play this game, all night long, and that's what it would likely last, all night long.

"So, Robbie, please set the scene for us," Tommy asked him. "It's raining Sunday night on White Plains Road, under the El and just outside the supermarket, correct?"

"Oh, it was pouring, and that little Sammy didn't have an umbrella," Campbell said. "I mean the rain, through the overhead tracks, was dumping buckets on that the poor girl's head.

"It wouldn't have been nice for me to leave her there to drown."

"What were you wearing and what was she wearing?"

"Now, isn't that rather personal?"

"Humor us."

"I was wearing a hoodie, and she had on a faux leather biker jacket with a hoodie under it," Campbell recalled. "What do they call it now, a pleather moto jacket?

"And we were both wearing face masks," he added. "I mean, we wouldn't want a cold to be the death of us. Now, would we?"

"Isn't it true that she declined your offer to drive her home?" Lou asked. The lack of her consent was a key element to kidnapping.

"Oh, kids today don't know what they want," Campbell said dismissively, "or what's good for them."

"She didn't want to get in your car. She knew that much, right?" Tommy asked. "So, you forced her."

"Is there a question in there, detective?"

"Did you physically force her into the stolen car?"

"I helped her, like a gentleman, by guiding her at the elbow," Campbell said. "And the car was not stolen. It was borrowed." His confidence was unyielding. His determination to steer his future was unwavering.

"So, you escorted Samantha into your neighbor's car while you held a blade to the back of her neck?"

"I was holding the keys in one hand and her elbow in the other," Campbell stated emphatically, not rudely but with firm intent. "There was no blade."

"Then why did you tie her up when you placed her in the front seat?"

"I didn't tie her up. Her scarf got caught on the broken door handle," he said. "I couldn't risk getting into an accident while driving in the rain just to untangle her."

"What were your plans for her that night?"

"To drive her home and see that she safely got inside her house."

"But you never made it to her house, why Robbie?"

"I thought I got a flat tire on Bronx Boulevard, so I pulled up to a curb and parked the car and got out to check the tires."

Campbell was almost believable in the details of his story. His narration was still, calm, without a ripple, and his body language offered no hint of uncertainty. His breath was not measured but natural as he spoke and he looked casually at the detectives, not away, not once, not ever. He had mastered the art of lying long ago as a way for him to gain and maintain control and manipulate most situations and people.

"What did you mean when you told her *next time say yes, although there won't be a next time for you?*" Tommy quoted Samantha's recollection, almost word-for-word, to see Campbell's reaction.

"I just told her that next time, she should plan ahead because there were a lot of crazy people on the street right now," Campbell said with certainty, as if he was looking out for the young victim. "I mean not everyone out there is helpful like me.

"I'm not sure why she bolted and ran screaming toward a truck when I got out of the car," he continued. "She must've untangled her scarf and ran. I just don't need that kind of crazy in my life, so I just left her there with the trucker."

He was enjoying his fifteen minutes of fame, invigorated by the attention, unaware of how his time in the spotlight could blow up in his face if he was identified as the killer of two frontline responders, the young nurses. He would be condemned by everyone rather than idolized by those twisted, closeted fans of notorious serial killers. That is a whole special kind of crazy. In this climate, New York is surviving only out of the bravery of the medical professionals, both local and visitors, like Susan Robbins, who were coming from all corners of the country to help.

"You know, we're searching your apartment right now," Tommy said to him. "We have warrants."

"Well, I hope you didn't break down the door," Campbell said facetiously. "It's a rental."

"Nah, the super let us in," Tommy said. "Nice guy!"

"Is that pretty Detective Flynn going to look through my undies drawer?" Campbell asked. "I get hard just thinking about it. I mean how do you guys work with her every day?"

He was trying, really trying, to rev their engines, knowing full well the camera was rolling and hoping to goad them into abrasive police behavior, recorded for posterity, but Lou and Tommy had been on the job way too long to allow any skank like Campbell to get on their last nerve.

"Are they going to find any surprises in your draws or anywhere else?" Lou asked.

"Do you mean souvenirs?" Campbell quipped. "I did buy a T-shirt in the desert on my way back to New York and a souvenir condom that said *The Gift that Just Keeps Coming.*"

Tommy had to quickly turn and face the two-way window because that was funny, although he refrained from laughing out loud.

"Hey, you're gonna be here a long time tonight, so get comfy," Lou said as he got up to stretch his back and read the urgent texts coming in from Hank and Maggie who were executing the search warrant at Campbell's apartment.

"We'll be back with dinner," Lou told him. Tommy was already out the door.

Campbell had never felt as painted into a corner as he did in this moment. Chained to a table, unable to leave, under the watchful eye of the young officer now standing in the corner of the room and under the watchful eye of whoever was hiding behind the two-way mirror. It was the reality check he needed to understand that he that may never see the outside world again, as he knew it. This was no longer his game, and the cops came to play.

Chapter Forty-Three

"Well, what do we have here?" Hank asked aloud to no one in particular as they entered the bedroom. The detectives and the rest of the forensic team had donned the requisite disposable shoe covers and gloves and stepped slowly through Campbell's almost too tidy apartment near Allerton Avenue. There in front of them, in plain sight, was a box of body bags. It was not something most people kept at home, not even coroners or morticians, much less a hospital transporter. They stopped searching immediately and called the assistant district attorney who was on duty and asked him to get an amended warrant based on probable cause for a more deadly crime like homicide, two of them.

After a quick inspection of the premises to be certain there was no one in danger anywhere in the one-bedroom apartment, they sealed the quarters up tight for the night. They would return in the morning with an amended warrant, much to the chagrin of neighbors on the floor who would be surprised to see the yellow police tape and seal across Campbell's apartment door when they woke up tomorrow.

Lou and Tommy were strategizing as they neared the holding cell. They had moved Campbell from interrogation to the guest suite at the rear of the station house after the team at Campbell's apartment alerted them to the cache of body bags they discovered.

Campbell could see them approaching. They were toting a take-out bag, presumably his deli dinner for the long night ahead.

Yet they were still too far for him to hear what they were saying, despite the eerie silence in the back cell inside this stone fortress.

"You know, it's not nice to whisper, detectives," Campbell mocked them. He had only been in isolation for less than thirty minutes when they returned, and his jocular acuity was still sharp.

They dared not ask him about the body bags in the short walk from the cell back to the interrogation room. If he said anything at all about the nurses, they needed to preserve the record.

With Campbell back at the table, Lou restarted the recording, while Tommy reminded him of his Miranda rights and his waiver of them, for a third time, while locking his cuffs to the anchor on the table. Tommy placed the ham and cheese sandwich on a roll in front of Campbell with a bag of chips and a cola. The handcuffs were connected to a chain long enough to allow any suspect to eat or drink during long, often mind-numbing sessions, as they anticipated that tonight's could linger into the wee hours of the morning.

"What? No vegan option?" Campbell asked sarcastically as he took a bite out of the sandwich, intentionally gnawing down on the roll like an animal, shaking his head like a dog wrestling for a bone and growling while he chewed.

He was taunting them. This was more fun than dragging the dead on their journey to the afterlife in the middle of the night. Yes, these guys were living, breathing victims and it would be an engaging battle of wits between him and them, all of them, once Hank and Maggie returned from his apartment.

"You're lucky we found a deli open this late on a weeknight," Tommy answered. "Blame it on Covid."

Lou scoffed down a wedge of roast beef and Swiss cheese with yellow mustard, dining in the observation room, taking notes, while Tommy sipped his lukewarm coffee not wanting to eat but merely form a casual bond with Campbell. He needed to stay alert and edgy.

"What's with the body bags?" Tommy asked.

"Oh, we're gonna have fun tonight, detectives.

"I was just helping the elderly," he continued. "Isn't that what the governor keeps telling us to do during his daily briefings? Check on your neighbors, especially the old ones."

"Helping them do what?" Tommy asked. "Hide a body?"

A knock on the two-way mirror alerted Detective Sergeant Tom Martin to stop. He guessed that maybe Hank and Maggie had just returned from the search.

"Enjoy your dinner. I'll be right back," he said to Campbell, stepping into the hall.

Maggie explained that they had called both Captain Bradshaw and the ADA and were waiting for an amended warrant to search for clues in the two homicides. Tommy yielded to her request to have an at-bat with Campbell since the two had bonded in the hospital elevator.

Tommy, Lou and Hank hung out in the observation room knowing this would be quite entertaining as Maggie was always laser-focused when she was pissed off. Her words often cut like a knife right through the bullshit of any suspect's lame-ass excuses. Let any guy threaten her with a scalpel and watch what happens next.

"Mirror, mirror on the wall, she's the fairest of them all," Campbell said, directing his comments at the male detectives he knew were hiding behind the mirror as Detective Flynn entered the interrogation room alone.

"What's the matter, boys?" Campbell asked the hidden detectives. "It takes a woman to do a real cop's job?" His beady eyes leered at Maggie, full of lechery and toxic masculinity. She could feel him raping her in his mind but deflected it with her strength like a sigma woman braced with an invisibility shield of confidence. This time she was in control, and he was restrained, anchored to a table, and with no way out.

Again, she read him his Miranda rights. Again, he repeated that he understood that anything he said could and would be used against him in a court of law for any new crimes discussed or revealed during the interrogation. And he repeated that he wanted to continue without a lawyer.

"So, why the body bags in your apartment?" she asked pointedly.

"I always help my neighbors, especially the elderly with no one around," he said. "I mean can you see a ninety-year-old using a food app to buy groceries when they have me?" He laughed without making a sound.

She wanted to slap the stupid grin right off his very ordinary face but instead she played nice hoping to eventually disarm him. He apparently felt like talking and she didn't want to shut him down prematurely by ramping up her Bronx sarcasm.

"The tricky part was the body bags," he continued casually, staring intently at her green eyes. "But once I got the hang of it, it got easier, just like anything else that takes time. It gets better with practice. As hard as it might be, it's always better with practice, don't you agree, detective?"

"You got better with practice killing people," she said in disgust. She was devoid of all emotion. She maintained steady eye contact with him no matter how difficult it was for her to refrain from reacting to his lustful innuendos with almost every answer that he provided.

"Can you explain why you needed body bags to help your neighbors?" she asked, now using every ounce of patience in her inquisitive body. She had to illicit a confession and was fully aware that you get more flies with honey. She didn't want to afford him any chance to flip the switch from cooperative to recalcitrant, nor open the door to him requesting a lawyer. That would shut down the interrogation before they had a chance to return to Campbell's apartment to search for clues in the Jenkins and Robbins homicides.

Campbell could still make her skin crawl, but she hunkered down. She was on familiar ground trying to delve into the minds of killers, especially serial killers. Maggie seemed to be a magnet for attracting social deviants and Campbell was about as twisted, weird and downright evil as she had seen in her four years as a Bronx homicide detective.

"You must've liked them?" Maggie stated in a way to pose a question through the fluctuation of her voice, inviting him to expand his story. Experience had provided her with the psychological tools to soft pedal the inquisition as required in the moment.

Campbell appeared to be a study in contrasts. On the one hand, he was empathetic to the plight of elderly neighbors locked away alone during a global crisis, unusual in itself for serial killers who rarely think of anyone else's feelings. While on the other hand, he was an egocentric narcissist who needed to be admired for the harm he did to others.

Maggie, along with the other members of the core four watching in the wings, understood that while serial killers exhibited similar behavioral patterns, no two were alike because their individual stressors and motivators distinguished them and kept them from being predictable. No two people experience life and death in the same way. No two people kill in the same way, even copycats have distinguishing traits.

"Of course, I liked them," Campbell admitted, "And I knew what it was like to be left alone, not knowing where to turn in an emergency.

"My mother left us alone to go to work, even when my sister was really sick."

He was opening up to Maggie. His guard was coming down, but he was still on edge. His anxiety remained hidden until his knee started bobbing up and down. Maggie could hear it tapping under the table, rattling the chain on the tabletop above. She ignored it and sat back in her chair, at ease and comfortable, hoping he would mirror her behavior and relax again. She knew that psychopaths often used the mirroring technique to charm their prey by copying their behavior and emotions before going in for the kill. It was not that psychopaths were empathetic. It was more like they possessed an internal switch to turn that emotion on and off to suit their needs in any given situation. Maggie was hoping the same technique that Campbell had likely mastered would work on him in reverse.

"Tell me about your sister," Maggie said. "Is she still alive?"

He explained that his older sister died of childhood leukemia a long time ago, when he was about ten years old. His story began slowly. His shoulders drooped and his chin tucked down as he started telling Maggie about the heartbreak of his childhood stress. His mother left them alone while she worked because there was no other family around.

Taking care of his sister was his responsibility. *That's what big boys do. They don't cry. They suck it up.* That was a lot of weight for a young boy to carry and he retained a lot of resentment for having done so.

Maggie understood immediately that his stressors, in part, were abandonment and helplessness and she used that to prod him forward. In the moment, the analytical mind of a detective needed to be as sharp as a killer's blade and she was on top of her game.

"I'm sorry to hear about your sister, Robbie. That must have been very difficult for you," she said, offering a breadcrumb of strategic compassion to this psychopath. She knew the duality of good and evil lives in everyone, and it's only an internal light that can erase the darkness. Yet in her short but intense career as a detective, she knew that some people are just born on the dark side and never leave anything but death and destruction in their wake. She, on the other hand, could turn her charm off and on, from dark and threatening to light and compassionate, when necessary, for the job, of course.

He appreciated her kindness at that moment. It was something he wasn't used to, not even at work, where kindness goes a long way toward healing anyone. Not for Robbie, though, since he didn't matter to anyone, or so he believed.

"Robbie let's get back to your neighbors," Maggie said redirecting the focus of the interrogation.

"How did you help them?" she asked. "Did you bring them food and medicine? Did you do chores for them?

"I know it's been very hard for the elderly right now."

He admitted running errands but said he felt totally helpless when Signora Genovese got so sick at the end of January.

He explained that the generally active woman was confined to bed, unable to take care of herself.

"She couldn't breathe, she couldn't speak, and she never talked about her family," he added casually. "There was no one to help her but me. Who could I call?"

"I mean she was a vibrant ninety-year-old until Covid, or what we thought was a really bad flu season back in January," he explained. "She walked the avenue every day and bought her own groceries," he continued his narrative. He was uncharacteristically chatty for a suspected killer.

"It must've been that last cannoli run that did her in," he surmised. All of the detectives realized that Campbell often used sarcastic humor to deflect his insensitivity, which came across as callous and unfeeling, typical of a psychopath. Yet that wit served to make the complex darkness of a killer's mind more accessible for most of us.

"I mean where else would she have caught the 'Rona, right?" he asked rhetorically, seeking validation from Maggie which was not forthcoming.

"Robbie, who is Signora Genovese?" Maggie asked, using his first name as if engaging a friend in conversation. She stretched behind her head, circling her pointer finger toward the mirror to have the team write this all down and find Signora Genovese. This name was new to all of them, and the squad was already checking the department's missing persons reports and online obituaries.

"You mean who was Signora Genovese?" Campbell replied confidently. "She died. I helped her."

"You helped her die, Robbie?" Maggie asked, realizing this interrogation was rapidly moving in a direction none of them had anticipated earlier in the day.

"Yes, Rita Genovese was a nice old lady who lived alone on Lydig Avenue in her own house," he said. "I asked her if she needed me to help her and she nodded her consent, so I gave her a shot of propofol, and she went to sleep peacefully. She was my first," he admitted. But his first what, no one was sure.

"I couldn't watch her shrivel up and die in pain," he said. "It's not anything you can understand until you hold the hand of a loved one as they take their last breath."

Hank heard that and was already on the phone, waking and notifying Captain Bradshaw and calling the same ADA they had spoken with an hour earlier to amend the warrant yet again since Campbell had just confessed to killing his neighbor. He asked the prosecutor to amend both the arrest and search warrants for the car theft since this case was changing by the minute. They would also need a new search warrant for Signora Genovese's house on Lydig Avenue.

Campbell explained to Maggie that getting the propofol was the easiest part of his job to helping his patients. He outlined how he would follow doctors and nurses around the hospital stealing their codes to use the drug vending machine.

"They never see me and I'm always there," he said confidently. "Or maybe they see me but never imagine that someone without an advanced degree could do what they are trained to do."

"Robbie, where is she? What did you do with her body?" Maggie asked, looking at the clock mounted on the wall behind Campbell's head. It was already the next day. "Did you put her in a body bag?"

"Oh no," he paused briefly. "Well, yes," he said, more as an afterthought, stumbling a bit and then felt compelled to clarify for Detective Flynn. "I mean I had to keep it neat and tidy like the rest of her house," he explained. "I did use a body bag to put her in the basement freezer. It didn't take much to move her, she was tiny, barely a hundred pounds soaking wet.

"It was back in January when nobody knew what was going on and I didn't have anyone to call for help.

"So, I took out a shelf in the freezer and she slid right in.

"I'm sure she hasn't moved," he suggested matter-of-factly.

Maggie was trying to process the revelation that this had just become a homicide interrogation, and she hadn't even gotten to the Jenkins and Robbins murders yet. The three detectives in observation were dumbstruck.

Maggie's head was spinning like a top. She could only imagine poor Signora Genovese stuffed into a basement freezer, as if The Bronx didn't have enough to deal with at the moment. It was nearly two in the morning and Maggie knew they would all need some sleep, even though Campbell looked wide awake. She would hate to shut him down while he was so willing to talk, but the four detectives needed to be just as alert when they executed the amended warrant at Campbell's apartment tomorrow along with the new search warrant at the Genovese home.

After stepping out to consult with the squad and Captain Bradshaw by phone and confirm the address and identity of Rita Genovese through public records, Maggie knew what had to be done tonight, for certain, before they could think about heading home.

Maggie returned to interrogation with Hank while Lou and Tommy remained in observation to make sure the recording did not stop on this version of unsolved mysteries.

"Robbie, you're going to spend the night here," she advised Campbell. "We'll need to check a few things out tonight and tomorrow morning before we continue.

"But before we go, Detective Sergeant Lopez asked me to follow-up with something about your trip with Samantha Gallo."

"Sure, go ahead, ask away," Campbell said. She surmised he was acting on a rush of adrenaline while the four of them were ready to drop on their desks for the night.

"You said that you were planning to return the car that you borrowed that night before your neighbor had breakfast the next morning," she summarized his earlier recantation. "Did you do that? Did you return the car?"

"Nope."

"Well, where's the car? What did you do with it?"

"I moved it up to Mount Vernon and left it near the railyard and took the subway home," Campbell revealed easily.

"Why didn't you just bring it back?"

"Who knows why I do most things?" he said, as if many had tried but none had succeeded.

"It's probably not there anymore," he suggested. "I mean, it's Mount Vernon along the tracks where anything can happen."

Maggie did not prod him for more or they would all be there until dawn. She trusted that Lou would be following up with the Mount Vernon Police Department in the morning.

Maggie asked Campbell to stand while Hank unlocked the cuffs from the ring on the table and held him by the elbow as Maggie again formally arrested him on the new charges.

"Robert Nathan Campbell, you are under arrest for the murder of Rita Genovese and the theft of your neighbor's car, John Doe's car," she said. "You have the right to remain silent. Anything you say can and will be used against you in a court of law. You have the right to an attorney before and during questioning. If you cannot afford a lawyer, one will be appointed for you.

"Do you understand these rights as I have read them to you?" She repeated the refrain read from the card but had lost track of just how many times any one of them had read him his rights since his initial arrest yesterday.

Campbell nodded, repeating his understanding of the rights which had now been read to him a handful of times in less than twelve hours, all but the first reading had been digitally memorialized and signed with Campbell's autograph on the Miranda card. The team had started writing the time on each card as soon as Campbell signed and dated it just to keep track of it more for themselves than for any recognized formality.

"Detective Flynn, who do I call tonight if I'm lonely?" Campbell asked. "Room service?"

Hank spun him around so quickly and returned him to the holding cell and locked him inside before unlocking his cuffs through an opening between the bars.

"You're going to be here overnight, so get comfy, choir boy," Hank said. "Look, we booked you a private suite all to yourself.

"A toilet with no seat. An electronically controlled faucet with no handles. And here's a blanket for good measure," Hank said, taking it from the young officer who retrieved one from the dark bowels of the building and tossing it to Campbell. "All of the comforts of home just for you."

Campbell was now starring in his own crime drama and loving every minute in the spotlight. Finally, someone was giving him the attention he had craved since puberty.

Chapter Forty-Four

Lou bolted once they called it a night, while Hank, Maggie and Tommy walked into the squad room like zombies, dead from their dark, empty eyes down to their tired dogs where the soles of their feet ached with exhaustion. Each of them slumped into a chair for a quick minute to organize and recalibrate the investigation.

Tommy barely had enough energy to make the drive home to the northern 'burbs. He actually toyed with the idea of taking a nap on his old, metal desk but dawn was just around the corner and catching forty winks in his comfy bed sounded a lot more appealing, even if only for three or four hours.

Hank checked his phone for any texts or messages and wished Maggie and Tommy a Happy Passover. It was an alarm notification on his calendar as was the news bulletin that on this April 9th, as of last night, more than eighty thousand people were hospitalized with Covid and nearly five thousand people had already died citywide.

"I doubt anyone will be gathering to celebrate this year, and anyway, we're all Christians here," Maggie reminded him. "But thanks. We need all the blessings we can get right now."

"Speak for yourself," Hank said. "I'm a savage heathen."

Yet despite his self-deprecating humor, Hank reached out to his wife, as did Tommy. It was for their spouses' peace of mind, as much as their own.

Maggie found a flurry of unanswered texts from Jax, Uncle Bobby and Lauren waiting on her phone, several from each of them. When she wasn't home by six o'clock, then by nine o'clock, and eventually by midnight, neither Jax nor Bobby were going to sleep until they heard from her, and she knew that.

She texted only Jax before heading up to the Genovese house with Hank. That was their deal. Jax would then report to Uncle Bobby and Lauren so they could all rest easy, and get back to sleep, if that was even possible at three in the morning.

Time was meaningless as one dark day rolled into the next. Most humans need contact with other humans and all humans need sleep. Covid was killing more than just the victims who succumbed to its grasp. It was killing the spirit of the city that never slept which was now in a catatonic state except for the NYPD detectives who stayed the course.

The PIO at headquarters was not answering the phone this late at night, or this early in the morning, depending on your viewpoint or critical need for information. He or she was definitely manning the desk but not eager to speak with overnight news vampires ready to suck the blood out of any crime or arrest for a soundbite. So as long as Campbell's arrest was not going to be on the books and officially processed until later in the day, all of them would try to catch some sleep. The unaware news crews would not be sniffing around overnight for an interview, or a perp walk, to satiate their ravenous desire to feed off New York's criminal underbelly for the morning drive news cycle.

Maggie took a long overdue bio-break and grabbed a cup of stale station coffee for the jolt she needed to search the home of Rita Genovese. What doesn't kill you makes you stronger, or in this case, hopefully more alert behind the wheel.

Maggie and Hank flew to Lydig Avenue with lights flashing but no sirens. There was no need to make a show at three in the morning or wake the dead. No criminals, no traffic, no rush! The scene was a short distance from headquarters. The ME's office and CSU were already en route to the Genovese home. They needed to learn tonight whether the suggested victim was in fact dead or still breathing. Even though they were armed with a search warrant, based on Campbell's voluntary confession, they had probable cause to take down the door if no one answered.

They didn't know what to expect at the Genovese house. Neither one of them had ever pulled a body out of a freezer before. CSU and the ME's office had already arrived and were waiting outside the house.

"We knocked but nobody's home," said one of the forensic techs.

"Well, there may be a body at home but not one that's breathing," Hank whispered to Maggie.

They needed a Halligan tool to pry open the heavy, sixty-year-old solid oak front door which was arched at the top and not squared off. It had a small inset window with iron bars covering the glass as if those who lived inside could see the ugliness approaching outside and fend off possible intruders with a metal barricade. It was not easy to break into one of those old brick homes from the 1940s. They were crafted as solid and strong as the Italian bricklayers and masons who built them decades ago, and this tidy home had been sealed as tight as a crypt for at least ten weeks, according to Campbell.

Maggie imagined that prying the door in this case would be a lot like opening an ancient tomb, releasing the demons and the musty air of the dead. She wasn't wrong. The thermostat just inside the living room had been left at sixty degrees and the house had taken on that stale odor of an old person's home. It happens slowly, over time, with the blinds drawn and the wall paint peeling and the same old dust-laden drapes hanging in place for fifteen years, having never been cleaned. The smell here was a cross between mold in the attic and dust in the basement settling on piles of old papers that no one will ever read, clothing unwashed because the laundry was in the basement down steps that were too rickety for an unstable senior citizen to safely climb, along with furniture stained and scarred by smoke. It was the smell that meant next stop death.

"Thank God for masks, eh, detectives," one of the techs said as they tip-toed their way to the basement. The CSU crew followed the assistant ME who followed the detectives down the wobbly staircase, in the dark, since the overhead light was in apparent need of a new bulb and logistically out of reach for anyone to bother changing it. The parade of them looked like a midnight funeral cortege, walking in silence, using their cellphone flashlights to illuminate their uncertain path.

"We may need more than an N95 mask down there," Hank said with one hand on the banister for guidance and the other holding his phone.

"Well, on the bright side, it's not summer and she's in the freezer as icy as a popsicle," Maggie added.

Cop humor got them through some of their darkest times, as with the assistant ME and forensic technicians too.

Hank approached the decades-old clunker of a freezer with trepidation. It was a Sears Coldspot, one of those chunky, top open, chest freezers found in nearly every home of the post-Depression era. It was the pride of every American family who survived World War II, and it stored everything from a year's supply of meat to enough fresh baked goods to host three block parties. Today, it was the final resting place of the lady of the house.

"How the hell did he lift a dead body up and into this tank of a freezer?" Maggie asked.

"Very carefully," the assistant ME deadpanned, "one limb at a time."

Oddly enough, the body of Rita Genovese was the only thing in the house that did not smell like death. Campbell had neatly placed her to rest in peace, almost with reverence. The pair of forensic techs carefully dusted the body bag and the freezer for prints and took the necessary photos before the assistant ME removed the body from the bag and started the preliminary on-scene examination of the remains.

"You think she's one of *those* "Genoveses?" Maggie wondered aloud as she and Hank carefully perused and inspected the home, room by room, looking for clues.

"Unlikely," Hank said unpersuaded. "Look at these family photos. They're from New York's mob era of the 1940s, '50s and '60s and I don't see Lucky Luciano, Big Vito or Vinny the Chin among them.

"They were the stars of the Genovese family back in the day, the alleged boss and the enforcer turned *caporegime*, the captain of his own crew."

"Poor thing, maybe she was the only survivor," Maggie said. "I mean Campbell said she had no one around."

"They're Italians, Flynn, you should know better," Hank chided her lovingly. "There's always someone around."

The three-hour long search didn't yield anything from the neat-as-a-pin home, despite the fact that CSU walked away with a few boxes of evidence, including samples of trace DNA, hair and carpet fibers and the fingerprints they hoped would confirm Campbell's uncoerced confession.

They removed the body and transferred the remains to the ME's autopsy center at NYU Langone and sealed up the door. That was it, another life lost in this pandemic but not to Covid.

Maggie couldn't wait to get home and snuggle with Jax, even if she was just getting in at 6:30 in the morning. The space between his arms is what drowned out the noise of the insanity which she confronted on a daily basis. She had to admit to herself, always with a smile, that Jax bunking at her place for the duration of the lockdown was the best thing that could have happened to her and to their relationship. Sometimes rushing down the path toward domestic bliss can stall forward progress in a new relationship but when it happens naturally, the path forward just opens gracefully, and the pieces fall into place. Just like a great interrogation.

Campbell's interrogation would continue later in the afternoon. He could wait, as could Signora Genovese's autopsy. She'd already been on ice for nearly three months. Another few hours would not make a difference.

Chapter Forty-Five

Showered and shaved and with about four hours of sleep under their belts, Lou and Tommy returned to Campbell's apartment bright and early in the morning with an amended warrant to include any evidence connecting their prime suspect to the murders of Brittany Jenkins, Susan Robbins, and Rita Genovese, as well as any Jane or John Does yet to be identified. The ADA was getting ahead of the curve, fully expecting Campbell might cough up the names of additional victims as his interrogation progressed, especially since he already admitted helping other neighbors with his stash of body bags.

Campbell was proving to be chattier than most serial killers. His signature was unique. His motive seemed almost altruistic in his warped interpretation of the new world order. He craved the spotlight and a chance to tell his story to a city trapped in the *mishegas*, the Yiddish craziness, of fake news and inadequate governmental oversight. After all, every real New Yorker knows a bit of Yiddish. His only stumbling block was that there was another serial killer with higher, much higher stats on the loose, grabbing all of the attention which he hungered for, stealing all of the headlines now splayed in the maddening news crawl across everyone's television. This was Covid's killing field and even Campbell was in its crosshairs.

"*Running out of Air*" as the city hunted down ventilators across the globe like they were chasing Bin Laden.

"*Test of Faith*" as New Yorkers prayed for help from anywhere and everywhere.

"*Brace for the Worst*" because help might not be coming.

These were the headlines in the Big Apple about the killer from the animal kingdom. New York was now the global leader in the total number of Covid deaths, more than any one country outside the United States.

Yet there was not one reporter in the entire city who had any clue of the evil locked away in the holding cell of the old Fort Apache while a virulent pestilence threatened everyone outside its walls. Just wait until the newspapers got wind of a serial killer, then the city would see real headlines. They would be the kind of captions generated by old newspaper rim rats, the copyreaders who sat around the edge of a newsroom, living on a diet of caffeine and tobacco, making them twisted and edgy enough to generate biting headlines to grab the city's attention. The dirty laundry and all of the sordid details would be hung out for the world to discover. For now, Covid was on the front page, as it had been the lead story for nearly six weeks, while the rest of the sleepy country, out west, was clueless.

This was springtime in New York but instead of life rising from winter's long sleep, the bloom of first love, new life, young innocence and seasonal uplifting were all dead on arrival.

The day started around noon for Maggie and Hank, as slow and dreary as any other day since the lockdown began. They were still on autopilot from the graveyard shift which they had pulled overnight while also pulling poor Signora Genovese out of her freezer.

With the expanded search warrant and the unrealized number of Campbell's potential victims yet to be identified, Tommy and Lou had started around eight o'clock at Campbell's place and would likely spend most of the day there, probing for clues. They would search every drawer, closet and box, and look behind and under every piece of furniture, as well as hunt down possible unique hiding spaces for evidence which could link Campbell to the crimes he had already admitted to, along with those Maggie and Hank hoped to obtain in a confession later today.

Hank nearly keeled over and his eyes watered as he went to retrieve Campbell from the holding cell. The guy smelled riper than the city during the Great Garbage Strike of 1968. It had been more than twenty-four hours since he was pushing dead bodies through the halls of Misericordia to sleeping on the filth left in the holding cell by every miscreant to have slept on that mattress since the precinct's infamous heydays.

Hank could not imagine Maggie sitting in the closed interrogation room and not passing out within five minutes. He went to his own locker to retrieve a clean shirt for Campbell and tossed him a roll-on deodorant between the bars. He did it more for his partner than for the poor soul before him digging his own grave, jailed in these wretched surroundings.

Maggie did a double take when Hank ushered him into interrogation. Her eyes squinted quizzically, just for a moment, as Hank invited Campbell to sit down and then locked his handcuffs to the table anchor. She recalled that when they arrested him yesterday, Campbell was wearing a blue button-down shirt with the hospital's logo on the pocket and wondered how and why he was now wearing a New York Mets sweatshirt.

"Don't ask," said Hank, responding to her quizzical look with a wave of his left hand through the stale air and a roll of his eyes in disdain.

"Just say, I took one for the team sacrificing my favorite Mets shirt this morning."

She had a coffee with a bacon, egg and cheese sandwich on a roll waiting for Campbell. Whether breakfast, lunch or just a snack, this guy could scoff down food like a lifer on death row.

"You take ketchup?" she asked him, placing a few packets on the table.

"Good morning, Detective Flynn," he said to her. "What New Yorker doesn't put ketchup on an egg sandwich, right? It's like asking if the Pope is Catholic.

"And today is Good Friday, if I'm not mistaken," he said, dissecting his sandwich to pull out the bacon. After all, observant Catholics do not eat meat on Good Friday of all days.

He thanked her for breakfast and started eating immediately, like he had not eaten since, what? Last night! Hank stepped out to start the interrogation recording and to look for a toothbrush for the guy. Again, it was more for Maggie's benefit because Campbell's morning breath could kill a horse.

She was getting right at it with Campbell and hoping he was still as talkative as he was last night.

"Good morning," she responded. "Sorry about the bacon."

She followed up the trivialities with a recitation of the date and time for the recording and a re-reading of his Miranda rights. Once again, he acknowledged that he understood and waived his right to have an attorney present. She didn't know that Captain Bradshaw had joined Hank watching from the observation room since the powers that be at One PP were demanding an update by two o'clock.

"Last night you mentioned that Rita Genovese was your first, your first what?" she asked.

"The first neighbor that I helped during this crisis," he responded. "Did you find her?"

Campbell wanted recognition for his delusional perception of being neighborly in this health crisis. He longed for acknowledgment from someone, anyone, that he helped these frail senior citizens by ending their suffering. He also imagined that the prosecutorial powers that be would consider his unwavering assistance in helping police locate Signora Genovese's body, or at least they should when he bargained with them for a possible plea deal. That's how it worked on all of those TV crime dramas he watched incessantly.

Maggie understood his desire for recognition and attention, but she was not about to give it to him. She heard his cry, absorbed it for the moment, and moved on to learning all she could from him before he clammed up again in this cat and mouse game. It happens with all serial killers. It's that moment when they realize they are giving and giving and giving but not receiving the recognition they desire. That is exactly when they flip the switch and pull back their cooperation. But for how long? Well, the retreat lasts until their ego commands the attention it pines for, and the cycle starts all over again. Stir, rinse, repeat or in this case, kill, retreat, repeat until they decide to end the cycle, and it happens in a flash.

"Did you help other neighbors?" Maggie asked him. She was almost afraid to hear his response. The idea of helping people by killing them seemed so commonplace for him that she shuddered to think there might be dozens of victims he had yet to identify.

"Oh sure, if not me, then who else?"

"I helped Mrs. DeLeon," he started a new chapter in his bizarre tale. "She lived in my building and asked me to help her, so I did," he confessed. "The same way that I helped Signora Genovese."

"What was Mrs. DeLeon's first name?" Maggie asked patiently, almost in a monotone voice so as not to indicate the gurgitation thrashing the acid around her gut like the agitator of an old washing machine tearing up the laundry inside the drum. She was confident that Hank was listening in the adjacent observation room and would jump on trying to track down and identify a Mrs. DeLeon in Robbie's apartment building.

"Her name was Helen," he said. "She was a nice old lady and a good neighbor. I hated to see her suffer."

"You don't like seeing people suffer, do you, detective?"

"How did you help her?" Maggie asked, ignoring his question. She was unaware that the ADA had joined Hank and the captain in the observation room behind the window. He immediately ran to amend the warrant yet again and expand the search area to Mrs. DeLeon's apartment. Tommy and Lou could, at the very least, make sure Helen DeLeon was not stashed in her freezer.

"Propofol, sleepy juice, just like Signora Genovese," he said casually, as if anyone helping a neighbor offers them a lethal hot-shot rather than a helping hand.

"Sleepy juice?" Maggie questioned, prompting him to elaborate.

"These poor people can barely breathe as it is," Campbell explained as if he were a trained medical professional and not simply a hospital transporter. "Their lungs are on fire because of the force they're using to grasp enough air just to survive. They're literally choking to death, and their lungs are inflamed making the process all the more painful.

"Propofol just makes them go to sleepy time and with a strong enough dose, they don't wake up.

"I'm there holding their hand the whole time," he continued. "It's actually a very peaceful way to go.

"Without me, they'd suffocate and die alone."

Maggie looked at his face. She was astonished at his calm demeanor. He seemed peaceful, content with his choices, not at all remorseful. His obvious mental disorder prevented him from feeling regret. Yet, he seemed almost empathetic in his desire to help his neighbors with their suffering. *Maybe the dark and light did live inside him, buried deep in his bowels*, she thought to herself.

"Robbie, is it appropriate for someone to play God, to decide who should die and when?"

He looked at her in disbelief. It was the first question he did not jump to answer. He could not process the outcome of his choices as being outside socially acceptable behavior.

She was puzzled as she sat with him in silence. Not even the air duct whispered a sibilant breeze. It was as if the world stopped in that moment, while everyone waited with bated breath for Campbell's answer. Maybe his heart was in the right place, but he could not comprehend that his behavior crossed the line.

"Robbie, people who kill other people go to jail," she said, as if talking to a child. "You understand that don't you?"

Again, no answer. His eyes remained downward while he fiddled with the chain on his cuffs. His drooped shoulders and his baseball sweatshirt made him look like an adolescent boy being scolded by his mother or a teacher. His knee started bobbing up and down again under the table. That was his tell when he was nervous, and it didn't take Maggie long to figure it out.

He never had a role model. His mother never taught him right from wrong. The only thing he knew was that he could not watch his sister die. That was just wrong, and it created an emotional deficit where his only option was to end the suffering which he did over and over and over again each time he saw someone in pain.

Hank had entered the room to whisper in Maggie's ear that Tommy and Lou were executing the amended search warrant at DeLeon's apartment, so the more information she could glean while they were there would be helpful. He knew she needed to get back on track since the captain and the ADA were watching. Their goal was to solve crimes and not analyze the killer's mental issues like the FBI.

"Robbie, what did you do with Mrs. DeLeon's body after you helped her?" Maggie asked.

That question alone appeared to jar Campbell back to attention and reawakened his ability to participate and cooperate in the interrogation.

"I had a hard time getting her into the car," he said, ignoring the five-minute gap which had just lapsed. Watching minutes tick away while you're waiting for key details in a murder case seems like an eternity but it's part of the process. Just like every killer has a trigger that gets them talking, they also have a kill switch that shuts them down instantly. For Campbell, probing his lack of remorse did it for him.

He explained the hardest part was logistically moving her body, sight unseen, through the apartment building, down the stairs and avoiding the elevator. So, he waited until after the nightly pot-banging ritual and then headed out through the alley near the dumpsters because kids had broken the exterior light, and that side area was in complete darkness.

"But where is she now?" Maggie asked. She needed to know whether there was still a danger to Mrs. DeLeon or to anyone else in her vicinity, or if there was an urgency in locating the body.

"I brought her to the hospital."

"You brought a dead woman, a woman you killed, to Misericordia?" Maggie questioned the veracity of his statement.

"Yeah. That was a no-brainer," he suggested. "I mean there's cold storage right outside the hospital and the victims are moved out as soon as the trucks are full."

The National Guard were staffing the perimeter of where the morgue trucks were parked and serving as temporary morgues just outside many city hospitals. Each truck held up to a hundred bodies, bagged, tagged and stacked inside. The city only purchased forty-five trucks and with about 600 people dying each day, New York would be out of space in a week. Nothing like planning for a rainy day in the nation's most densely populated city which was now in the eye of the storm. All he needed was space for one more casualty, and logistically, this was war.

Campbell explained that he moved the body the night he killed her because it was his night off work. He brought her to the hospital because he was playing on his turf and he knew exactly how to navigate moving a body, any body, through the streets and across to the morgue trucks. He was an inside man, and he knew that gurneys were often lined up outside the emergency room doors and at the basement door which led from the hospital's on-site morgue to the street for the convenience and transfer needs of funeral directors. Maggie knew that much to be true from her close personal encounter when they nabbed and arrested him.

He felt sorry for the unwitting pawns he recruited to assist with his mission. The orderlies and guardsmen were a united front to facilitate his disposal efforts and more than obliged him. He kept his head down. He rolled out her body just as he would for patients who died while hospitalized. He asked for help, routinely, politely but not friendly. He didn't need to be identified as the friendly transporter by any one of the guardsmen or hospital workers doing the work of God. One more victim would be loaded onto the forklift and deep into hell without a question.

"I carried Mrs. DeLeon from the car to a gurney near the ER door," he confessed. "She wasn't heavy. I'm sure she weighed less than a 110 pounds when she took her last breath."

"And not one person questioned you?" Maggie asked.

"Why would they?" Campbell replied. "It's hell outside just like inside.

"Every day I roll bodies to the trucks, sometimes two at a time," he continued. "And every day they're lifted onto the loading platform and carried inside the fridge, loading back to front, toward the door.

"Mrs. DeLeon had a toe tag. I did it myself and created the same transfer document as with every other patient.

"The loaders aren't checking for visas, if you catch my drift.

"Everyone's in a moon suit. Everyone's in a face mask and everyone just prays they'll get through their shift to live another day.

"We're all helping each other survive, so the guys helped me load her inside without any questions just like every other body.

"I remember it clearly."

Hank and the captain marveled at Maggie's poise in handling the man who nearly took her life less than forty-eight hours earlier. The young ADA was getting aroused at the possibility of a career-making case so early in his employment and called the district attorney to talk about offering a plea deal which was above his pay grade to authorize.

"You have to be nice to people," Campbell continued. "I made sure that I always asked the guys outside how they were doing?"

"They'd answer with a silent nod or a shrug of their shoulders," he said. "That's all they could do.

"We're all exhausted and beyond our emotional bandwidth, as they say, to handle much more loss and suffering."

Maggie sat back, exhausted herself from listening to his detailed chronology. Campbell held nothing back, explaining how the bodies were loaded deep in the truck and stacked until it was completely full. At first victims were tagged, covered and moved on gurneys. Then they were pushed on gurneys, covered only in sheets. Then they placed two bodies on one gurney at the same time. There just was not enough equipment or space on the trucks to accommodate everyone who was falling.

"The bodies inside are like travel buddies to the afterlife," he said to Maggie as he recognized the look of pain on her face. He was trying to make it all better.

"I'm surprised they didn't lose or mislabel lots of victims," Campbell suggested. "It's ungodly chaos out there, which only helped my mission."

He described the nightly routine as a well-choreographed death march, with everyone being as respectful as possible while pushing bodies across city streets. Hospitals became bastions of last rights amid a sea of used surgical masks and gloves which littered residential neighborhoods.

"This is as close to hell as New York City has ever witnessed," he said.

Maggie feigned indifference, not registering the hurt she felt deeply in places she didn't even know that she could feel.

"Do you know which truck she was on?"

"No clue," he said. "It doesn't really matter at the end of the day, does it?" he asked. "She was out of pain and on her way to Hart Island, most likely."

Captain Bradshaw had seen a lot in his thirty-seven years on the job, but this was incomprehensible. A multitude of questions danced through his head and not one of them had an answer that the commissioner or the mayor would find palatable.

God save this guy's soul and the souls of all of his victims, was the first thought that came to his mind this Good Friday.

Bradshaw's immediate concern was guessing how his detectives could locate the body of Helen DeLeon. The trucks were routinely being moved to Hart Island where victims were being buried in mass graves. Was poor Mrs. DeLeon among them? If not, was anyone really going to start searching through truckloads of Covid victims? It was ghastly. It was unlikely. And it could be deadly.

His department was already fighting with the health commissioner to get face masks for members of the NYPD. The commissioner claimed she did not care about cops. Imagine if he now had to ask her for hazmat suits so they could scour trucks, hunting down the victims of a serial killer. If this was the end-of-days, he certainly was not about to order his detectives to walk into the dragon's den without proper battle gear.

Hank stepped in to give Maggie a break. He said he needed to speak with her outside for a minute. Even Campbell rested his head on the table. It was too much. It was all too much for everyone. He had been talking with Maggie for nearly five hours and knew that he had barely scratched the surface of coughing up all of his sins.

Hank and Maggie returned with a mushroom pizza about twenty minutes later and found Campbell had nodded out for a nap in their absence. They could both use a nap right about now since a long vacation was not even remotely possible with commercial travel grounded across the country.

Refed, refreshed and ready to dig in, they got back at it. Hank took the lead as Maggie stayed on to observe. It was pointless for her to leave the room. She was Campbell's drug in this game, and they feared he would start jonesing for her and completely shut down in her absence.

"We're going to eat while we work. OK with you?" Maggie asked him, further endearing herself to the man who once held her captive.

"Sure," Campbell said. "This is good pizza, and you remembered about meatless Friday."

He was savoring every bite like he was already convicted, and this was his last meal but fortunately for him, New York abolished the death penalty years ago. The hardest punishment he could face now would be consecutive life sentences for each murder. He would never see the light of day again outside the prison walls.

"I need to clarify something you said earlier about moving Mrs. DeLeon," Maggie said after confirming they had restarted the recording in the observation room.

"Whose car did you use to move her body?"

"I grabbed one off the street up in Mount Vernon," Campbell said without hesitation.

In for a penny, in for a pound. He knew he was all in at this point and would lead and prolong the dance only as he saw fit, not with any objective goal toward being released. Right now, he was the center of attention. He would continue as such until he imagined there was nothing else for him to gain beyond bargaining for the best prison hospitality the DA would agree to coordinate.

He walked Maggie through his night, of taking the subway north to hotwire a car in the next suburban county and then driving down to his neighborhood and finding a good parking spot on the street at the rear of the building near the dumpsters, before going upstairs to help Mrs. DeLeon. He laid it all out and confessed again to the premeditated murder of another senior citizen who relied on him for help.

"She stayed in the trunk for about an hour after I brought her down," Campbell revealed. "I had to check on my friend, Manny Ortiz. He was the first neighbor I met in the building."

"Who is Manny Ortiz?" Hank asked to take the volley from Maggie who had tapped his knee under the table upon hearing the new victim's name. It wasn't for any other reason except that she needed to digest that there was another life gone and this guy was enjoying pizza like he was swapping stories at a class reunion.

"Oh, Manny, Manny, Manny," Campbell whispered his name a few times, wearing his grief openly for the first time, moving his eyes to his hands which he seemed to unknowingly clasp together, almost in prayer.

Maggie noticed that and so did Hank.

"I can see that he must've been a good friend, Robbie." Hank said, observing a brief glimpse into Campbell's hidden humanity. Whatever spark of sensitivity existed inside him was buried quite deep.

Campbell, however, used the display of sadness as a calculated strategy to gain further accommodations from police and the DA he imagined was hiding behind the two-way mirror.

"Oh Manny, Manny, Manny" he repeated. "He was a really good egg. I'm gonna miss the old guy.

"I had called him during the day, and he could barely whisper. By the time I got home and checked on him, it was too late. He was already gone."

"What did you do then?" Hank asked the next logical question of the totally irrational suspect before him.

Campbell remembered his only friend when he spoke to the detectives. He told them how they would play chess and smoke cigars and joke with each other, mostly about hookers. Hank tried to hide a faint smile recognizing that was exactly what old-timers did in the 'hood, whether it was in his old Queens neighborhood or in The Bronx.

Yet inside, Campbell felt nothing, he acted solely for the benefit of his audience. He was anything but mournful and was actually relieved that he did not have to dispose of the man's body. It was all too exhausting. Let the cops believe what they want. Each side was waiting to see how this would all play out.

"So, Robbie, how many neighbors have you helped, into their freezer, the morgue trucks or anywhere else?" Hank asked hesitantly. He was hoping the fate of Mrs. DeLeon and Mr. Ortiz were the last two victims but he was unsure. The detectives were certain of only one thing, Campbell still had more to tell.

"That's it," Campbell said, pausing, hesitating whether to enlighten them beyond the scope of Hank's question.

"I can't watch people suffer and die, can you?" he asked the detectives, looking directly at both of them across the table. Again, neither detective answered his question.

There was a stillness in the windowless room. No one knew whether the sun was out without looking at the wall clock behind Campbell's head or peeking at their phones which were set to vibrate mode. Time seemed to stand still inside the void of this dark, grey space but it hardly mattered during lockdown, which took on a whole new meaning for every New Yorker and not just the city's inmates. Detectives knew the clock was ticking on the time to get Campbell arraigned within the usual forty-eight-hour window. Lucky for them, Covid had turned the whole system upside down and it was highly unlikely that Campbell would be arraigned at six o'clock on a Friday night.

He had not yet confessed to the initial charges for Samantha Gallo's kidnapping or Maggie's kidnapping. He didn't really need to. The DA knew those charges were rock solid. Instead, Campbell issued an invitation to murder and freely admitted to killing two neighbors and lifting at least one car. Yet they still had nothing to tie him to the Jenkins or Robbins murders and there would be no deal coming from the DA until Campbell confessed.

Chapter Forty-Six

Lou and Tommy, looking a bit rough and tumbled, ties loosened and askew, hanging off necks too tired to hold up their heads, returned from the daylong search of Campbell's apartment. They hauled several boxes of evidence into the squad room as Hank and Maggie discussed arraignment possibilities with the ADA on the phone.

"You guys still going at it?" Lou asked, not expecting to find anyone still around this late on a Friday, especially Good Friday. The senior detectives had called in from the DeLeon apartment, before returning to headquarters, to say it was all clear and the lady of the house wasn't at home. They would return in a day or two to complete a more thorough search. Nothing was being rushed. The city which normally vibrated at warp speed had slowed its pace to that of a metronome, clicking time and not going anywhere.

"That's some payload you've got there," Maggie teased them upon seeing their haul of boxes. "Looks like you guys will be busy this weekend."

"So will you," Tommy reminded her that they were all in it together. "It's actually a whole lotta nothing. More junk than probative evidence."

"Has Campbell been arraigned?" Lou asked.

"Well, we've been a little busy," Hank replied. "The guy's been killing off his neighbors left and right."

"Are you kidding? Did he confess to killing the nurses yet?"

Unfortunately, he had not, frustrating the ADA's goal to get this a guy a plea deal and maybe go straight to sentencing. Wishful thinking on the part of the new assistant prosecutor, Kevin Kennedy. There was a backlog in criminal courts across the boroughs, stretching from The Bronx and Manhattan and over to Queens, Brooklyn and Staten Island, as if any serious crime happened in that suburban outpost.

While courthouses were closed citywide, staff worked from home and arraignments were up in the air, taking place virtually or in-person if the case was severe enough. Grand juries were not being convened so indictments were not coming down and there were lots of inmates clogging an already over-crowded jail system.

Yet in the case against Robert Nathan Campbell, it was apparent to everyone that the case was more than severe. It was downright deadly!

"We just don't have enough space in this room for all of the white boards we need for this guy and all his victims," Hank said to the stymied group. The captain was just as baffled as his squad, and Kennedy could not amend the search and arrest warrants fast enough.

Captain Bradshaw advised Hank and Maggie to handle the virtual arraignment with the young prosecutor in the morning. The court was also coordinating to have a public defender on standby even though Campbell wanted to represent himself.

"This is all such a puzzle," Maggie said. "There's nothing here except a case of body bags that would lead me to think he's a serial killer."

"His apartment was as neat as a monk," said Tommy still shocked that his kids' bedrooms were a hot mess compared to this suspected serial killer. "It was tidy and clean and there was nothing unusual except for those body bags from the other day and a few items of women's clothing hung in the back of the closet as if they were forgotten.

"You know, how you push the old clothes into the back of the closet, hoping they'll make their way to sock land, never to be seen again," Tommy added.

"What?" he said, looking at their droll faces, shrugging his shoulders with open arms, hands held up in surprise, realizing the three of them had stopped to look at him.

"You know we all do it!"

"And we did find a few vials of propofol in a shoebox and some women's jewelry scattered in his dresser," Tommy added without missing a beat. "Maybe they're souvenirs."

"Oh, we also found his lucky souvenir condom but that's it," Lou chimed in with a lift of his brow.

"If we get lucky, we'll keep a lid on the deaths of the nurses until after his arraignment for the murders of Genovese and DeLeon, at least for a while longer," Bradshaw suggested. "Maybe the scanner scavengers and beat reporters are home where all smart people are tonight and not listening to the police radio."

"So, Covid's essentially nailed the coffin on news coverage of the killing of two nurses in The Bronx?" Hank questioned how the deadly virus was changing the city on a fundamental level. His sarcasm was often his weapon of choice in his rhetorical arsenal.

"That's about it," the captain said. "If there's a silver lining in any of this mess, it's that reporters aren't hounding us, lurking at precincts waiting for perp walks, and roaming through night court because proceedings are now held virtually,

"We may even be able to continue Campbell's detention here if the DA doesn't object," Captain Bradshaw suggested to the core four, intentionally loud enough for ADA Kennedy to overhear it.

The ADA, busy typing the new warrants on his laptop in a corner, heard the background chatter and signaled his agreement with a thumbs up. It would serve everyone much better to keep this close to home. If there was anything that was a sure bet in these uncertain times, it was that Robbie Nathan Campbell wasn't done talking and he wasn't going anywhere on bail.

"If he keeps coughing up names, we could be here until the pandemic's over," said Hank.

The young prosecutor accompanied Hank and Maggie back toward the holding cell with the newly amended arrest warrant. It was difficult to prosecute a case for murder without a body, but Campbell had already confessed, and they fully anticipated a plea deal would be forthcoming, if and when he also confessed to killing Brittany Jenkins and Susan Robbins.

"Robert Nathan Campbell, you are under arrest for the murder of Helen DeLeon." Hank began reciting the Miranda rights again in front of his partner and the ADA, placing the cuffs on Campbell through the locked cell door.

"Anything you say can and will be used against you in a court of law. You have the right to an attorney before and during questioning. If you cannot afford a lawyer, one will be appointed for you.

"Do you understand these rights?" he asked Campbell.

"Yes, sir," he stated clearly. He remembered Detective Summer's reprimand for merely nodding with a mumble when he was arrested for Sammy's kidnapping. He signed and dated the waiver once again and Hank noted the time and initialed on the corner of the card.

"Courts are closed under an Executive Order, so you'll be arraigned virtually tomorrow on all of the charges before you," Maggie explained.

Campbell was a bit dumbfounded because he knew he had so much more to say but he was not rushing the process. He knew what hell awaited him in any one of the jails in Bronx County, especially Rikers Island. At least at the station house he was getting pizza and egg sandwiches instead of prison slop. The bars which held him captive here also held Covid at bay.

The captain coordinated with the desk sergeant to look into getting a change of clothing for their new house guest tomorrow after his arraignment. He then praised all of his detectives for toughing it out and said he would see them all Monday morning, if not sooner.

Tommy decided to stay behind to organize the boxes before they all returned tomorrow to comb through Campbell's life and hopefully uncover more of his secrets.

"It's better than coloring Easter eggs with five bored kids and a stir-crazy labradoodle," Tommy said.

"No argument from me. I'll join you," Lou added. Between the two of them they just wanted to put the workspace in order instead of leaving a hot mess to sort through before actual work could begin tomorrow.

That old saying *"cluttered desk, cluttered mind,"* was never more true than in a squad room where busy detectives were investigating one suspect for at least four murders.

Chapter Forty-Seven

In the past, virtual arraignments and court proceedings had been reserved for hospitalized suspects, but the whole world went virtual at the push of a button almost overnight. New Yorkers now referenced their lives in two stages, pre-Covid and Covid, anointing the pandemic with its own name like The Great Depression. Judges and their clerks sat at home, suspects appeared from jail and lawyers and prosecutors appeared from wherever they were located, even if that meant from their beach house, deciding life and death questions in Hawaiian shirts with a dog or toddler roaming through the background.

"Good morning, everyone," Judge Horatio B. Sanderson addressed the invited guests appearing on their assorted devices from six different locations.

With greetings exchanged, Judge Sanderson began the record and reserved criticism of the court stenographer's apparent location in her daughter's bedroom. She hadn't realized the child's favorite princess lamp was in the direct line of sight of her laptop's camera and so the arraignment began as formally as possible in this now emerging casual context.

Campbell repeated his desire to represent himself at the arraignment. A public defender remained on standby in case the judge decided otherwise after questioning Campbell about the significance of waiving his right to an attorney. This wasn't just a snatch and grab robbery. This was murder many times over!

"Robert Nathan Campbell, the district attorney of Bronx County has charged you with two counts of murder in the first degree for the deaths of Rita Genovese and Helen DeLeon; two counts of kidnapping in the first degree for the kidnapping of Samantha Gallo and Detective Margaret Flynn; menacing and assault on an officer in the first degree for the assault of Detective Flynn; and other related charges under charging instrument number 1657 of 2020. How do you plead, sir?"

"Not guilty," Campbell said confidently, or about as confident as a New Yorker in a Mets sweatshirt can be in the throes of an aborted baseball season. He looked at the judge, eye-to-eye in this virtual proceeding, not up and over the judge's bench as in a courtroom. All appeared equal in their square little boxes on the screen as if on a celebrity game show. Campbell was not cowering before anyone as most guilty defendants would during an arraignment, hanging their heads low in that come to Jesus moment, realizing their lives were over for taking the life of another person. Except for the team sweatshirt which he wore from yesterday, Campbell appeared as confident as a Mafia boss in proclaiming his innocence when everyone else knew he was delusional.

He had just confessed to two murders prior to his arraignment while numbered notes found on Brittany Jenkins and Susan Robbins indicated there were at least eight other bodies to be discovered.

"Mr. Campbell, it is your Sixth Amendment right to waive representation by counsel, as you have stated here this morning," Judge Sanderson explained. "It may not be your best move considering the charges. However, we have Attorney Louis Pinto here from the public defender's office. The court will provide you with his number should you change your mind at any time so that you may call him directly.

"Do you understand?"

"Yes, your honor."

"Attorney Pinto, is this your cell number?" the judge asked the hesitant legal aid counsel. He wore his inexperience like a too-tight tie choking his airway when the judge questioned him.

"Uh, uh, yes, your honor," was all he could answer. He was glad he was coddled in that moment by the comforts of his own living room. The anxiety of the black robe syndrome which plagued many new attorneys was hidden by the limitations of the new virtual reality.

"Mr. Campbell, you are facing multiple counts of murder and kidnapping, along with the assault on Detective Flynn. While you have pleaded not guilty to these charges, these crimes are serious, violent acts against many people, including a police officer," Sanderson continued. "As such, I am ordering that you continue to be remanded and held without bail.

"Do you understand?" the judge asked, not expecting a response from Campbell who sat firm in his power and complied politely to any and all directives with a nod and a pat reply.

"Yes, your honor."

"It is my understanding that due to the nature of this investigation, and the fact that it's ongoing amid the current health crisis, the district attorney and the police department have coordinated and agreed to continue your remand at the Simpson Street precinct rather than transfer you to jail.

"Is that correct, Mr. Kennedy?" he asked the eager prosecutor.

"Yes, your honor," he replied. His tie was off-kilter to the left, his hair disheveled, his outer appearance reflecting his inner turmoil. He had been amending search applications so feverishly in the past forty-eight hours that he forgot to shave the peach fuzz which appeared to be a beard sprouting on his otherwise cherubic face.

"I trust that as part of this agreement, you will make certain accommodations at the Simpson precinct for Mr. Campbell's personal hygiene and meals, etcetera?"

"Yes, your honor."

"Mr. Campbell, do you understand that this proceeding and the resultant accommodations are due to the extraordinary limits imposed by the current pandemic and the parties believe it to be in everyone's best interest to continue your remand at Simpson Street?"

"Yes, your honor."

"Detective Flynn and gentlemen, we will reconvene here in our new virtual courtroom one week from today if not sooner. That will be a status conference where I expect reports from both the NYPD and Mr. Kennedy as to whether it's practical to continue Mr. Campbell's remand locally or whether he will be transferred elsewhere.

"That is all," Sanderson proclaimed. "Have a good day."

"The host has ended the meeting" electronically signaled to everyone on their screens to disconnect.

Chapter Forty-Eight

"Look at how much time we just saved," Hank said returning to the squad room after the arraignment. "No lights and sirens, no traffic, no reporters and the judge started on time," Hank explained to his captive Saturday morning audience. "Miracles happen!"

Tommy and Lou had arrived while the arraignment was going on and started digging into their haul from Campbell's apartment and the Genovese home.

"By the way detectives, while you kids were lollygagging at the virtual arraignment of our house guest, we managed to do some real sleuthing," Lou volunteered.

"I tracked down a distant relative of poor Signora Genovese in Arizona," he said. "He's arranged for a direct-to-cremation service with a local funeral director since New York is no longer hosting in-person funerals."

"What a piece of work," Tommy added. "He wanted to know how soon he could come and sell the house. I think the desert must have fried his brain and his compassion."

"I thought the Easter miracle was that you two were gonna help sort this evidence," Tommy yelled after Hank and Maggie, but they were already out of the door heading toward the interrogation room where Campbell had remained following his arraignment.

"Don't you two worry," Tommy yelled after them. "When we're done here, we've gotta return to DeLeon's apartment for a more thorough search but you kids go play footsie with the psycho next door."

Maggie and Hank were probably the first in the squad to attend a virtual arraignment and they had to admit that it did make their lives more manageable. Getting from point A to point B is such a time drain for any New Yorker, not just the police.

"What's for lunch today?" Campbell asked as though his cell was the guest suite at a luxury resort and the interrogation room was its posh restaurant.

"I tell you what, why don't you place your order with room service," Hank said. He was ready to get to work and had enough of Campbell's charades.

"Do you like baseball, Robbie?" Hank asked, seething as he stared at his old Mets sweatshirt on the killer before them.

"Yankees all the way, Bronx born and bred," he answered, fully aware of the loyalty Detective Summers held toward New York's other team.

Hank, however, thought there was no breeding in Campbell's childhood, and while he may have been hatched, he certainly was never nurtured.

"I tell ya what, Robbie, this is a holiday weekend but no one's celebrating anything this year, so we've got all weekend to hang out with you but first we have to take care of a few things."

Hank removed the cuffs and escorted him back to the only holding cell in the building. The cell's stark environment was meant to accommodate one or two prisoners for a few hours. But when they had to accommodate Campbell overnight, the sergeant had a patrol officer bring in a folding cot that had been stashed in the dark corner of an old supply closet.

"Remember what Ben Franklin said about the three-day rule?" Hank asked aloud to no one in particular. "Guests, like fish, begin to smell after three days."

Maggie hid her face by turning toward the door and choked back her giggle. Campbell, on the other hand, simply ignored the comment as both detectives stepped down the hall.

"Hurry back. I'm hungry," Campbell said. "And we're only getting started."

Hank and Maggie decided to let him stew while they took a New York minute to review the mounting evidence with Tommy and Lou. The boxes of evidence had been neatly labeled and color coded with different markers for DeLeon, Genovese and Campbell occupying separate tables which they had dragged in from the precinct's kitchen. The rickety legs of each metal table could easily buckle under the weight of the boxes but there was no other option.

"Wow, I'm impressed," Maggie said, reviewing the scene and looking straight at Tommy. She knew that his household was supervised by an elementary school teacher who managed her kids, and her husband, like boot camp in order to hold it altogether. "You paid attention in marker class," she chuckled, and he couldn't hide his smirk.

"We gave Campbell a timeout," Hank chimed in. "He cooperates better after he's been fed later in the day. I think four o'clock is like his witching hour."

There wasn't much evidence from their first pass at DeLeon's apartment. They had rushed there yesterday, more to check for a body than to search for evidence. CSU had taken fingerprints and collected some trace evidence, but they sealed it tight with yellow tape and a police warning notice. They fully expected to find Campbell's fingerprints around the apartment since he admitted being there. DeLeon's life came down to one neat and tidy, half-full evidence box and her body was now freezer-packed, somewhere in The Bronx or Brooklyn where the city had relocated many of the refrigerator trucks once they were full.

The haul from Rita Genovese's home didn't yield much more than three boxes, largely family photos and correspondence which Lou had used to track down her surviving family. There was no point hauling the freezer out of the basement, it was logistically impossible without a crane, and it weighed as much as a tank. Photos and swabs would support Campbell's story as the prosecutor took it all into consideration toward forming a plea offer.

Tommy had boxed the women's jewelry and clothing they found at Campbell's apartment and set it aside for Maggie's review while the three guys inspected and catalogued the boxes and boxes of other evidence from Campbell's place. Yet despite the sizable haul, at least twenty-four boxes, there were no obvious kill souvenirs as they sorted through his secretive world.

It was nearly 4:30 when Maggie and Hank found Campbell eating a wedge of sausage and peppers which the sergeant had ordered for him. Keeping him fed and comfortable was the way to ensure his cooperation. Keeping Maggie front and center for questioning was the way to satiate his darker appetite for her. Dangle the carrot and get the pony to perform. Cops used that technique frequently hoping to draw more info out of a recalcitrant or hesitant suspect who held his secrets close.

Maggie had spread out photos of the women's clothing and jewelry they found at the back of his bedroom closet on the table, as both detectives watched Campbell's reaction. There was none. He did not flinch. He did not offer a sarcastic sexual reference. He stared at all of it blankly.

"Robbie, whose clothes and jewelry are these?" Maggie jumped right into the interrogation.

"I don't know," he said. "Whose are they?"

"Wise guy, we found them in your closet," Hank said. He was a bit hangry himself and had enough of Campbell's altar boy routine.

"Oh, they've been there forever," he said as if having a sudden epiphany. "I drove cross country from New Mexico with a girl I met about a year ago. She stayed with me for a week or so before moving on."

He suggested that he met her in the desert town, and she offered to share the ride, using her car if he paid for gas all the way to New York. It sounded like a good deal to him.

"Where did she go?" Hank asked.

"I don't know," Robbie replied. "I really don't. One day I came home from work, and she was gone along with most of her things.

"She must've forgotten these because they were in the back of the closet."

"And the turquoise and silver necklace on the hanger?" Maggie asked about the jewelry, wondering if the girl was a victim and he held onto it as a souvenir.

"Again, hers," he answered. "If you found it in my closet then you know how far back it was. I had forgotten about it myself."

"Did she take her car when she left?" Hank asked.

"No, she left the keys behind, and I used it for a while," Robbie said. "It was old, so I got rid of it.

"It wasn't yours to get rid of," Hank reminded him.

"Nor was it mine to worry about either," Robbie added.

"Look I called her, and she didn't answer and changed her number," he continued. "The girl is good at disappearing and reinventing herself. She did it in New Mexico, left everything behind at the gas station and jumped in a car with me, a complete stranger.

"I don't need to chase crazy," he added. He advised Hank that he wasn't certain if the name she used with him was her real name.

"She went by the name of Melody Chalmers," he said. "Does that sound like the name of a Native American to you?"

"How, where and when did you get rid of the car?" Hank continued asking the mundane but necessary questions.

"I left it on the street. It was no longer my problem," Robbie said. "Who needs the headache and the cost? That was nearly two months ago.

Hank knew the timeline worked because it had been six weeks since the murder of Brittany Jenkins.

"The car wasn't in my name. Some kids probably took it to a chop shop or maybe they torched it after a joy ride."

They had been going at it for hours, moving in circles, round and round, not getting any closer to making more of a connection to the Jenkins murder or the Robbins homicide. Campbell could see the weariness on his opponents' faces and seized the moment to windmill them in this ongoing imaginary game of chess.

"Which street did you leave it on?" Hank asked.

"I really don't remember," Robbie answered, staring down at the handcuff anchor and not looking Detective Summers squarely in the eye. Hank barely noticed that Campbell's knee was bobbing up and down under the table, yet he knew immediately that he was lying. It was Campbell's other tell to avert eye contact while painting himself into a corner of untruths.

"What's your recollection? Where was it? I mean was it near your apartment? Yankee Stadium? Jerome Avenue?" Hank offered him multiple choices to see if he would grab the bait.

Campbell was intimately familiar with the windmill tactic. He had used it many times in his chess games with Manny Ortiz. He could seize a lot of ground by making his adversary move repeatedly back and forth helplessly, tiring him out toward an eventual checkmate. Playing the windmill, he was in complete control of the conversation, and he knew it. The longer he moved them around the board, leading them this way and that, he could delay his eventual incarceration at a preferable prison. It boggled his mind that these two geniuses had yet to realize his cunning strategy. He decided to give them something to sleep on when they called it a night around eight o'clock.

"Detectives, you're smarter than this," he said, cocking his head to the side while giving them a bit of side eye. "You're just not asking the right questions. See you tomorrow and don't forget my jellybeans, piña colada, please."

Chapter Forty-Nine

Hank and Maggie found the squad room empty. Tommy and Lou had cleared out while they were in interrogation.

"We're not asking the right questions?" Hank asked Maggie. "What the fuck?" he wondered with just the two of them around. His face scrunched up like a week-old peach, unpleasant and wrinkly. "How many people did this guy kill?"

"No clue but tomorrow's another day," Maggie said heading home. "Go get some rest and have a good night."

She was much too exhausted to think about making *pizza rustica* for four hours as she headed up the West Side Highway. Uncle Bobby would understand if she picked up a loaf from Boiano's tomorrow. Easter would not be Easter without the heavy egg, cheese and traditional Italian meat pie.

Jax was nearly perfect except for his foul temper when he angered himself for not doing something perfectly perfect, anything really. He was just too hard on himself, as was Maggie. They were emotional twins in that regard.

She could hear Pavarotti singing "Perfect" in Italian as she stepped off the elevator. It was one of her favorite songs to listen to while cooking, but Jax rarely played it, preferring the music of Al Green and old rhythm and blues instead. The aroma of true love beckoned her as the scents of good food floated overhead, calling her in like the mythical sirens of the Amalfi Coast. She knew he was cooking something behind the apartment door, but she couldn't imagine what delights waited for her inside.

Her man had found her nonna's recipe for *pizza rustica* in her cute, old-fashioned metal recipe box which she kept front and center on a shelf over the sink. He started making the time-intensive delight hours before she returned home. He saw cheese, and lots of it, and meat, and definitely imagined it was worth making. He never imagined that all of the chopping and stirring would give him a rigorous upper body workout.

She snuck in quietly and watched him, covertly from the foyer, as he messed up the kitchen, clanging pots and pans, tossing spoons with abandon into the stainless-steel farmhouse sink.

He had lined up a row of disposable tin foil pans on the kitchen island to pour the batter into when it was ready after what seemed like three hours of non-stop chopping of no less than four kinds of meat and two kinds of cheese plus ricotta, followed by an hour of stirring over the stove. She did not have the heart to tell him that she had a few springform pans in the bottom cabinet.

How did I get so lucky? She thought as she grabbed him from behind in a tight hug which released most of the tension in her back and jostled the loosely tied apron strings around his ripped core.

He turned toward her, hugging back and kissing the top of her head, without missing a step, still holding a cheesy spoon in one of his hands. She was more important than the mess. Neither of them let go until he whispered, "Go sit down. I've got this. Dinner will be ready in ten minutes."

He loved watching her undo her bra with one hand while placing her gun in the nightstand in their bedroom. Yes, it had become *their* bedroom in her condo, but he hoped that would change by the end of the year.

He brought her a glass of merlot to wash away her day as she settled into the sofa to watch a rom-com. Jax loved cooking and he had mastered *Pasta Finocchio con Sarde*, one of his girl's favorites. He had watched her make it often enough, just like her nonna used to, adding *pignoli* nuts and raisins, since every self-respecting Sicilian-American puts raisins in almost everything.

By the time it was ready, his sexy crimefighter in a Yankees blue t-shirt, with the image of a dad holding his young, pony-tailed daughter's hand had fallen asleep on the couch, *like father like daughter*.

Chapter Fifty

Maggie slept late this Easter morning. Captain Bradshaw told the squad to take the day off after working nearly a week straight. There was no longer the sense of urgency to catch a killer. No one was reported missing. No other bodies had dropped. And the judge allowed the prime suspect to spend the next few nights at headquarters.

She stretched herself awake and felt the note Jax had left on his pillow next to her which she had unknowingly rolled into and held in her sleep.

"Out for a run. Coffee made. I've got breakfast when I get back. Hoppy Easter. Xoxo"

This would have been their first holiday waking up together, but he missed it. Maggie prayed a lifetime of other celebrations would make up for it. She knew that as certainly as she knew that she was a damn good detective. It was the first time in her life that she didn't have to explain herself, her passion, her job, her independence and that was supremely comforting and empowering.

"Look what I grabbed at Boiano's," he said, holding up a boxed *colomba* as he returned home. It was the Italian cousin to the Christmas easter bread *panettone* except orange zest replaced the raisins in the light and fluffy bread. "And I grabbed half a pound of *sfogliatelle* in case this new French toast recipe doesn't work out."

"Are you trying to satisfy all of my cravings or just get me pregnant?"

"Practice makes perfect," he said sheepishly.

"Well, the only *woo-lee* I have is for you!"

"A what?"

"A *woo-lee* is Sicilian for *voglia* which is Italian for craving but Sicilians slur words together and that's now a *woo-lee*."

"Mamma mia," he said placing the bakery box on the counter and getting to work in the kitchen.

Maggie was about to call Uncle Bobby to wish him a Happy Easter and see what time they were getting together for a casual lunch when a text from Tommy popped up on her screen. He thought the holiday would be better spent at Bobby's with the three of them hashing out the nefarious mind of their latest serial killer.

Tommy knew the legendary Detective Lieutenant Bobby Stonestreet from his years on the force, but he was only introduced to the family's board game analysis of a killer's mind during the case of the Binky Killer who left a trail of dead clergy in the path of Maggie's first year on the job. The brainstorming session helped them catch a killer then and he was hoping a new session now would help them seal the lid on Campbell's end game.

Jax took the opportunity to travel to his place in Manhattan to grab additional clothes. The seasons had changed since he first started playing house with Maggie in Westchester. The wet cold winter had danced on the edge of an early spring, but everyone was still in hibernation around New York.

Maggie met Tommy at Bobby's around four o'clock where dining on Bobby's homemade pizza was first on their agenda. Paper plates and cups pushed aside, they sat around the dining room table like it was their war room. The killer was in custody, but his story was far from over and they needed more than a board game analysis now.

Maggie explained that before leaving last night, Campbell suggested they were not asking the right questions, prompting each of them to wonder what they had been doing wrong. Taking a step back is sometimes the best strategy in any chess match to reassess the field and their opponent.

"Campbell is a smart, organized, narcissistic sociopath," Maggie described him in a nutshell.

"And he cooperates more with Maggie because he fantasizes over conquering her," Tommy stated what the squad knew but what Maggie likely held back from her godfather.

"The odd thing is that he has an empathetic side too," Maggie said shaking her head. Her green eyes squinted when she didn't understand something.

"Don't let him fool you with that, Maggie," Uncle Bobby cautioned her. "He uses sympathy to endear himself to his prey so that when he kills them it softens the blow."

"Yeah, if he really cared about Signora Genovese he wouldn't have stored her like a slab of meat in the basement freezer," Tommy added.

"Each kill energizes him," Bobby continued. "It's that craving to feel that power over and over again like a junkie who needs a high.

"One kill will never be enough since he lacks remorse."

"He wants to direct the show," Maggie said. After all, she was the only one out of the three of them who had spent so much time with Campbell, questioning him and carefully dancing herself away from the edge of his scalpel in the elevator.

"He's been playing on Hank's last nerve for three days."

"Ahh, don't worry about your partner," Tommy said.

"Wait, you're my partner."

Tommy looked over at Bobby and they both knew what she didn't seem to realize. After nearly thirty years on the job and now Covid, Tommy was looking at retirement sooner rather than later. He avoided addressing her concern and continued their strategizing session.

"Empowerment is his sole motivation, whether he's killing a sick patient or a nurse who rejected his advances," Tommy said. "And since his surge of power only lasts until his victim takes his or her last breath, he needs to refuel more often to feel that high."

"The gratification for him is instantaneous," Bobby added. "But the only person who ever witnesses his high is the victim, so he needs to relive that moment to feel that power, over and over and over again like a stage actor feeding off the audience's reaction."

"His emotional wound of abandonment and rejection by his mother planted the seed for him to constantly seek approval elsewhere," Maggie said. "So, it was more than a desire to help people. He needed to prove his worth and that will never be enough for him, especially when he's rejected."

"Exactly," Bobby said. "Until he's fully empowered, he will never stop seeking the attention that fuels that fire, yet ironically, he will never be fully empowered.

"His high never lasts longer than the time it takes him to snuff out someone's life and bodies will continue to drop."

Chapter Fifty-One

"New week, new day, Robbie," Maggie greeted him as Hank walked him into the interrogation room. "How are we gonna start this one?"

"Together, Detective," he answered, without missing a beat. After all, Detective Maggie Flynn was the first woman in a long time to give him the attention he craved. He played out new fantasies in his head with each visit to the interrogation room. Except for the shackles which bound him to the table, he wanted to grab her with one hand and pleasure himself under the table with the other. It was a thirst he could never quench, a hunger he could never satisfy, a desire that was never reciprocated.

After nearly a week together, slow dancing, destination unknown, the relationship between the detectives and their suspect was fraught with tension, tighter than wearing pantyhose on Thanksgiving. The mayor called the commissioner who called the Bronx DA who advised Captain Bradshaw to tighten the vise they had around their only suspect and close this case sooner rather than later as the city's Covid death toll multiplied by nearly 500 percent a day. In the grand scheme of things, a serial killer on the loose in New York would garner headlines for weeks or months until he was behind bars, but now the media was hardly aware of the other evil hiding in The Bronx.

Hank tilted his head back, staring blankly at the yellowed ceiling tiles. He knew they had to ply Campbell with the right questions to kick this session into overdrive. He gritted his teeth and turned his head from side to side, trying to stretch and roll out the tension building across his shoulders while he waited for either

Maggie or Campbell to blink. His patience had run its course, and it was only ten o'clock in the morning.

"Listen," Hank said, slamming his hand down on the table close to the anchor which restrained Campbell in place. The loud bang jolted Maggie from the morning's slow roll, but Campbell barely flinched.

"You've got four days to get your story together before you're back in front of the judge and likely rolled out to Rikers, where they're dropping like flies," Hank said sternly. "The DA's not playing around. The city's got a noose around its neck with a killer more important than you. So, let's cut to the chase. Stop breadcrumbing us and start giving us names, dates and details, everything," Hank thundered. He was barely two inches from Campbell's face and the guy didn't blink, twitch, react in any way that would indicate he yielded.

"Who else did you help with your sleepy juice, Robbie?" Hank asked, lowering the pressure a few bars.

"Well, now we're getting somewhere Detective Summers," Robbie said shaking his head in recognition and appreciation. He was impressed the detective ran with the clue he had provided them Saturday night. "You're finally asking the right questions.

"You just hit the proverbial nail on the head," he added with a smug grin.

"Covid's the killer we all have to worry about, not little old me. I'm helping my neighbors, my friends and my patients without playing favorites."

Hank and Maggie just stared at him, trying to hide the shock they internalized as breakfast bubbled in their stomachs. It was not such a large analytical leap to think Campbell could kill patients. If his twisted rationale was to help people in pain who were suffering and he already admitted to using drugs to kill his ailing neighbors, then his workplace was the grand buffet to feed his insatiable hunger for control. The sterile but often deadly milieu of the hospital was familiar to him, and it served up a desperate and helpless population to prey upon.

"Robbie, are you saying that you killed patients here in The Bronx?" Maggie asked, playing the good cop in the room.

Even Hank knew that his bad cop performance needed to be taken down more than just a few notches since Campbell had opened the door to more kills and the death toll was rising.

"You're not listening, dear Maggie," Campbell admonished her like a headmaster with a wave of his pointed finger. "I expect more of you."

"I didn't kill anyone," he insisted. "I helped them transition to the next plateau."

"At Misericordia?" Hank asked.

"Yes."

"All of them?"

"Yes."

"How many patients were there, Robbie?" Maggie asked.

"Oh, I'd say more than a few but less than a dozen."

Campbell had just dropped a bombshell, and he was going to play this day into a very long night. It was as though his internal clock said *"It's evening. Let's have some fun."*

Maggie laid it all out, as much as she could, for Captain Bradshaw while Hank called Lou and Tommy and asked them to return to the precinct. It was all hands on deck as the investigation took a turn to an even darker place on the already blackened highway to hell.

They would need to hunker down, get every last detail that Campbell would or could provide before breaking the news to the hospital. There was no doubt the apocalypse had truly just arrived at its doorstep and there was no way out but through the firestorm.

"Robbie, we're going to take this nice and slow, and we'll stay here all night if we need to," Maggie advised him.

Hank stayed in the observation room with Tommy, Lou and the captain as Maggie picked up where they had left off this morning and the others started the recording. She needed to remain vigilant in her questioning, pacing herself so as not to miss any crucial detail, remaining calm so as not to agitate Campbell, and above all else navigating Campbell's responses with balance and precision. After five days and nights, she was learning how his sick but calculating mind worked. His need for power and control and the techniques he implemented to disarm his gullible targets made him a master at his game.

"Who was the first patient that you killed since arriving at Misericordia?"

"*Tuh, tuh, tuh,*" Robbie said while shaking his head in the negative and clicking his tongue. "Detective Flynn, I've told you many times in the past few days that I didn't kill anyone. I helped my patients the way I helped my neighbors and friends."

"You drugged them and killed them," she answered calmly, trying not to sound accusatory to the man she needed to steer toward confessing completely.

"I helped them cross over to the next dimension," he said. "We are not going to get anywhere if you keep telling me that I killed them when I didn't."

"Robbie, for clarification so that anyone listening to the recording now, in the next room, or later for the district attorney, please describe exactly how you helped each patient as we discuss them today. Will you do that?"

"Yes," he agreed. "You asked nicely."

"Who was the first patient that you say you helped at Misericordia?"

"Her name was Thelma Ondrovich, a lovely lady who came to us in a terrible state."

Instantly, Hank focused on the name which he recalled early in the Jenkins case. Ondrovich was the woman who died in the hospital while they were speaking with Brittany's co-workers. He made a note for Maggie to ask a follow-up question but would not interrupt her rhythm now.

"The poor woman had been connected to life support for nearly a week," he started explaining the story of her demise. "She couldn't breathe on her own and was so uncomfortable."

"How did you know that, Robbie?" Maggie asked. "Do you have medical training?"

"You don't have to be a med school graduate to observe when someone has a tube down their throat and they can't breathe or eat and imagine that they must be uncomfortable," he started. "She was lying in the same position for days on end. Existing becomes superfluous to actually living."

"How did you choose to help Mrs. Ondrovich that night?"

"I didn't choose her, she chose me," he said. "And I didn't say she was married. You called her Mrs."

Maggie did not react to his criticism. Her Bronx DNA wanted to get all up in his face and scream and slap him into next month, but that would not get her the result she needed, confessions not only to his neighbors' and patients' deaths, but also to the homicides of Brittany Jenkins and Susan Robbins.

Campbell paused long enough to allow her to react but continued his monologue after seeing she was nonplussed.

"I would often visit the patients on the Covid isolation floor, stopping in just to say hello and let them know that someone sees them, and they weren't alone in their time of greatest need and despair.

"Thelma would often make eye contact with me when I stopped in her room. That night, however, she looked more uncomfortable. She wore the pain on her face. She could barely open her eyes, but she did for a brief second when she heard my voice.

"I was telling her about the wet snow that fell and quickly melted the night before and I wasn't sure whether she could hear me since the ventilator's whisper valve was making that steady exhalation noise.

"*Sss, huh, sss, huh, sss, huh,*" he added his own sound effects to the saga playing out in the most bizarre way in front of the most jaded detectives who thought they had seen it all until now.

"I asked her if she'd like me to make it all better and she said yes."

"Well, Robbie, how exactly did she say yes with the ventilator tube down her throat?" Maggie asked.

"I understood her without words," he continued. "I directed her to squeeze my hand once if the answer was yes and she did just that.

"Sometimes a response is more powerful when they say nothing at all," he suggested.

The idea itself gave Maggie pause, realizing that silence is an answer, as is a gesture.

"And you assumed that someone who wanted their condition to be made better meant that she wanted to die?" Maggie asked. "That's a big leap, isn't it?"

She was pacing herself, taking baby steps toward the finish line which was further away than she ever imagined.

"Detective Flynn, maybe it's not something that you can understand," Campbell said. He wasn't minimizing her but deferring to the fact that maybe she had never experienced that type of grief and loss, that complete sense of helplessness that comes from watching someone creep toward death, slowly, uncontrollably, and inevitably.

Everyone moves at their own pace, and everyone is broken in the places where the hurt sneaks in and imprints on their soul. In this moment, although focused on the retelling of a most deadly story, the detective's reality did not match her suspect's. How could it? She had never taken a life, but she most certainly suffered loss. On the other hand, Campbell had suffered loss but processed it much differently. He was a person who continued to grieve internally until it bubbled through his pores, and each and every breath, affecting others like a deadly virus spread by the mere act of breathing so closely to another that it kills one and not the other. The silence, in that moment, in the small confines of that room, was unnerving, disturbing not just for the two engaged in the uncomfortable discourse but for anyone in observation.

"Detective Flynn, have you ever seen someone exist in the gloaming, in that void where there is no sense of time and space?" He did not wait for her answer and continued justifying his actions. The silence troubled him more than the details of his dark journey. Once the gates of his personal hell opened, there was no holding him back.

"They pray for relief from the pain and the monotony of that empty awareness, lying there, knowing they're dying which is the only certainty in their future."

The entire team was spellbound. They marveled at Campbell's distorted sense of importance mixed with his perverse ethical code in the treatment of patients.

"I had grabbed two vials of vecuronium to keep in my pocket just for these kinds of emergencies."

"Why vecuronium?" Maggie wondered. "You said that you used propofol, or sleepy juice as you called it, with Signora Genovese and Mrs. DeLeon."

"The propofol drawer was empty that day," he said matter-of-factly. "It needed to be refilled." It was as simple as that for him, like swapping orange marmalade for grape jelly when the cupboard is bare.

"Excuse my ignorance but is there a difference in doing what you do when using propofol versus this drug vecuronium?" Maggie asked. She wanted to keep him talking. The longer he was in the spotlight, the more he would reveal.

"They're two different kinds of drugs," he said as if he was a pharmacist. "Propofol is a sedative and an anesthetic to help people relax and once it's administered through an intravenous tube, it takes about forty seconds for someone to lose consciousness.

"It lowers blood pressure and suppresses breathing, so if you use a high enough dose in a patient whose condition is already compromised, they never wake up. But if they do, there's always a pillow nearby," he added sheepishly. His warped humor failed to incite a smile on Maggie and had the group in observation just rolling their eyes and calling this guy exactly what he was, a sick fuck!

"And vecuronium is a comparable substitute?" Maggie wondered. She had never heard of the drug before and her ignorance played right into Campbell's need to dominate and control her.

"It's a neuromuscular blocker," Campbell said. "It's amazing the information you can collect in hospital hallways where doctors and nurses discuss life and death without noticing who's walking by in the same hall.

"They use vecuronium to relax vented patients who may be agitated by the tube in their throat," he explained the practical usage. "It relaxes and paralyzes the muscles making it difficult to breathe naturally, preventing shivering or contractions that could actually harm them while vented.

"The problem is that it takes at least ninety seconds to kick in, but beggars can't be choosers, and desperate times call for alternate measures."

He explained how he had injected the drug into Thelma's IV tube and waited for her breathing to slow down to nothing, tripping the automatic death alarms, alerting nurses and doctors to run toward the danger. There was nothing left to elaborate. Death is the last act that needs no epilogue and Campbell assumed Maggie would move along to the inquiry on other patients.

"Robbie, was anyone else in the room when you administered the vecuronium to Thelma Ondrovich?"

"'Atta girl," Tommy said proudly, getting fist bumps and agreement gestures from the others in the observation room. Hank tore up his reminder note for follow-up. Detective Maggie Flynn didn't miss a beat and remembered everything.

"Oh yeah, some doctor came in after I had pushed the drug," Campbell admitted without hesitation. "Why?"

"Well, did he help you or did you help him?"

"He wasn't sick. He was just a nuisance."

"So, this doctor didn't help you with the patient?" Maggie asked, slow stepping this great reveal into another confession.

"There was nothing for him to do."

"Was Thelma Ondrovich dead or alive when this doctor came into the room?" Maggie asked.

"Barely hanging on is the only way to describe it," Campbell said.

"Did you know this doctor? Had you seen him before?"

"Yeah, it was Dr. Levy, but he didn't know me. I just knew him from around the hospital," Campbell said, trying to distance himself from the dead medic.

"Did he check on the patient?"

"No."

"So why did he enter the room?" Maggie was painting him into a corner.

"I have no idea," Campbell responded. "Like I said, he was just a pest. He thought I was too close to a Covid patient or that I was doing something to her when I was only holding her hand for comfort.

"I went to introduce myself and shake his hand, but he collapsed and dropped to the floor when I approached him."

"Robbie, did you help him the way you helped the patient that night?" Maggie didn't mince words.

"No, like I said, he didn't need help," Campbell was prolonging the inevitable. "Ask me the right question Detective Flynn?" He leaned across the table, staring at her, intimidating her with his heavy, lustful breathing and close proximity.

It took a lot to rattle Maggie, but ice was creeping down her spine, causing her skin to prickle and not in the joyous way of getting goosebumps of watching your first sunrise over the ocean.

"Robbie, did you inject Dr. Levy that night with vecuronium or any other drug which could have caused his fatal collapse?"

"'Atta girl," Campbell praised her like a puppeteer pulling the strings on his favorite marionette. "Yes, I did. He was in the way, and I had to make sure he was gone.

"I was out of the room as the alarms sounded and before the nurses came running down the hall to find a dead twofer in the room.

"Hey, any chance we can order a pizza?" Campbell asked casually. "I'm starving and we've been going at this for quite a while."

Maggie didn't have an appetite, but she certainly needed a break.

Hank stepped in for round two, letting Maggie sit on the sidelines alone. She appreciated the space to decompress. The captain had left at the dinner break, along with Tommy and Lou who would get an early start tomorrow morning, drafting the tedious but necessary victim reports for ADA Kennedy to use in putting together a formal plea deal. They were hopeful Campbell would confess to killing Jenkins and Robbins because the entire deal hinged on him doing so.

"So, where's Detective Flynn?" Campbell wondered. He upped his game when confronted by his beautiful nemesis.

"Ah, we're giving her a dinner break," Hank replied. "It's just me and you shooting the breeze for now.

"So, you told Detective Flynn that you helped more than a few patients but less than a dozen." Hank quoted his earlier admission, allowing the suspect to think he had the upper hand because they were listening to him. In reality, they just needed to know how many bodies to chase down, whether in the refrigerator trucks or in the morgue.

"Do you know the exact number, Robbie?"

"Yes?"

"Listen bud, I'm not playing games here. The clock's ticking toward your status conference and while I don't have a crystal ball, I predict the judge won't allow you to remain here in our posh surroundings.

"That means unless you stop your antics and start telling us what you did to whom, when and where and how that you're going to Rikers and that's gonna be a real party for the likes of you.

"They're dropping like flies in that overcrowded hellhole. They're not wearing masks and you'll likely be dead before you go on trial while you wait and wait and wait," Hank told him.

"Rikers makes Attica look like a lux resort, so stop with the one-word answers and start talking," Hank hunkered down, leaning into Campbell across the table as he started rolling up his shirt sleeves. First one and then the other, with conviction, as if he were warming up in the ring.

"You comfy?" he asked Robbie. It was Hank's best verbal skill. He majored in it at John Jay.

"Well, maybe if you asked better questions that can't be answered yes or no, then we would move this conversation along." Campbell bit back and his sarcasm was not lost on Maggie who was listening more than watching in the observation room. She tried to block out the noise by closing her eyes, but Hank could not temper his acidic, sharp edge with a milder, dull monotone. She knew that Hank's temerity only fueled Campbell's resistance and if Hank thought she took a long time drawing out the first two deaths, it would take him days to get to the next one if he didn't dial it down a few notches.

Maggie gingerly opened the door to the interrogation room, holding two cups of coffee and placed them on the table. Her goal was to make both men think she was bringing them some refreshments but her true intention, in that moment, was beyond their ability to project outside the ring. She needed to break up the warring couple and hoped that Hank would either take the coffee to go and leave the room or leave the coffee and remove himself to observation under the guise of needing to use the restroom. He chose the latter.

"Ahh, my favorite is back," Campbell winked and exhaled as Maggie took the seat warmed up by Hank.

"Robbie, you must be exhausted," she said, allowing herself to recognize that even killers are human and allowing him to feel seen.

"You want to get out of here and we all want to go home," she continued. "But that's not gonna happen until you start taking this seriously.

"Do you think we can wrap this up tonight before tomorrow gets here? Can you do that? For me?" She added the flourish, bending without breaking to support the fruit of his low-lying ego.

"Just because you asked nice, I'll try my best," he said.

Maggie trusted that Hank was still recording in observation.

"After you helped Thelma Ondrovich and got rid of Dr. Levy, who was the next patient or person in the hospital who you helped transition?" She used precise references to his lethal prescription for his victims to frame her questions, leaving little room for doubt in his confession. Robert Nathan Campbell could call it whatever he wanted to, but murder is murder and the intentional transition of taking another's life is simply lethal madness.

"There were so many starting around Saint Patrick's Day into the third week of March," Campbell jumped right in. "I think there were three, but I truly don't remember dates and I can barely recall names.

"Everything was happening so fast when the city went into lockdown and people were coming to us in waves." His mind seemed to drift as Maggie watched his eyes stare blankly into the corner of the room, from time to time.

"I've worked in many hospitals across the country, but I've never seen anything like this before.

"I know the next person I helped was Mrs. Rodriguez," he said. "I never knew her first name and no one could locate her kids."

He explained that they had jumpstarted her heart at least three times in five days since she was admitted because she didn't have any advance directive instructions on hand as to her end of life wishes. Absent those authorizations or a court-appointed surrogate or a loved one in place to act as such, most hospitals were ethically bound to keep them alive, even if that meant mechanically.

"I had to step in," he muttered almost humbly, looking like a lost boy. "I held her hand as she took her last breath after pushing propofol through the IV. No one should be alone when they take their last breath."

Maggie was not a psychologist but reading people was her superpower when trying to probe a killer's mind. It was generally a dark web of tangled neurons which triggered random thoughts that made sense to no one but the killer's ego. In this case, Robbie Campbell was a lost boy, abandoned by a mother whose validation he continued seeking long after her passing. He was trying to prove his worthiness for love by caring for the elderly in their darkest hour.

"I couldn't stop myself," he admitted.

"The nurses had me sitting with so many people and helping families say their final goodbyes on tablets and telephones, that one day rolled into another and one death was just like the next.

"John Doe was next," Campbell confessed. The known and admitted death toll was now up to six, not including Brittany Jenkins and Susan Robbins.

"This guy was a homeless guy they found up on White Plains Road, slumped on a corner," he continued. "No name and no family that they could find in such a short time and the guy was dying, so I helped him."

Campbell explained that as patients died in their rooms, doctors signed off on the death certificates as Covid-related and nurses asked him to transport the bodies down to the morgue. After that, he had no idea what happened to them. The refrigerator trucks did not arrive for another two weeks.

Maggie and Hank had no idea how many bodies would drop tonight before Campbell ran out of steam but as long as he was talking, they were still playing. They had to continue or run the risk of changing his mind if he slept on things for another night.

"Who was the next patient or person that you helped, as best as you can remember?" Maggie remained calm, steady to keep him on track.

"I think that was Lottie Martin," Campbell said without hesitation. "I remember her because they had asked me to sit with her for a minute and I helped her with a shot of propofol just as the evening nurse came in holding a tablet. The woman's daughter in Washington State was on the screen and wanted to say goodbye to her mother. She literally watched her mother cross over as I held the tablet and then she thanked me for helping her say a final goodbye, virtually.

"That was a bit of an unexpected rush," he admitted. "No one had ever thanked me before for what I had been doing privately.

"She was going to die anyway. At least her daughter was able to be there thanks to my help."

Hank observed Maggie in action and realized in that moment just one reason that women made great detectives. In social settings they talked and talked and talked, sometimes passionately and overly emotional, without ever getting to a point and men listened without hearing. Yet when push came to shove and a detective needed to focus and home in on what mattered to the investigation, women came alive, working their analytical, multi-tasking, multi-level thinking without getting flustered. It was in their DNA, and they lacked the surge of testosterone that made men, in similar situations, fight or debate or defend their turf like pit bulls.

"Who was the next, patient or person?" Maggie heard Campbell's comment earlier and tailored her questions to encompass much with only a few words. He liked to talk, and he especially liked to talk to her.

"That would be Mary O'Neill who was brought in by her son," Campbell recalled. "Poor thing had just turned ninety-five.

"She wasn't going to last the night, and the nurses had advised her son that it wouldn't be much longer.

"So, shortly after the son left, I went in and assisted her."

These were cold, calculated killings. He was on a mission to rid the world of pain, the pain he watched his sister carry as a helpless child. Campbell was powerless then but empowered now making life and death decisions with forethought, but randomly, as the need presented itself.

Maggie looked up at the clock and noticed it was nearing tomorrow as they appeared to be slowing down. She was hesitant to stop the interview since Campbell was in his zone and cooperative, so she pushed on, already certain they would be back at it tomorrow to push for a confession on Jenkins and Robbins.

"Robbie, did you help any other patients or people at Misericordia or anywhere else in New York City and the boroughs between the time you helped Mrs. O Neill until the evening you were arrested?"

"Just one," he admitted. "That would be Arthur Goldberg, a nice old man."

"A nurse asked me to sit with him while she got his family on the line," he recalled. "Fortunately, I happened to have two extra vials of propofol in my pocket since I had just come from the meds closet.

"He couldn't respond, so I didn't need to ask him anything," Campbell said. "He was gone by the time the nurse returned, running toward the alarms coming from his monitors."

By the time the clock struck midnight, Campbell had confessed to killing six patients and a doctor at the hospital, bringing his total confessed death toll to nine. He said that was all, but tomorrow was a new day and Maggie hoped she could close this case where it all started, solving the murders of Brittany Jenkins and Susan Robbins. Or would another body drop?

Chapter Fifty-Two

ADA Kennedy joined Hank and Maggie to start the day with Campbell. They all looked slightly bedraggled. It had only been six days since Campbell was arrested but for all of them it felt more like six weeks. At least the detectives and Kennedy could sleep in their own bed and take a shower before coming to work. As for Campbell, there were no facilities for prisoners at local precincts. Captain Bradshaw had arranged two days ago for two officers to stand guard while Campbell took a shower in the officers' accommodations much to their chagrin, and they hoped to ship him out before another wash and spin cycle was warranted.

"Good morning, Mr. Campbell," Kennedy said calmly but frustrated. He was tired of this case. He had only joined the DA's office in February after he was sworn in as a member of the bar. In the past six weeks he had floated around from bureau to bureau, wherever he was needed, mostly drafting or researching motions and appearing in court to prosecute minor offenses. Coming face-to-face with a suspected serial killer was unsettling for most people, especially a twenty-five-year-old who was still wet behind the ears. The enthusiasm he had for catching this big case nearly two months ago was tempered by twenty-four-hour days and endless paperwork.

Cordialities dispensed with, Kennedy wanted to make quick work of wrapping up this case as his bureau chief had mandated.

"Mr. Campbell, we know you've been discussing a plea deal with Detectives Summers and Flynn, but the clock is ticking on this," Kennedy said, bringing a new reality check to the investigation. "Unless all is done and wrapped up with a bow in the next forty-eight hours, you're moving out of here and all hopes of a deal are off."

Maggie and Hank knew Campbell was ready to crack. His greatest fear was going to Rikers, and once you know a man's greatest fear, controlling his mind is child's play.

"It's nine o'clock now," Kennedy said, looking at the old wall clock. A circle of dust and soot outlined where it hung until it was obviously jolted off-kilter by unknown forces.

"I'm leaving you with Detectives Summers and Flynn," he continued. "I'll be back at one o'clock and I suggest you work really hard to answer all of their questions by then.

"Before I go, would you like me to call the public defender, Louis Pinto, who Judge Sanderson assigned to you, to review any questions or concerns you may have before entering into a plea deal agreement?"

Robbie Campbell just shook his head from side to side. His exhaustion was beginning to show. He had always answered vocally since being reprimanded at his arrest and he was starting to slip at observing the investigation's formalities.

"Mr. Campbell, we need you to respond orally for the record," Kennedy reminded him.

"No, I don't need an attorney," Campbell answered, still shaking his head, losing the spirit which had him fighting, more like competing, for days.

ADA Kennedy spoke with the detectives in the hall, advising them he would place Attorney Pinto on notice to be available for the next two days. Even though Campbell did not want counsel, they thought they should cover all bases in a case of this magnitude. They needed to make sure that each of Campbell's confessions and his plea agreement were clear and that each time he waived his Miranda rights he did so knowingly, voluntarily and intelligently. The DA and Kennedy did not want an eventual deal overturned on any perceived failures by a higher court because

Campbell did not understand his rights before entering into a probable life sentence agreement.

"Robbie, how ya doing this morning?" Maggie asked him. She could read his face almost as well as she could predict his terse answers. Exhaustion and exasperation were the emotions he displayed openly in the lines of his face, now shadowed by a two-day-old scruffy beard.

She started the morning with a brief rundown of yesterday's homicide confessions, six patients and one doctor in three weeks. That, along with two of his neighbors, placed Robbie Campbell's admitted death toll at nine. If they got him to confess to the Jenkins and Robbins homicides, the numbered notes stuffed inside their mouths would make sense and that would make Robert Nathan Campbell the most prolific serial killer in New York City's history since Joel Rifkin nearly thirty years ago.

Maggie was refreshed, ready to start the day after a good night's sleep. Jax was staying out of her way and had gone back to Manhattan to let her focus. When they were in the same space, all they did was focus on each other, pleasantly uncharacteristic for both of them, the career-driven, analytical, laser-focused dealmaker and the alert, analytical, people-reading detective. They were on opposite sides of the legal spectrum but shared a brilliant wit to make each other relax and laugh, hard, really hard, on their worst days.

"What would you like to talk about today, detective?" It was odd for Robbie to lob the first question across the table.

"Robbie, we have to talk about Brittany," Maggie explained. "We know you knew her. You worked with her at Misericordia, right?"

He chided her for asking softball questions when he knew she already had the answers. Yet he also knew she was laying the foundation for his eventual arrest on additional charges, and she was crafting the plot like a well-written true crime novel.

"Let's go back to that wet, slushy night in March when Brittany was killed," Maggie steered him where he needed to go if a deal was to be had.

"It was raining, right?" she asked him.

"You would already know it was," he said, slumping into his chair for the first time in days. She was losing him and herself, in part, as this dragged on.

"What was your relationship with Brittany?" Maggie asked. She didn't offer up suggestions or descriptions. She wanted him to use his own words to describe his perception of a relationship that didn't seem to exist for Brittany outside of the workplace.

"I started at the hospital the same week she started her nursing internship, or whatever they called it. She hadn't graduated yet and was waiting to take her licensing exam," he explained.

"We became more than co-workers or friends. We trusted each other. We told each other everything, or so I thought," he said. His face was able to hide the resentment which singed the tone of his voice with the burnt taste of disappointment. His flat-faced appearance showed no outward signs of the inner turmoil which churned in his gut. For the first time he folded his cuffed hands together, tightly, as if to stifle an outburst and quash any turmoil from bubbling to the surface.

Maggie took it all in, as did Hank in observation.

Campbell described himself as a helper because he did not like seeing anyone in pain. *Especially himself*, was the first thought in Maggie's mind. There was a dark crevasse somewhere in Campbell's cerebral cortex where that desire to help others, when rejected, triggered a primal switch to kill and eradicate any challenge to his omnipotent urges.

"Here I am being nice to her, offering her a ride home on a slushy, wet, late night, and she lied to me," he said. His disbelief mixed with outrage. "She never told me that she had a boyfriend or that they lived together," he continued. "She was leading me on the whole time, the stupid bitch, she thought she was too good for me."

He had opened the emotional floodgates. There was no point in corking the dam now. It was a deluge of anger, hurt, rejection, resentment, fear, loss of control, all rooted in his childhood and pouring forth now like Niagara Falls.

Maggie just watched him, expressionless but unconsciously nodding her head from time to time, sometimes in awe of how the deranged human mind rationalized the most bizarre psychopathic behavior, while at other times empathizing with a man so utterly torn up as a boy.

"It was her time to go," he said emphatically. "You can't treat people that way.

"Shame on her as a first responder," he continued. "You don't help people by lying to them."

"Did you help her, Robbie?" Maggie asked not wanting to accuse him of killing since that accusation had previously angered him and she could not risk that so close to the finish line.

"*Phhh*," he offered an expression of disgust. "I helped myself. I killed her."

There it was. The first of two confessions needed to close this case.

He explained that he had a vial of propofol in his jacket. He always took a few spares to aid his mission. It was just enough to get her to stumble into the wooded baseball field and then he finished her off with her own scarf.

"At that point, with her boyfriend, the only way I could have her all to myself was to kill her."

"But why the hidden note in her mouth, Robbie?" Maggie asked.

"There's a lot of hurt going on right now, in hospitals and behind closed doors," he started down a path which came as a surprise to Maggie and Hank.

"She was different, different from my patients and neighbors," he said. "My mission was to help them, and she was just a bump in the road.

"You can't compare someone like Signora Genovese with Brittany," Campbell continued. "Signora Genovese needed help, but Brittany needed to learn a lesson.

"The numbered notes kept it straight in my head," he said. "It took you guys long enough to pick up on that."

Maggie was masterful. She let him believe he was in control. She allowed him to live under the delusion that detectives are ignorant fools while killers are in the driver's seat. She knew there was only one killer all along and they all knew they'd catch him because most of them always make a mistake. In the case of Robbie Nathan Campbell, it was the one who got away who led to his downfall.

"And what about Susan Robbins in Shoelace Park?" Maggie asked.

"Oh, that was her name?" Campbell asked. He had never met her, so there was no reason that he should know her name before that fateful night.

"Why her? You have a thing for nurses?" Maggie asked, wondering if he had a type, as most men do.

"Why not?" Campbell replied. "She was another one who thought she was too good for me.

"I was walking down that old roadbed, which runs parallel to the back of the hospital, and she was coming from the opposite direction, and I noticed she had scrubs on.

"I saw her grab a seat on a bench and asked how she was doing out of concern." He seemed to be sincere as he retold the story of the crime's genesis.

"She got squirrelly when I grabbed a seat next to her on the bench and she went to leave, but I couldn't let her do that.

"I was on edge from frisky Sammy the night before and this woman just pushed the wrong button," he said. "I couldn't leave her behind."

"And what about her note?"

"What about it?"

"Who wrote them, Robbie?" Maggie asked, still wondering if Campbell had a helper.

"A friend, that chick Melody from New Mexico," he said without hesitating.

He explained that she had no idea why she was writing these notes. She had written a few of them, at his request, before she left his apartment, and he simply added the numbers for Jenkins and Robbins later.

"This ain't my first rodeo, as the saying goes, and I need to keep it organized in my head," he said. "I only had two of the original posties left," he added. "Good thing you caught me, or I would've run out!" He offered a maniacal laugh that came from out of nowhere, making its presence all the more haunting and disturbing.

Hank struggled with whether to ask him how many other rodeos he took part in but feared opening the door to murders in other state jurisdictions and losing this case to the feds. The FBI would be sure to rush in and sweep it away as *their* investigation for profiling serial killers when the jurisdiction to prosecute crimes lies with each individual state. Either way, they didn't want a turf for prosecution rights when they were closing in on locking Campbell away for life.

Maggie signaled Hank with a tap on his knee under the table. She realized they had a job to do and, at the very least, an obligation to the Guadalupe County sheriff based on their prior discussions and the help of his department.

They asked a patrol officer to take Campbell to the men's room for a break while they regrouped in the hall to discuss the new bombshell Campbell had just dropped. The man was an unending reservoir of tales from the dark side which he used to arouse the morbid curiosity of his audience as he saw fit, dragging out his inescapable imprisonment yet again.

ADA Kennedy didn't expect much when he returned at one o'clock sharp, but he was pleasantly surprised when Hank advised him that Campbell had confessed to killing the two nurses and said he didn't kill anyone else since returning to New York. The detectives, however, did reveal the new stunner that while there were no open murder investigations in ViCAP with similar signatures across the rest of the country, Campbell just indicated that New York was not his first rodeo. They agreed that Hank should call the Guadalupe sheriff while Kennedy needed to inform the DA himself.

The three observed Campbell through the window in observation, eating his lunch and appearing relaxed and not on edge for the first time since his arrest. We all have our breaking point and once we hit it and the weight of our secrets is lifted our shoulders ease into our new reality.

Campbell wanted his new reality to be located at one of New York's best prisons and certainly not at Attica, Sing Sing or Dannemora. He was hopeful he'd be shipped upstate to the Eastern Correctional Facility, a newer, cushier, maximum security prison and made that his top demand as they started negotiating his plea deal.

Hank was typing up all of the details Campbell had confessed to for his eventual signature, while Maggie was arranging a photo array for Campbell to identify his victims, all eleven of them.

"Robbie, we have a bit of housecleaning to do to get this deal finalized," she explained, after letting him eat his lunch alone with just an officer standing guard outside the room.

"I would like to show you these eleven photos," she said as she laid out the photo array on the table before him.

"Please identify each photo to the best of your ability."

"Awe," he said looking down at an older photo of Signora Genovese. He remembered it used to sit on the fireplace mantel at her house.

He paused for a moment after identifying her as his first victim and went down the line of photos, each time identifying the victim by name and eventually shuffling some around the table when he noticed they weren't in sequential order according to the dates he took their lives.

Maggie had him confirm that these photos were of the eleven people he identified as his victims and that there were no others since he returned to New York more than a year ago.

"Just three last, short questions," she prefaced what she was about to say so that he didn't anticipate a long, drawn-out discussion.

"Did you kill anyone else in New York State?"

"No," he said firmly.

"Have you killed anyone in any other state?" she asked hoping the list would not be long.

There was an uncomfortable silence in the room. She could hear the heat kick on as the radiator spit out steam. The buzz of the overhead light indicated no one had fixed the ballast which had been broken months ago, buzzing with the irritating hiss she presumed was part of sound torture.

Campbell was thinking of what to say. He recognized his future in a New York prison was limited but if he told the truth, maybe another state would be more suitable to his desires and needs.

"Detective Flynn, you've played it straight with me so I'm going to do the same for you," he said looking across the table to her in what could quite possibly be one of the last times.

"Death became overwhelming while at my first job at a hospital and that was in New Mexico," he said. "I found my life's calling there and that's where this all began.

"My first time helping a patient transition was in Guadalupe where I worked for a short time," he said, "I'm not quite sure that she actually died because I didn't hang around long enough to see the final results before heading back to New York.

"I've learned a lot since then."

"Sit tight," she advised him. "ADA Kennedy is typing up your plea deal and the public defender wants to review it on your behalf."

"No worries," Campbell said. "It's not like I'm going anywhere for a long time.

"By the way, Detective Flynn, you missed one."

Maggie's back was already to him, and she was one foot out the door, when he pitched that curveball in the air.

Hank and Kennedy were at the door quicker than a fastball from Yankees' pitcher Masahiro Tanaka.

"What the fuck are you talking about?" Hank asked in the only way he could, confident the recording was not running, so as not to jam him up with a rip for inappropriate language. In instances like this, it was the cop equivalent of the swear jar, a reduction in pay with more serious consequences.

"Again, it comes down to asking the right questions," Campbell said knowing he still had a secret up his sleeve.

"Explain right now or this deal is off," said Kennedy who had joined the party in interrogation, as did Attorney Pinto.

"There was also a girl in seventh grade, right here at home, but that was an accident," he revealed for the first time. "I didn't mean to kill her. Actually, I didn't kill her at all. The bus killed her after I pushed her into the street. It was just an accident and that was nearly twenty years ago."

The detectives and Kennedy were confident their deal would stick in New York and would let the feds and New Mexico decide how to proceed after Campbell signed on the dotted line and was shipped off to Eastern Correctional. Their headache was over, at least for now, while the hospital's was just beginning.

The plea deal spared this psychopath the death penalty for taking lives but no one in the room was certain they would ever find all of the bodies.

"You know what the amazing part is?" Hank asked the group in the squad room, after notifying the hospital of the murders under their roof and speaking with Sheriff Gallup in New Mexico.

"What? That we get to go home before midnight for the first time in a week?" Maggie wondered.

"Well, there's that but we also did all of this during the worst crisis to hit the nation in decades without one reporter getting in our way. Maybe there is a silver lining in all of this insanity."

Maggie and Hank headed north in separate cars. They had an important stop to make before heading home, actually two stops. This police visit would be as emotionally charged as the death notices delivered six weeks earlier.

"Six weeks ago, Mags, just six weeks ago," Hank said as they walked up the path to the neatly kept white house on the corner. He could not believe they put a serial killer away in such a short time without the media catching wind of it.

They rang the bell just once as someone inside opened the door. Mrs. Jenkins didn't need to ask the purpose of their visit. She knew exactly why Detectives Summers and Flynn were on her front porch. They assured her they would return when they caught Brittany's killer. Her life would never be the same, but she could sleep a lot easier now, or at least try.

It was the same for Mike Scavi when they delivered the news to him. The death of one life changes the lives of many in ways that few can imagine.

Epilogue

"Where are we going?" Maggie asked Jax who jostled her out of bed early the Friday morning after the arrest. All she wanted to do was sleep late this weekend. She deserved that and much more, but he had other plans.

"I packed a bag for you while you were sleeping, princess," he said, sounding in charge and delivering a directive she could not ignore. "We're getting out of Dodge for a few days, and before you open your mouth, we'll be back Monday afternoon, so you can get back to the grind which makes you vibrate.

"I already checked your schedule with Tommy and Hank and Bradshaw," he assured her.

She had pulled the comforter over her face to hide from the day and from him but peeked demurely out of the corner with the one eye that was awake.

"Do I need my passport?" she asked, smiling coyly.

"Wow! That didn't take you long," he said. He pretended to look amazed, when in reality her sharp mind and ability to cull anything down to its roots was what drew him to her like a magnet.

"Well, we're not leaving the country, but we are leaving the mainland."

She hopped in the shower, quick like a bunny, and guessed they were heading to a nearby island, somewhere like Long Beach Island or Long Island, since commercial airlines were barely flying. She didn't care where as long as she was with Jax and out of The Bronx and Westchester, hell, out of the whole metropolitan New York area.

"No, no, no, you don't," Jax warned her not to answer her ringing phone as they got into the car, destination known only to him. But that warning fell on deaf ears.

"What's up, Hank?" Maggie identified who it was so Jax wouldn't leer at her until she coughed up the name.

He apologized knowing that she was on her way out of town but thought she would want to know of the bizarre call he had just fielded from a homicide detective out on Staten Island. He explained that a newborn was dropped off overnight inside a Safe Harbor box at a firehouse in Tottenville. There was a note wrapped in the baby girl's swaddling that piqued the interest of the detective who now caught the case.

"I'm sorry but why are homicide detectives in any borough now getting caught in Safe Harbor baby drop-offs?" Maggie asked. "And not to be callous but why the hell are you calling me on my weekend off to be swept away by tall, dark and handsome who is sitting next to me and sending virtual daggers your way through my phone?"

"Sadly, the mother was found dead next to the firehouse," Hank replied. "And hi, Jax," he added after hearing Maggie place the call on her speaker.

"I still don't understand why this lands on our doorstep," Maggie wondered. She was rolling her eyes, frustrated that she couldn't just escape and angry with herself for answering the damn phone. Jax's emotions echoed hers.

"It looks like she died from childbirth after dropping the baby in the box," Hank continued. "The detective texted me a photo of the note to see if it means anything and you'll see why.

"Stand by."

It didn't take him long and the note appeared on Maggie's phone as well. She knew that handwriting as well as her own. It was a match for the notes left inside the mouths of Brittany Jenkins and Susan Robbins and she had studied them for nearly two months.

"The invisible pain is unbearable. Please hide my baby. Don't let that monster destroy our daughter's life too."

Maggie and Hank sat together in silence, in joint shock across the ether. Jax sat there as well, not privy to their inside secret. The thrill of a weekend escape was muffled as all three of them took a minute to absorb the final development in a case that just kept giving.

"The mother was using a phony ID, Maggie," Hank continued. "The name on it was Melody Chalmers and the fake address she used was Campbell's. This poor baby is that killer's kid."

They knew that the city's child services agency would likely do DNA testing to confirm the baby's parentage as they processed her into the system. Since they now had a sample of Campbell's DNA in evidence and uploaded to their database, along with the poor mother's DNA which they would get from her autopsy, it would not take long to validate what the deceased woman wrote in her last desperate plea to escape her worst nightmare, her dying wish. Yet it would be a long while before any of that would be processed.

"With any luck Melody's family will welcome this poor baby into their tribe and that will be the beginning of a new life for her," Maggie prayed as she said it.

Hank assured her that his next call was to Sheriff Gallup to notify the family of the woman, otherwise known as Melody Chalmers.

"At least there's family out there," Hank said. "While child services here may have a legal obligation to notify Campbell of his new offspring, he'll never get close enough to touch her."

That's what they all hoped. That's all they could do.

The death of one life changes the lives of so many in ways that few can imagine, especially when it's murder.

"Please, let's just go," Maggie begged Jax to leave the condo's parking lot. She didn't care where they were headed. She just needed to escape. She turned off her phone and tossed it in Jax's bag because it was closest to her in the back seat. She barely noticed the tickets lying inside his opened bag or the gift box alongside them.

He took a deep breath and prayed that his eagle-eyed detective was too tired to see what waited for her on the other side of tomorrow.

"What are we doing at the airport?" Maggie asked. "Who's flying?"

Jax ignored her and drove straight to private parking at the Westchester County Airport, the lot where private charters and jets are stored and where the owners park their luxury cars as they fly off to wheel and deal or take the kids to Orlando.

"Are you kidnapping me, Mr. Spencer?" Maggie asked. "You know what happened to me the last time I was kidnapped? I almost died."

"Awe, baby, trust me, you're about to start living," he said, grabbing their bags and guiding her to a small private jet which waited on the runway.

"Do you have more money than I thought?"

"No, just friends in high places," he smiled. "We're flying to Jekyll Island for the weekend."

Maggie was nonplussed by the trappings of wealth but more impressed with Jax for the romantic gesture and his big, loveable heart, the safe space where she could curl up and just be Maggie. The safe space in between his arms and tucked just under his chin where the outside noise dared not enter.

"Down there doesn't look so scary ugly from up here," she said peeking out the window.

"My girl isn't scared of anything," Jax said. "Except maybe me."

She laughed, turning from the clouds outside to find him kneeling on one knee beside her, ring box in hand.

"Maggie Flynn, you are the love of my life, this life and every other life. Will you fly with me into forever?"

Her eyes said it all and their kiss was their eternal bond!

Acknowledgments

As an author, I get to weave a fictional web of dark, twisty tales created solely in my imagination. I visit the places no one is brave enough to enter from the safety of a cozy room with my laptop and a good cup of coffee. In reality there are lots of people who have influenced, nurtured and supported that creativity along the way.

For all of my friends, colleagues and relatives who have supported me, I thank you from the bottom of my heart, especially Andrew C. Quinn, Esq. who is always one text away to iron out procedural glitches or take my calls from the back of a patrol car; to all of the cops, top cops and foot soldiers, whom I've had the honor to work with – stay safe out there and thank you.

I am also fortunate to have worked with the best of the best in my broadcasting career. I am honored that two of those radio legends from WCBS-AM continue to push me to be a better writer on a daily basis – Gary Maurer, I am shocked that you still take my calls? I lost count of how many there were as you edited Dead Cold, from finding typos, oh my, to letting me know when the clues just didn't add up; and to John Cameron Swayze, Jr., who pulled no punches in telling me what needed to be redone.

To all of my fellow Bronx natives and those grammarians who feel compelled to call out punctuation and street slang, The Bronx is a place, and we capitalize "The" accordingly and with reverence. However, when we use Bronx as an adjective, such as the Bronx homicide squad, *the* is not capitalized.

Thanks also to Chris LoBue for his creativity and patience on our treks to Asbury Park to capture my many moods in his viewfinder while tolerating the moods left in editing.

Art has inspired me since my first trips to The Met and The Guggenheim as one very lucky child. It is an absolute privilege for Detective Maggie Flynn to discover the talent of new artists like Aaron Westerberg. I am running out of wall space!

The last Detective Flynn Mystery, the Costa Affair, was written during the pandemic, while Dead Cold was written about the pandemic when life did go on as The Big Apple was collapsing. To all of the known and unknown first responders, grocery store employees and postal carriers who held our world together, one thank-you will never be enough.

To our libraries, especially Mamaroneck and Mount Pleasant in New York and Beach Haven in New Jersey, kudos to you. You continue to provide new and creative ways to keep our libraries open in the digital age.

And where would Detective Maggie Flynn, and her author, be without the Boiano Bakery? Grazie tante to Pat, Anna, Teo, Marisa and everyone who works there, including the morning espresso paesani who unknowingly add color to starting my day.

About the Author

Lisa Fantino is an award-winning journalist and attorney whose best-selling travel memoir, "Amalfi Blue - lost & found in the south of Italy," has been Number One in the U.S., Canada and Australia and Top Ten on three continents.

As a broadcaster she spent a career on the air as a reporter, writer and tape producer at New York's top news stations, WCBS-AM and WINS-AM, and as an anchor at the NBC Radio Networks. As an attorney she has represented clients in both state and federal courts.

Lisa's passion for reading and storytelling is in her DNA. While her dad taught her a great love of reading, her mom created stories so that she wouldn't have to read. It was the best of both worlds for a budding author.

In "Dead Cold," Lisa continues on the case with Detective Maggie Flynn, a no nonsense crimefighter with a New York City street edge, seasoned with just enough Italian to make life passionate and exhilarating.

Visit her website:
AuthorLisaFantino.com

Other Books by Lisa Fantino

Detective Maggie Flynn Mysteries
THE COSTA AFFAIR

"If you're after a good mystery thriller, this one is perfect." ~ Amazon & Instagram

"I've found my new favorite author! Thoroughly enjoyed the read and can't wait to see it on the big screen." ~ Amazon

"Fantino fills in the gaps nicely while keeping the mystery on high boil. I'm looking forward to the next offering in this series with open arms. Bravo, Fantino." ~ NetGalley

"Detective Flynn was knowledgeable, funny and incredibly sharp!" ~ NetGalley

FRACTURED

"I couldn't put this book down! I loved it! It's a page-turning thriller with an ending I never saw coming. You've got to read it!" ~ Barnes & Noble

"A gripping serial killer mystery that keeps you on the edge of your seat." ~ Amazon and Instagram

"Maggie's thrust into this classically seedy Big Apple crime drama. To the reader's eager satisfaction, she's going in fists first." ~ Amazon

"Hair-trigger suspense…with chilling insight and prose as incisive as the sharp end of a stiletto, the author takes you through the looking glass into a dark and sinister place you've never been--the cold, calculating mind of a psychopath…Touch it if you dare. The shock will keep you looking over your shoulder in the dark." ~ Amazon

Mickey Malone Mysteries
SHROUDED IN POMPEI

"I can recall few other books I have read recently that treat the topic of political corruption with both intellectual seriousness and a touch of charm. This book has the necessary suspense and mystery to keep us reading, but it's fun." ~ Amazon

"An exciting and suspenseful mystery and a savvy political thriller. The story had me hooked from the first page and never let me down…I think it would make a great movie. Looking forward to the next Mickey Malone mystery." ~ Amazon

www.ingramcontent.com/pod-product-compliance
Lightning Source LLC
Jackson TN
JSHW020353170225
78973JS00002BA/45